THE CABERNET CLUB

A NOVEL

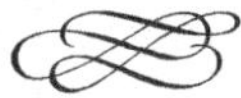

RONA S. ZABLE

MARGIE ZABLE FISHER

Empress Editions

Typeset in Baskerville in Cambridge.
Printed and bound in the US by Lakeside.
ISBN 979-8-9995270-7-3

Note to Reader: This book is a work of fiction. Names, characters, places, and incidents are either a product of the author's imagination or are used fictitiously. Any resemblance to actual persons, living or dead, is entirely coincidental.

For Rona S. Zable, my mother, my best friend

"It is never too late to be what you might have been."

— George Eliot

CHAPTER 1

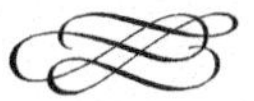

I turned up the radio when I heard one of my favorite songs, "How Do You Like Me Now?" by Toby Keith. As I took in the sunny day and scenery, the song seemed just right. "How do you like me now, now that I'm on my way…"

For the last twenty minutes, I'd been driving down palm-tree-lined streets with bright red and pink hibiscus flowers in front of big, beautiful houses and impressive condo communities. BMWs and Teslas kept whizzing by, but my 2012 Toyota Corolla suited me just fine.

Just then my cell phone rang, interrupting my reverie. It was Lori.

"Hi Mom. Are you okay?"

"Of course I'm okay. I spoke to you a few hours ago when I crossed state lines. Florida's looking pretty terrific so far."

"You could have had an accident or something," said Lori. "I still can't believe you drove down there by yourself.

I thought you didn't even like to drive on the highway. I was so scared something would happen to you."

My daughter was right. I hated driving on the highway. But driving was cheaper than flying and sending my car on the car train. Plus, by loading my car with things I needed, I saved money on shipping. And it was about time I got over my fear of driving, especially since Banyan Beach didn't have a whole lot of public transportation. So I did what any strong, sensible woman over sixty would do—I packed my weight in snacks, white-knuckled my way through the two-day drive, and stayed overnight at a Best Western in North Carolina.

"I told you. This is the beginning of the new me, and my new life." No need for Lori to know how scared I actually was on the trip. "And despite your worrying, I'm almost at Palmetto Pointe. I'll call you tonight. Love you."

I ended the call and felt something unfamiliar in my stomach. Excitement. It had been a long time since I looked forward to anything.

~

Up ahead on the left, I saw a sign. I pulled into the visitors' lane and read the blue-on-gray letters:

PALMETTO POINTE

An Over-55 Active Adult Community

The *e* on Active was askew.

As I waited behind the cars ahead of me at the gate, I looked around. The lush, tropical trees and colorful flowers I saw showcasing the fancy communities on the way to Palmetto Pointe were nowhere to be seen. Instead, I saw an endless array of gray, aging, two-story, flat-roofed buildings that looked like army barracks. Instead of well-dressed women laughing and chatting (à la *The Golden Girls*), the only people outside were white-haired men and women with walkers getting into a white transport van with a sun-faded Palmetto Pointe decal.

"Excuse me, miss. Please pull up to the gate," a voice said from the guard shack.

I'd been so busy looking around that I hadn't realized I had made it to the front of the visitors' line.

"Sorry about that," I said.

"No worries. Welcome to Palmetto Pointe," said the security guard in a strong Jamaican accent. He was short and round, maybe in his fifties, and a big smile dominated his face. His name tag said "Tommy."

"Thank you, Tommy," I said, smiling back. "And you can call me Debbie. I'm a new renter here."

He smiled broadly. "Nice to meet you, Miss Debbie. I also work security sometimes at the pool."

"The pool!" I exclaimed. "We never had pools where I was from—"

Impatient honking behind me interrupted our conversation. Tommy's smile disappeared.

"I need to see your license, please."

"Oh, sure." I searched around in my pocketbook. More honking.

"The sign says 'have your license ready,'" came a voice from the car behind me.

"Sorry, I'm new here," I yelled back and handed my license to Tommy. "I'm picking up the key to my rental. I'm supposed to get it from the condo director, Harriet Bertulli. Can you tell me how to get to her place?"

He chuckled as he handed me a parking pass. "Miss

Harriet. Our own 'Black Widow.' You bet. Just go straight down this street…"

I nodded along at his directions, but my mind was frozen on "Black Widow." What the heck did he mean by that?

I took a deep breath and drove through the open gate.

~

I NOTICED THE SAME ROWS UPON ROWS OF GRAY, OLD-looking buildings. The only greenery was occasional small patches of lawn.

I hated to admit it, but I was disappointed. Oh well, I thought, psyching myself up. Does it really matter what the outside of these condos looks like? The inside is the most important thing.

After a few wrong turns, I got to Harriet's building. I found a guest parking space, then walked up to Unit 729 and knocked. A few seconds later the door opened and—

I shrieked.

The woman in front of me was dressed in a floor-length black caftan with a hood that covered her head. Her face was painted entirely white, except for small circles around her eyes. She frowned, causing cracks to spread throughout the white around her eyes in a way that made her seem like she was disintegrating in front of me. "Why are you yelling? What—you've never seen a face mask before? You gotta take care of your skin when you live in Florida."

"S-sorry. Um, hello," I said, still nervous. "You must be Harriet Bertulli. I'm—um—Debbie Gordon. I'm renting 758 and I need to pick up the key. I spoke to you earlier."

"Oh, yeah. I forgot about it. You caught me right in the

middle of my beauty treatment. I got avocado oil on my hair, too."

Harriet looked past my shoulder. "Where's your stuff?"

"In the car. I didn't need much because the condo is furnished."

"I have to get this crap off my face, and then I'll meet you at your condo and show you around." Harriet slammed the door in my face.

As I walked back to my car, I realized it was actually three months to the day since the wake-up call that led me here—to Florida.

CHAPTER 2

It was a cold New England afternoon; one minute my neighbor was waving to me, and the next minute she was on the ground.

"Are you all right?" I said, running up to her.

"Yes," Janet said shakily.

"I saw you from the window," said Janet's husband, out of breath. Slowly, he helped her up.

"I was heading to get the laundry in Building D," she said.

"To hell with the laundry," he said. "This damn ice. It's dangerous."

"Let me put my groceries away, and I'll get the laundry," I told them.

"You're an angel," he said.

As I drank my chamomile tea that night, it hit me. That could have been me. And I didn't have a husband to help me up.

Winters in New England were not fun for me. I never

liked winter sports, and snow and icy roads increased my stress level as a nervous driver.

So why did I live in Winslow?

Until recently, I would have answered that I stayed because my family and friends lived here. But now my daughter and her family had moved away, and my one remaining friend had a new boyfriend she spent most of her time with.

I also worked as the office manager of a law office, but I was old enough to retire with my full Social Security benefit. And boy, was I ready to retire.

How many years had I dreamed of living somewhere warmer? Where instead of worrying about falling on the ice, my biggest concern would be whether I should lounge by the pool or at the beach? And where I could make plans any time of the year to go out to a movie or dinner, and maybe even have a glass of wine or two or four.

Most importantly, I wanted to own a home of my own. I wanted to paint the walls blue and have new appliances and floors without carpeting. I could never afford a place in our suburb outside of Boston.

In my heart of hearts, I wanted to find a sunny place that I could call home, with friends and fun, while I still felt healthy enough to enjoy it.

So what the hell was keeping me here?

Janet's fall provided the wake-up call I needed. Or, really, a wake-up fall. I needed to wake up from my humdrum existence and finally live the life I wanted to live.

I moved to my computer and pulled up my bank account, then took a look at my retirement savings. I would have to watch my spending, but I should be able to rent for a short time and then buy a place.

I took a deep inhale and opened up a new tab on my computer. In Google, I typed in "inexpensive rentals in South Florida."

CHAPTER 3

My daughter wasn't a fan of my idea.

"Seriously Mom, you'll be all alone in Florida…no friends, no family. Why can't you retire to Delaware and live with us?"

The microwave beeped and my stomach started gurgling in anticipation of the lasagna.

"Nobody retires to Delaware," I scoffed. "It doesn't even sound like a real place. I never knew anyone from Delaware. Besides, it snows there, too. I want more sun."

Lori started talking about the hot Florida summers, and how I would miss having all four seasons. Even though she had a point, I didn't want to give her any more ammunition.

"Lori, I'm done with living in Winslow. I'm tired of typing out appeals and motions. I raised you, worked, and saved enough to retire, and I'm weary. After more than fifty years, I want a change. A chance to live a new life, on my terms, and a year-round tan. Is that too much to ask?"

Silence. And then Lori tried a new angle.

"No, but I'm worried you're setting yourself up for disappointment," said Lori. "You do realize that in real life it's not easy to make new friends at your age, right? It's not like in *The Golden Girls*. And you won't be living in a beautiful home with a killer wardrobe, going out all the time. Don't forget—you're on a budget."

In addition to being a helicopter daughter, Lori was also an accountant. Money always seemed to be part of the conversation. Granted, money had been scarce when she was growing up as the daughter of a single parent and a deadbeat dad. And legal secretaries weren't known for amassing fortunes during their careers. But I had scrimped and saved for years.

"Thanks, Nancy Negative. I understand that." Secretly, though, I kind of hoped my experience would be like *The Golden Girls*. Or, at least a version of *The Golden Girls* who lived on a budget. Maybe *The Bronze Girls*.

I decided to come clean. "Besides, I've already signed the lease."

Silence.

"Hello? Lori? Are you still there?"

"I'm here," she said, in a flat voice. "I can't believe you signed a lease. You didn't even ask me to look it over?"

"Oh for God's sake, Lori. I've rented and dealt with leases my whole life. And I worked in a legal office, where I've seen hundreds of them."

Silence again.

"And this isn't your decision. It's mine," I added.

"I guess you've made up *your* mind about *your* new life, on *your* terms."

I sighed. "Please be happy for me, Lori." I decided to play the sympathy card. "I sure won't miss lugging the laundry to another building. They have washers and dryers in every condo there."

That didn't work, as Lori reminded me that she had a washer and dryer in her house, too.

Lori tried a new tack. She was like a dog with a bone. "What about your furniture?"

"I'll sell it." In fact, I couldn't wait to part with my furniture—heavy, dark pieces left over from my brief marriage years ago. "This rental looks amazing, and it was such a great price. Everything is so new and modern. I always wanted a bright, airy bedroom."

"But you'd save so much money living with us, and you can decorate the guest room however you like. And the kids miss you so much."

"I'll miss them, too," I said, ignoring her whine. "But you'll all have a great place to come visit during school vacations."

What I didn't say—while I loved my grandchildren, I wasn't looking forward to becoming their unpaid nanny.

"In fact, you can all come for Thanksgiving. I'll even make dinner."

Lori laughed. "Please, Mom. We don't want to get food poisoning."

I laughed too. I'd rather have Lori laughing than arguing with me any day.

"By then my lease will be up, and I'll hopefully be able to show you where I'll be living permanently."

"Wait—what?" Lori asked.

"I said my lease will be up then and I hope to have bought a place by then—"

"So—you're only there for six months?"

"Yes, Lori." This wasn't exactly rocket science. "That's

the term of my lease. I want to start looking for a place to buy—"

"So really you're just having an extended vacation in Florida, right?" Lori's voice was giddy. "You'll be horrified by the brutal summer heat, you won't find any new friends, you'll be lonely and sad, and you'll be ready to come live with us. In fact, when we come down for Thanksgiving, we can help you pack up your clothes and things to come to Delaware."

I had had enough.

"Lori, by the time I see you at Thanksgiving, I will have survived the summer, made friends, and enjoyed myself." I said. To make the point stronger, I added, "And I will have bought a condo or rented a place for the season."

Lori snickered quietly, but I still heard it.

"Okay, Mom, let's make a deal."

Seriously? This was my life, not a game show. But I decided to humor her.

"Okay, what's the deal?"

"If you're not happy in Florida by Thanksgiving, you'll come live with us."

Wow. Just wow. I was supposed to find happiness in six months? Then I realized—*why not?* I had been living in the slow lane my whole life. It was time to get going.

I decided to call her bluff. "You've got a deal."

When we hung up, I ate my cold lasagna and watched the snow fall.

I would prove my daughter wrong, and find my happiness in Florida. How hard could it be?

CHAPTER 4

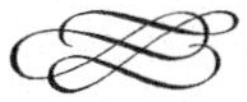

As I trudged up the steps, a suitcase in each hand, I wasn't so sure. I was sweating hard. I hadn't used my leather American Tourister luggage in years, and the bags were heavier than I remembered.

"I haven't seen that kind of suitcase since the '70s," Harriet said from the end of the hallway. "Haven't you heard—luggage now has wheels?"

"Yes, I know that, but this luggage is perfectly good and I didn't want to waste—"

"Look how you're sweating. How come you didn't use the elevator?" she interrupted.

"I didn't know there was an elevator."

She snickered. "Of course there is. You should use it. It's always getting stuck, though."

I stopped in front of the door. "I can't wait to cool off and relax in some nice air conditioning. It's so hot out. Plus, I really have to go to the bathroom."

"The air conditioning's gonna take a while to get cool,

but—" she unlocked and opened the door—"Ta-da. Here we are—feast your eyes on Buckingham Palace."

~

EVERYTHING WAS WOOD-CHIP BROWN. MORE BROWN EVEN than my apartment in Winslow, if that was possible. The couches were brown, the shag carpeting was beige, and the "entertainment unit" was a dark brown table with an old-fashioned TV that probably weighed fifty pounds.

Where is the light and bright furniture I saw in the online pictures? I walked down the short hallway and peeked into the bedroom.

My heart sank. No light and bright furniture here, either. The headboard, dresser, and end tables, were—of course—brown. The bed didn't look like the queen-size one from the photos, and I guessed that it was a full size. It was covered by a brown and yellow wool crocheted blanket like my grandmother used to make, and that we only pulled out on the coldest days in Winslow. The carpet was the same beige shag I had seen in the living room.

"Are you done looking around?" Harriet yelled from the front of the condo. "I have things to do."

Shaking my head, I walked out of the bedroom. "Just let me check out the kitchen," I said.

Peeking in, I didn't see any stainless-steel appliances. Instead, I saw an old white refrigerator (finally, something was light and bright in this place) and counters made of brown Formica. The kitchen table was small and round, and made of wood, with four wooden chairs covered with dark brown seat covers. Next to the kitchen table I noticed something on the wall—

I let loose a blood-curdling scream, a sound I hadn't heard myself make since I saw *Jaws*. My arm had flown up at the same time, and Harriet looked where I was pointing.

"That's what you're screaming about?" Harriet rolled her eyes. "What—you've never seen a palmetto before?" I shook my head. "You'll get used to them," she said.

"A palmetto?" I asked, still horrified. "I thought a palmetto was a little tree."

"That too," said Harriet, snickering. "But everyone in Florida knows when you say 'palmetto,' you mean the palmetto bugs. Sometimes they fly."

I shuddered and noticed that the dark brown (of course), three-inch cockroach, was moving. "Oh, my God, it's crawling up the wall. How am I going to get rid of it?"

Harriet looked around. "Jeez, they didn't even leave you with paper towels or anything." Then she looked at me and said, "Give me your purse."

"Wh-what?"

"Just give me your purse," she said.

"I used all of my Kleenex on the ride down—" I said.

Harriet grabbed my handbag from my arm, and I wondered if she'd planned to catch the bug inside of it, thinking how gross it would be to have its buggy germs all over my stuff.

Thwack.

"That's how it's done," Harriet said, lowering my purse from where she smacked the wall with it. "You'll learn. This place has been vacant for a while but once the exterminator starts coming every month, things'll get better." She tried to hand me back my purse, with the bug stuck to it. "You might want to clean that off."

I backed away from her. "I'm not sure it'll come off," I

said, my voice cracking. "It's the new fabric bag from Coach. The girls at the office chipped in when I left, and I've been really careful with it since the background color is so pale."

Harriet sighed and, still holding my purse, fished what looked like a well-used Kleenex from her pocket. Why the hell hadn't she used that instead of my purse? I thought, my frustration quickly shifting to anger. She wrapped the bug in the Kleenex and dumped it into the garbage disposal.

"Harriet—wait—you're not supposed to put Kleenex in—"

Harriet turned on the garbage disposal and it *roared.* She shut it off after a few seconds and gave a self-satisfied smile. "It works for me."

I looked around again. "This place doesn't look anything like what I saw online. The pictures showed light modern furniture, stainless steel appliances, and—"

"Oh, you probably saw Betsy Jamieson's condo. She has a nice place, so they might have used photos from her unit to market these condos."

"Is that legal?" I fumed.

"What? Do I look like an attorney?" asked Harriet. "Besides, why do you think you got such a good price on the rent?"

"I figured because it was the off-season."

"That's true, but still, prices have been going up. But lucky you. Mrs. Altman's kids couldn't decide whether to sell the condo or not, so they asked the rental company here to rent it out 'as is' during the off-season. Everything is just the way Mrs. Altman left it."

I sighed. "This is so depressing. It reminds me of my place back home."

"Back home is Bah-ston, huh? I figured out the accent."

"Actually, I'm from Winslow. It's a small town about—"

"So, how many times have you been married?"

"How many—oh, only once. I'm divorced."

"I'm from Long Island," said Harriet. Her accent was so heavy it sounded like "Lon-guy-lin."

"Been married three times. My last husband, Carmelo, was a saint, may he rest in peace." She made the sign of the cross.

"Speaking of men," she said, "I know how to cheer you up." Her eyes went so wide with glee that the tips of her false eyelashes superimposed onto her eyebrows. "You can come with me to the Mature Singles Dance tonight. I'll come by for you."

"A dance?" I shuddered. "I haven't been to a dance in years, not since Parents Without Partners. I'm really not into dances. To me, they're like meat markets."

"So they're like meat markets, so what? That's why you have to go early—to get the best cuts." Harriet elbowed me and I flinched. "Besides, you told me on the phone you don't know anybody down here. Maybe you'll meet Mister Right."

"No really, I'm exhausted, and I've got so much to do—get groceries, unpack. I don't even know where the supermarket is and—"

"Listen, I gotta go," Harriet interrupted, already breezing toward the open door. "Take a left at the stop sign down the street and keep going for about a mile to get to the shopping center. You can't miss it. Anyhoo, see you at 6:30 p.m."

I sighed. "6:30? But why so early?"

"Yeah, they go out for early-bird specials and they don't

want to go home after and wait until eight or nine o'clock for the dance to start." She started to shut the door behind her.

"Well, okay, but what should I wear?"

Harriet rolled her eyes. "Whatever. Just dress like you're going to a dance. What is this—high school?" She smirked and walked out of the condo.

Well, I wanted to get out of the slow lane and experience the Florida lifestyle. I might as well get started. Besides, I didn't have to get up and go to work tomorrow.

Even though Palmetto Pointe was not what I expected, for now I had a place to live, sun, and maybe even a new friend.

My cellphone rang. It was Lori.

"How's the place, Mom?"

"It's great," I said, putting my big-girl pants on. "Just what I need to start my new life. In fact, I'm going to a dance tonight."

CHAPTER 5

Luckily, my favorite blue jeans, short-sleeve white cotton sweater, and blue pumps were easy to find in my suitcase. I had lost some weight over the last few weeks, probably due to the excitement of moving to Florida, so my jeans looked really nice. I smiled at myself in the mirror and began putting on my lipstick.

Then I heard a horrendous pounding on the door. I jumped and smeared my lipstick. My heart in my throat, I looked through the peephole and saw that it was Harriet. When I opened the door, Harriet practically fell into the condo. She was dressed to the nines, and all in black—skintight dress, black heels, gold jewelry, and bracelets clanking. Her long black hair was down, she wore full makeup, and she reeked of perfume.

"Harriet, you scared me. Why didn't you ring the doorbell?"

"Hmph, you sure are a scaredy-cat. For your information, the doorbells here never work." She looked me up and down and frowned.

"You're not ready? Hurry up and get dressed."

"Um—I am dressed. This is what I'm wearing. I figured the dance would be kind of casual, being on a Tuesday, and—"

Harriet shook her head and sighed. "Well, I guess anything goes these days."

She waved her car keys around, the clatter as dramatic as her tone.

"I'll be glad to drive, Harriet. Just tell me how to get there."

"Nah. I'd rather take my car. Come on. Move it."

A few minutes later we were coasting along in Harriet's Toyota Camry.

"So—you've heard of Monday Night at the Movies, huh? Well, this is Tuesday Night at the Temple. Once a month, Temple Shalom has this Interfaith Dance for Mature Singles."

"Thanks for inviting me, Harriet. I just got off the phone with my daughter and told her I was already going to a dance. Do you have kids?"

"Two sons. They're on the West Coast. I don't hear from them much unless they need money. No grandkids. What about you?"

"My daughter, Lori, is married, with two kids. My son-in-law was offered a job in Delaware so they moved there a few months ago. Lori wanted me to retire and move to Delaware near them."

"Dela-*where?* Who retires to Delaware? It doesn't even sound like a real place. Anyhoo, here we are."

~

The parking lot was full of beige and white Toyotas and Honda sedans a few years old, with some late-model Hyundais and Cadillacs.

"Last time I went here, I met this guy, Barry. He's such a bee-yoo-tee-full dancer." She pointed at a black Cadillac sedan and nodded. "Oh good, he's here." Then she frowned. "Huh. I wonder how he got a handicapped sticker. I wanna get one, too."

"A handicapped sticker?"

Harriet just ignored me, and continued circling the parking lot, looking for a space.

"Look, Harriet, there's a spot," I said, pointing to a space in the next row.

"That's too far away. I can barely walk in these heels."

She drove around for a few more minutes and accelerated when she saw a car backing out of a space near the temple. After parking, she checked her lipstick, sprayed on more perfume, and turned to me.

"Do you think I need more perfume? It's the new one from Avon. *Far and Away Infinity*."

"No, you're fine," I said, choking on the smell.

Harriet shrugged, and bolted out the door. Then she stopped short.

"Say, you got a breath mint on you? I taste like I gargled with shit or something."

I came around to the other side of the car, fished in my purse, gave the pack to Harriet, and heard a thunk. Did I drop something?

I started looking around for the source of the noise when Harriet grabbed my arm.

"Come on already. While we're still young."

"I thought I heard something drop—"

"Nothing dropped. Let's go."

Harriet dragged me out of the parking lot so fast that I had trouble keeping up with her.

"I thought you said you couldn't walk in your heels," I said, breathlessly.

~

"Unchained Melody" was playing as Harriet pushed open the heavy door with the sign saying "WELCOME TO THE TEMPLE SHALOM INTERFAITH DANCE FOR MATURE SINGLES."

It was pretty much what I expected. The lighting was supposed to be flattering, but everyone looked strangely hollow-eyed. The haze of perfume and aftershave. Clusters of women everywhere—sipping diet soda, nibbling on tortilla chips, talking, laughing, preening—dressed in outfits ranging from tailored pants to clingy dresses like Harriet's. And, of course, hardly any men.

A few couples were out on the floor, their moves so smooth you could tell they had danced together often.

From out of nowhere, a man in a Barney purple shirt grabbed Harriet and pulled her onto the dance floor. She followed his moves perfectly as he whirled and twirled her, dipping her low, and then, as a grand finale, pulling her up so she sat on his knee. I figured this was probably the amazing Barry that Harriet had told me about.

Suddenly I felt a tap on my arm. I turned to see a short, stooped man with a comb-over. He jutted his chin toward the floor. "Wanna dance?"

Before I had a chance to reply, he grabbed my hand and brought me to the center of the dance floor. "This your first time here?" he asked. His breath smelled like garlic and I jerked backward, which he apparently took as not being able to follow his steps. "Relax," he told me, "go with the music."

I kept trying to turn away from him, since he had started singing along with Paul Anka, "Put Your Head on My Shoulder." At last, the song ended. Before he had a chance to say anything else, I hurried over to one of the few empty seats on the other side of the room. Luckily, Garlic Guy asked another woman to dance.

Sitting there by myself with nobody to talk to, watching Harriet, Barry, and the other couples cha-cha across the dance floor, I felt a wave of loneliness. Years back I had gone to dances with my best friends from back home, Roz and Judy. The Three Musketeers we called ourselves. Now that Judy had passed away, it was just me and Roz. And now that Roz was with Cy, I felt like a third wheel most of the time.

And I wouldn't mind someone to dance with, someone who didn't have garlic breath, and could carry on a conversation. But who was I kidding?

Maybe I'm too old to start over. Maybe I should never have left Massachusetts. Maybe I should pack up and move in with Lori and Greg and the kids in Delaware.

The music changed, and I snapped out of my reverie. Enough of this pity party, I told myself sternly. Feeling restless and bored, I fled to the ladies' room just to kill time.

As I stood in front of the mirror fixing my hair, Harriet rushed in. "Oh, there you are," she cried, "I was looking all over for you. What's your name again?"

"Are you kidding? You invited me to this dance and you don't even know my name? It's Debbie. Debbie Gordon."

"Whatever." Harriet shrugged. "I'm not good with names. Anyhoo, Barry wants to go to this new jazz place by the beach. It's on the other side of town so you need to find a ride home."

"Find a ride home? But—but I don't know anybody here."

"Oh, pul-eeze." Harriet waved a dismissive hand. "I'm sure you can find somebody here from Palmetto Pointe. Why don't you ask around?"

"Ask around?" I repeated dumbly. Did she actually expect me to go up to people I didn't even know and ask for a ride home?

Harriet rolled her eyes. "Isn't there anyone you could call?"

"No, I just said—"

"Oh, crap, look at the time," Harriet said, after glancing at her watch. "Barry's gonna be pissed. You'll just have to call a taxi or Uber—whatever."

I wasn't happy about it, but okay, I could do Uber; my phone had the app. I fished in my tiny purse for my cell phone, and to my horror, I realized it wasn't there. Crap. I must have dropped my phone when I was looking for breath mints. I knew I heard something drop. I felt like crying.

Humiliating as it was, I would have to borrow Harriet's phone. Which, as it turned out, wasn't an option because Harriet didn't even own a cell phone. "I can't be bothered with all that tech stuff," she said airily.

Trying to keep my voice steady, I said, "Couldn't you just drop me off at Palmetto Pointe and have Barry follow you or something?"

"It's out of the way and Barry wants to leave now. You're on your own, kiddo."

That got me crazy. Harriet had pushed me too far.

"Harriet Bertulli, you cannot leave somebody stranded in the ladies' room of a temple," I thundered. "This is a house of worship, and you are committing a sin before God."

Harriet didn't say a word. That got me even more worked up.

"God will punish you," I ranted on. "Think about those plagues in Egypt … pestilence, frogs, locusts …" For the life of me, I couldn't remember the other plagues. "Locusts," I repeated wildly, "and—um—bedbugs."

Harriet just stared at me. Finally, she opened her mouth.

"It's your own fault," she shot back. "You shoulda taken your own car."

I choked. "Taken my own car? I offered to, but you said no, you'd rather drive."

"Well, I figured you'd probably meet someone, but not the way you're dressed, like the Farmer in the Dell." Harriet walked into a stall and slammed the door. "Who the hell wears denim to a dance?"

"I do, Harriet Bertulli," came a voice from another stall. The toilet flushed and a moment later, out came a plump, pretty woman with silver curls. She wore a denim skirt and blouse. "It's me, Maria, your neighbor. I recognized your voice."

Maria went to the sink and washed her hands vigorously as though she were scrubbing up for surgery. "I heard the whole conversation. You should be ashamed of yourself, running off and leaving this poor girl," she waved a soapy hand at me, "to fend for herself. You tried to pull that on me at the Palmetto Pointe barbecue, remember?"

"And you dumped me, too," came a strong New-England-tinged voice from the third stall, "At a Friday morning pickleball clinic."

"Hah—another country heard from," Harriet snapped. "Who's that?"

"It's Fran." The toilet flushed and a tall woman with a redhead's fair complexion emerged and joined Maria at the sink.

"You know, Harriet, just because you meet up with a guy doesn't mean you can dump whoever you came with." Maria yanked at the paper towel as if for emphasis. "It's a girl code."

"Well, if you're such a Mother Teresa, then you can give what's-her-name a ride home," Harriet retorted. "She lives right near you."

"I was just about to offer. I'll be happy to give what's-your-name a ride home," Maria smiled at me.

"Oh, thank you. I really appreciate it. And I do have a name. It's Debbie Gordon."

Harriet flushed the toilet and flounced out to the full-length mirror. She examined her hair, putting a finger in her mouth to make a spit curl.

"Ewww, Harriet, that is so gross," Maria cried. "You didn't even wash your hands."

Harriet gave us a withering glance and stomped out of the ladies' room.

We laughed and left the bathroom, Maria leading the way to the dance area. More and more women were leaving, and the few men there had already been scooped up, so we had our choice of seats.

As we sat down, I said, "You know, we New Englanders have to stick together."

"Yes," said Fran, laughing. "I noticed that we all have New England accents, too. I'm from New Hampshire. Where are you from, Debbie?"

"I'm from Massachusetts. And you, Maria?"

"Rhode Island," she said.

We watched the dancers, and after a few minutes, I leaned over and whispered, "Isn't this better than having a good time?"

Maria burst out laughing. "You're right. Let's get out of here."

"How about stopping off for a glass of wine on the way home? It's "Twofer Tuesday" night at Applebee's. They have discounts on appetizers, too," said Fran.

"I'd love to, but I really need to get home to check on my mom," Maria said. "Raincheck?"

"That sounds really fun," I said. "And I can't thank you guys enough for rescuing me."

"I'd have spoken up sooner," Maria said, "but you were giving such a great performance I didn't want to miss a word."

The soft Florida evening felt like a welcoming hug as we walked out to the parking lot. "Oh, look," Maria cried, "is that a cell phone over there near the grass?"

Sure enough it was my cell phone, none the worse for wear. I held it up triumphantly. "The miracle at the temple," I sang out. "Thank You, God."

I was feeling giddy. "I can't believe you're my neighbors," I gushed. "I hardly knew my neighbors up north."

"It's kind of the same way here," Maria said. "One day I noticed this couple coming out of their place a few doors away. I'd never seen them before, so I asked, 'Are you new here?' And the woman said, 'We've been living here for seven years.' Well, actually they were snowbirds, but still… you know?"

"I'm kind of embarrassed to say that I didn't even know Maria's name until tonight," said Fran. "I've seen her around, but I never spoke with her."

"Well, even though she ditched all of us at some point, I guess we have Harriet to thank for meeting each other. Let's exchange numbers." We pulled out our cell phones.

"And I'll drive you home, since Maria has to get to her mom," said Fran.

"Thanks, Fran. Would you mind pointing out the grocery store? I was too busy chatting with Harriet on the way here."

"Sure thing."

I smiled as Fran drove. She wasn't a big talker, which was fine with me. Both women were interested in going out for wine and a bite to eat. We already had a lot in common.

CHAPTER 6

I smiled as the Paul Newman lookalike asked me to dance. How lucky to get to dance to my favorite song. I heard the melody to "I Got Friends in Low Places" and then realized I couldn't hear the words. Oh, it was my cellphone ringing, waking me up from a nice dream. Darn.

"Hello," I said drowsily.

"Mom, you didn't call me. It's 9:30 a.m. You always call me by 8:30 a.m."

"Oh, sorry, Lori. I was exhausted from yesterday, and I guess I slept late."

"Well I've been worried. You never sleep past eight o'clock.

Uh—hello, I thought. I'm retired. I can sleep as late as I want.

"Anyway, did you have fun at the dance?"

"Actually, yes, kind of," I started. But I didn't really want to get into all of it then, because I hadn't had any coffee.

"Would you mind if I called you later? I haven't gone

shopping and I don't have coffee or anything for breakfast. And I'm starving."

"I'll call you on the way home from work." I knew Lori was busy with work and her family, so I usually spoke with her on her way to or from work. It wasn't always convenient for me, but at least I got to speak to her every day.

"Okay, love you."

"Love you. And watch out for those Florida drivers. I've heard they're awful."

Yeah, I had heard the same thing. But Massachusetts drivers were pretty bad, too, I thought.

On my way to Publix, the nearest grocery store, I saw a McDonald's. Fitting, I thought, Golden Arches for this Golden Girl. I bought my cheap, perfect coffee and an Egg McMuffin, scarfing it down in record time.

Turning into Publix, I saw diagonal rows of parking. Each row faced the opposite way. Huh, I thought, each row only allowed one-way driving. Interesting. That's different than Winslow. Probably safer.

Maneuvering to one of the rows, I saw a space up ahead on the right. Out of the corner of my eye, I saw a car turning into my row, going the wrong way.

"Stop," I yelled, but my windows were up and the air conditioning was on.

The car was about to hit me, and I slammed on the horn. It finally stopped inches away from mine. Then it slowly backed up to let me park.

Shaking, I pulled into the space. What the heck was wrong with these drivers?

When I got out of my car, a woman next to me in a color coordinated yoga outfit was loading her groceries into her SUV.

"I saw what happened," she said. "Are you okay?"

"Yes," I said crisply, now more angry than shaken. "I'm new here, and I've never seen anything like this before."

"I'm from New York, and I've never seen crazier drivers," she said. "Last year, someone drove through the front entrance of the store, through the glass and everything. It took them months to repair it, and they closed the store. We had to go to the Publix out east."

"Wow. Okay, I guess I'll have to bring my A-game every time I go shopping," I said, and we laughed.

Once inside, I was pleasantly surprised to see a light, bright store. Back in Winslow, we had an old Stop & Shop. A newer one was built in the next town over, but it wasn't convenient.

I started in the produce section, my eye drawn to the Sale sign proclaiming "Red Delicious Apples, $6.39 per pound."

What? I had never paid more than three dollars per pound for apples, and that was rare. And this was supposed to be a sale price?

I heard a number being called, and I saw a growing line of people at the deli counter. Not wanting to wait forever, I abandoned the produce and grabbed a number.

Lori called me "The Wolf" because I loved all kinds of meat and protein. The deli was my favorite place. Looking closer, I checked out the prices. "Turkey for $14.99 per pound," I grumbled. "Provolone for $8.99 per pound? Am I in the Twilight Zone?"

"You can get prepackaged deli much cheaper at ALDI," said a lady whizzing by in a motorized shopping cart.

"What's ALDI?"

The woman clapped her hands gleefully. "Let me tell you about it..."

After ten minutes, I had learned all about ALDI. Which was good, because it made the wait go faster.

When my number was called, I limited myself to half a pound of Publix turkey breast and provolone, instead of the Boar's Head brand that I liked but cost more, and I was so hungry that I had a couple of slices of turkey while I shopped.

My second favorite section was frozen foods. First, because I hated to cook and made frozen dinners almost every night. But also, because I love ice cream. Luckily, the Publix brand of ice cream was Buy One, Get One Free (BOGO according to the sign), so I got a chocolate chip and a coffee flavor. When I got to the Cool Whip section, I was delighted to see that they were on BOGO, too. Except that the only containers were on the highest shelf, and I couldn't reach them.

Looking around, I noticed a man a little further down the aisle, looking at frozen vegetables. He looked to be in his early seventies, wearing gym clothes and a baseball cap. I went up to him and asked if he could reach two Cool Whips for me.

"Sure," he said.

He was only about 5'8" or so, but he grabbed them easily.

"You should get some, too," I said. "They're on BOGO," proudly using the new term I learned.

He shook his head. "I make my own whipped cream, thanks."

"You mean—all the time? Or just for special occasions?"

"All the time," he chuckled.

"Wow, your wife sure is lucky," I said, enviously.

"No wife," he laughed, and looked at his phone. "Sorry—I've got to run. I have a coaching session soon."

He smiled, and I sighed as he walked away. No wife, not bad looking, and cooks. Too bad I didn't get his name, I thought. But one thing was for sure. I'd continue visiting my nearby Publix, even with the high prices, and I hoped I'd see him again.

CHAPTER 7

On the way back from picking up my mail, I heard a wheezing voice say, "You know, you got a lot of mail for one person."

I turned around and saw the same eighty-something man I'd seen whenever I picked up my mail. Every day he would sit in front of his condo on a piano stool and sun himself like an old lizard.

"They're mostly ads and early-bird coupons," I replied.

He sat up straighter, and looked up at me, with his New York Giants baseball cap pulled firmly over his head, and his trifocals winking and blinking in the bright Florida sun.

"You like to go to early birds?" he asked, sounding hopeful.

"I haven't been yet, since I just moved in."

"Well, I don't think I'm ready to move in together," he said. "But we should at least know each other's names. I'm Stanley Stein."

I didn't really want to get into a conversation with him, but I was raised to be polite.

"I'm Debbie Gordon."

"I have lots of early-bird coupons, Darcy. I even have a two-for-one coupon for Wendy's. They give you a nice hamburger. We could go there later—"

"Uh. I have to get home. I've got something in the microwave," I told him, and ran off as fast as I could.

As I walked up the stairs to my condo, I heard my cell phone ringing. I ran to the door and grabbed the phone from the kitchen table. "How come you're all out of breath, Mom?" my daughter teased. "Got a hot young stud with you?"

"Right," I snickered. "Although actually, I was rushing away from this guy who hit on me when I went to get my mail."

"Would he get my stamp of approval?" Lori asked innocently.

I groaned. "Ha ha."

Secretly, I was glad Lori was joking around with me. This was the Lori I remembered enjoying so much. It was just the two of us against the world, and we were more than mother and daughter—we were best friends. When she married and had kids, we still spent a lot of time together. Now that she had moved to Delaware, it was almost like our roles were reversed. She was the mom, and I was the daughter. But she still had a great sense of humor when she wasn't focused on worrying about me or talking about me moving to Delaware.

After I finished telling Lori about the mail guy, I said, "And that, my darling daughter, is why I was out of breath when you called."

She laughed. "Wow, Mom, you're a real guy magnet.

Oh, and you're meeting those nice women from the dance today, right?"

"Yep, I'm meeting them at the clubhouse pool after lunch. Anyhow, enough about me. How's everything with you guys?"

Everything was fine, Lori told me. The family was adjusting to their new life in Delaware. Greg liked his job, and the kids were making friends. Zoe, always the social butterfly, was busy with birthday parties and sleepovers. "Oh, and Zack says he can't wait to go to high school because first grade is too hard."

I smiled, picturing my grandkids. How I loved them.

"Look, Mom, I hate to cut you short," Lori said, "but I have to drive the fashionista to the mall. Have a great day. Love you."

"Love you, too. Be safe." Sometimes when I talked to my daughter, it was like a hug across the miles.

Right after I hung up, I got another call. It was Roz. I had told her about meeting Maria and Fran at the dance and figured she'd be happy I had met some new friends. But I was wrong.

"Oh, sure, now that you've got some new people to pal around with, you don't have time for your old friend who's known you through thick and thin," Roz huffed when I told her I couldn't talk too long because I was meeting Maria and Fran. "Well, excuse me, Miss Popularity. Give me a call sometime when you're not so busy."

Roz and I had been friends since the second grade, when I picked her to help me wash the blackboard at school. And even though we had some different interests (she liked Mah Jongg, and I liked reading books), she always had my back and invited us to holiday meals. I realized with a start that this would be my first Thanksgiving in over thirty years without her.

I knew that Roz missed me, and I missed her, too. "Aw, come on, Rozzie-ola, you'll always be Numero Uno."

That mollified her somewhat. "Well, okay then, I'll let you go. Have a good time."

I knew what Roz meant: Have a good time, but not too good.

Palmetto Pointe boasted two Olympic-sized pools at the clubhouse, one for residents only and the other for residents and their guests. I had already been to the resident pool, so I decided to check out the guest pool facilities, for when Lori and the family came for Thanksgiving.

Today the guest pool was crowded, as was the small wading pool for infants and toddlers. I guessed that schools had let out for summer vacation. Kids of all ages were shrieking and splashing in the water, fussed over by grandparents in broad-brimmed hats.

A prominently displayed sign stated, "CHILDREN WEARING DIAPERS ARE NOT PERMITTED IN THE GUEST POOL."

"Come in with Grandma," said a gray-haired woman, holding the hand of a little boy about five years old. A sour-faced man on a nearby lounge chair called out to her, "Hey, lady, is that kid wearing a diaper?"

"No—are you?" she shot back.

The bystanders laughed a little. One thing is for sure, I decided—Palmetto Pointe was certainly not dull. I was enjoying it all, the bright sun, the warm breeze, the sound of kids laughing and playing. On a day like this, anything seemed possible.

After a while, I headed to the residents' swimming pool, which was a misnomer, because hardly anyone did any swimming. Even though I had only been to the pool a few times, I always saw the same thing. Groups of people walked back and forth across the width of the pool, some using full plastic water bottles to do arm exercises. In fact, if you watched them long enough, the motion of the water gave the appearance of a small tsunami. I guess pool walking was the exercise of choice in Palmetto Pointe.

As I waited for Maria and Fran, I settled myself on a plastic lounge chair and reached into my tote bag for the newest issue of *News and Schmooze*, the Palmetto Pointe newspaper. I scanned the listing of various clubs and activities: Pottery Workshop, Long Island Club, Dance-Your-Heart-Out Class for Beginners, none of which grabbed me. I really ought to get involved in some activity. Now that I'm retired, I have the chance to try some new things.

Then, on the last page, a small notice caught my attention: Join the Palmetto Pointe Creative Writing Group. I caught my breath. I had always loved to write, but I had stopped after breaking up with Sam. The excitement I felt just reading about the writers' group made me realize that I still had my passion for writing. And wasn't moving to Florida all about doing what I wanted to do? I tore out the notice carefully, filled out the form, and put it into the special mailbox for residents.

I spotted Maria hurrying over. "Sorry I'm late, Deb." She plunked down on the lounge next to me. "I had to pick up a prescription for Mom, and I stood in line forever. Oh, and Fran can't make it. You know she volunteers at We

Care, and they asked her to work this afternoon. But she's coming tonight to happy hour at Applebee's. I'm really excited."

"Me too." I said.

Maria slathered on sunscreen, then stretched out on the lounge. "The water looks great, but I just want to sit here for a while. Oh, that sun feels so good. Maybe it's not healthy, but I like getting a little color, you know?"

"I sure do know. I look like Casper the Friendly Ghost."

Maria laughed.

It was easy being with Maria. Warm and down-to-earth, she talked about the fact that she was a widow and had moved down here with her mother. Maria spent a lot of time bringing her mother to doctor appointments and making her favorite meals. But today her mom agreed to go on a trip with the Young at Heart club.

"They're going to the outlets in Palm Beach Gardens and having dinner up that way, so they won't be back until 9:00 p.m."

"Great. Then we can have a leisurely happy hour," I smiled. "Tell me more about your family."

I listened to Maria's stories about growing up in Woonsocket, Rhode Island, the only daughter after three boys. "When I was born, the doctor told my mother, 'Well, now you've got your old-age insurance.'"

"Sounds like that policy certainly paid off."

"With dividends," she agreed. "Anyhow, here I am, babbling about myself and I want to know about you, Debbie."

I talked about my daughter, son-in-law, and grandkids, leaving out the fact that Lori was hounding me to move to Delaware. I just wanted to relax and enjoy the day.

"And your condo is nice?" Maria asked.

Oh well, so much for stress-free sunbathing.

"Actually, I think I got stuck with Palmetto Pointe's crummiest rental. It's so dark, with old-fashioned furniture. And I think it needs a good cleaning."

"That stinks," Maria made a sad face.

"Luckily I'm only renting it for six months."

"Six months? Oh no. You're missing the best weather," said Maria.

"Yes, but I got it for a great price, since it's the offseason. Then I was hoping to buy an inexpensive place in the area."

Maria nodded. "You picked the most affordable place. Palmetto Pointe isn't fancy, but it's fun, and comfortable."

I nodded and smiled. I didn't need fancy. Fun and comfortable sounded just right to me.

"And I'm happy to help you look for places. I'm also really great at cleaning if you want me to help spruce up your rental."

Cleaning? Wait—that wasn't a subtle request for help. "I can clean it myself. I'm sure you have better things to do."

"Not really, but if you change your mind, I'm happy to help."

Maria laid back on the lounge chair and closed her eyes.

Then I started second-guessing myself. Maybe I said no too quickly. I was just used to doing things on my own, but it would have been nice to have some help cleaning my place, and someone to commiserate with about its ugliness. If I was going to live my best life in Florida, I would need to get better about asking for help.

"I was just at Publix the other day," I said, hoping to continue our conversation. "The prices were crazy. It seems like prices are going up everywhere."

Maria nodded and opened her eyes.

"I think I'm going to look for a part-time job. I don't want to work at Starbuck's or in retail. I'd like another office job, so I'm not on my feet all the time."

Maria sat up and looked excited. "It just so happens that I was speaking with Joyce Davis the other day, and she said they were looking for part-time help at the Banyan Beach city offices. I don't remember much, other than you need good typing skills."

"Who's Joyce Davis?"

"She's actually in your building, but she never leaves her apartment. She's in her nineties and seems to know about everything and everybody at Palmetto Pointe and in Banyan Beach."

"How is that possible if she never leaves her apartment?"

"It's a mystery," said Maria. "But I check in with her every week to make sure she's okay, and she gives me all the latest news. I'll call her later and get you more details."

"That would be fantastic, thanks, Maria. I'm a really fast typist, and good at technology, too, since I managed our legal office for the last few years before I retired."

Maria looked intrigued. "Do you know how to get viruses off a computer?"

I nodded.

"That's amazing. If you could help me do that, you'd be a lifesaver."

"Of course I'll help you. But right now, I'm sweating. Let's go cool off."

We went into the pool and walked back and forth like everyone else, chatting about all kinds of things. After about an hour, we headed back to our lounges to get more sun.

Maria's cell phone was ringing and she dug it out of her bag. "Hello. What?" She sat down heavily. "Where are you? *Mãe*, please stop crying." Silence. "Let me talk to the driver."

More silence. "Yes, all right. I'm sorry, too. I'll be there as soon as I can."

She clicked off the phone. "My mother had a meltdown on the trip. I have to go get her. By the time I get back and get her settled, it'll be too late for happy hour. I'm so sorry. But you and Fran should go." She looked as if she were about to cry.

"No, please, it's okay." I forced a smile. "We'll do it another time. I hope your mom is all right." We packed up our stuff and walked to our cars. Maria hugged me.

I sat in the car and called Fran to tell her about the change of plans. Then I drove home, disappointed. Oh, well, as a great philosopher once said, Shit Happens.

But as I neared my condo, Shit Happens took on a more personal meaning.

I could hardly believe my eyes.

CHAPTER 8

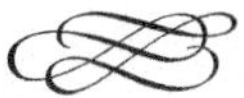

For a moment, I thought maybe I had misread the numbers. But no, my eyes had not deceived me.

Somebody had taken my parking space. A cardinal sin.

Who would do such a thing? Everybody knows that the First Commandment of the Florida condo lifestyle is "Thou shalt not take someone's assigned parking space."

Or at least that's how I felt. I had never had a parking space before. My apartment building in Winslow had limited parking, most of it a long, cold walk from my building. My parking space here was something I treasured, especially when it was hot and during the occasional afternoon downpour.

Yet there, big as life, sat a black Lexus with New Jersey license plates in parking space Number 16, the permanent parking spot assigned to me.

My space had been hijacked. And it wasn't as if the perp had simply made a mistake. It was so obvious. The assigned parking spaces had bright red numbers and said,

"Reserved for Residents Only." The parking spaces without numbers were outlined in bright green and said "For Guests."

Not sure what to do, I parked right in back of the Lexus so the owner couldn't get out, then tooted my horn nonstop, hoping somebody would come and see what the commotion was all about. But not one door flew open, which was not surprising, since it was around four o'clock and most of the residents of Palmetto Pointe were probably dozing in front of TV sets or off to early-bird specials.

I sat there in shock, wondering who the Lexus belonged to.

Spotting a man and woman by the mailbox, I got out of my car and hurried over to them. "Somebody's in my sparking space," I cried breathlessly, "a black Lexus with New Jersey plates."

"That's terrible," the woman said, shaking her head. "Why do people do that?"

"Do you know who might have someone visiting from New Jersey?" I asked.

The man spoke up. "I saw two people with suitcases going into Mister High—I mean Stanley Stein's place. You know Stanley, don't you? The guy who sits outside on a stool?"

"Oh, I certainly do. Thanks so much."

I scurried down the walkway to his condo and rang the bell. I had to keep ringing it because the TV was so loud, and then I remembered that most doorbells in Palmetto Pointe did not work. Finally I began to pound on the door.

"Hold your horses, I'm coming," called a familiar voice from inside. Stanley Stein unlocked the door and squinted up at me. "Oh, I thought you were the delivery guy. We ordered Chinese from China Palace."

I was in no mood for small talk. "Listen, do you have someone visiting you with a black Lexus?"

"What—did you hit my car?" A burly man wearing a sweat-stained I Love Banyan Beach t-shirt lumbered over.

"Somebody hit your brand-new car?" a woman shrieked, "Elliott, I told you they don't know how to drive down here."

"I hope you got good insurance, lady," Elliott growled. "What happened?"

"Nothing happened. It's just that you're parked in my space. You need to move your car."

Stanley stared at me. "Oh, now I recognize you." He turned to the woman who was his mirror image only much heavier, with the same tufts of white and ginger-colored hair and poached-egg eyes. "She's the one I told you about, Freda."

"Oh, the lady who gets a lot of mail." She smiled archly at me. "Don't worry, I'm not Stanley's girlfriend, I'm his sister, Freda. And this is my son, Elliott."

"How do you do?" I said, as politely as I could while gritting my teeth. "But please, Elliott, you're parked in my space, and that's against the rules."

"What's the difference? There are other spaces."

"But you're in my space, the one assigned to me. It's clearly marked Number 16 in red." I tried to stay calm. "And it so happens I'm sixteen."

"Funny—you don't look sixteen," Elliott said. The three of them howled.

"You won't be laughing when you try to get out," I told

him. "I'm parked right in back of you. Come outside and I'll show you."

Elliot's tiny eyes narrowed into slits. "What'd you pull? I bet you did something to my car." He followed me out to the parking area with Stanley and Freda trailing behind.

"Okay, now do you see what I mean? Red spaces are for residents; green are for guests," I explained. "You can park in plenty of other places."

"If there's plenty of places, what are you bitching about?" Elliott was busily checking the Lexus for dings and scrapes. "My uncle Stanley is a resident here, too, but he's not making a federal case out of it."

"That's right. And I don't even have a parking space." Stanley sounded aggrieved. "They never gave me one."

"Maybe it's because you never learned to drive," Freda offered.

"So what? Then my nephew could have my space."

"But that isn't your space, it's mine." They were making me nuts.

Just then a silver Mercedes Benz pulled into the adjoining residents parking space. A tall, striking blonde wearing big wraparound sunglasses got out. I had never seen the woman before, although I had noticed the car in the lot and idly wondered who in Palmetto Pointe drove a new Mercedes.

In desperation, I cried, "Oh, I see our new condo director now," and ran over to the woman.

"Please help me," I stage whispered, "I'm Debbie Gordon from 725 and this jerk from New Jersey parked in my space and he won't move his car and—" With that, I burst into tears.

Oh God, why did I do that? I tried to keep my emotions

under control, but sometimes when I get frustrated, I cry. It's so embarrassing.

"Aw, come on, what's the big deal?" Elliott bellowed. "So I accidentally parked in her space."

"But he's not supposed to, and he knows it," I sniffed. "And he won't move his car."

"So I'll move my car tomorrow when we go out to breakfast, okay?" Elliot had this shit-eating grin on his face. You could see he was awed by the blonde stranger, who was certainly not your typical Palmetto Pointe resident.

She stared at me for a moment. Then, looking very imposing in her crisp white blouse, navy linen slacks, Gucci purse, and oversized sunglasses, she strode over to Elliott.

"You move that goddamn car, and move it now, mister," she told him.

"Gimme a break. I'll do it later. We got Chinese food coming."

She looked at her watch. "I'm counting to ten. One two—"

"I'll do it after we—" Elliott started to say but she cut him short.

"I am not only the condo director," she said coolly, arms folded in front of her, "but I am also a retired prison guard. So do not fuck with me, fat boy, or I promise you will wind up in the South Florida Penitentiary with a broomstick up your ass."

"Okay, okay." Elliott gulped and fished the keys from his pocket. He glared at me. "You gotta move that heap of yours so I can get out."

I never moved so fast and Elliott probably never did either. He found a guest parking spot halfway down the street. The three of them hurried back to their condo.

By now, I had stopped crying. I went over to the blonde woman and thanked her profusely. "Oh, my God, that was amazing."

Just then, a horn tooted and a van pulled up with a sign, CHINA PALACE. YOU GET SPECIAL ALL DAY LONG. A young Chinese man got out, carrying three large brown paper bags that had started to soak through.

"Do you know where is apartment number 740?" he called to us.

"That must be the Chinese takeout they ordered," I said.

"Oh, right here." The woman waved the delivery guy over. "We've been waiting for you."

She whipped out some bills from her purse and handed them to him. He thanked her and drove off.

"Wow, that was so cool," I said. "And they were really lusting for that Chinese food. Wouldn't Elliott be pissed to know you intercepted their dinner?"

The woman shrugged. "Look, I don't even want it. It's the principle." She handed the bags to me. "Here, you take them."

"Me? Oh, no I couldn't."

"Sure you could. Bon appétit."

The aroma of the food was so tantalizing I couldn't stop myself from peeping into the bags. Yum—containers of what looked like shrimp lo mein, cashew chicken, pork fried rice.

My mouth watered. When I finally looked up, the woman was gone.

But which way did she go? Where did she live? Who was she? And why would she not only come to the rescue of a perfect stranger, but also pay for all this food?

Later on, after I sampled all the items (my favorite was the cashew chicken), a thought kept nagging at me. Something was familiar about that woman.

Oh, well, another of life's unsolved mysteries. Right now, it was time for dessert. I brewed a cup of green tea and reached for the fortune cookies. Not that I liked them, but I liked to read the sayings, even though they were usually pretty sappy.

The first one said, "Life is a bowl of cherries." The second, equally dumb, said, "Nothing succeeds like success."

The third fortune cookie had a different color paper and a different typeface, as if someone decided to hire a new fortune cookie writer.

I read the message, and a shiver came over me.

The message said, "Someone from your past will come to your aid."

CHAPTER 9

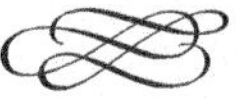

My head swiveled to the left and right as I looked at mansions, with the ocean shimmering between.

I had heard of A1A, the South Florida road that ran along the beach, but it was even more breathtaking than I had imagined.

"That one sold for twenty million last year," Maria said, pointing at a huge, modern-looking house that seemed made of all windows.

My jaw dropped. We had some fancy homes in Winslow, but nothing like this.

Today's beach adventure was a spontaneous activity. One of the best parts of retirement, I decided then and there, was the opportunity to take part in unplanned fun.

Fran had texted us this morning saying she was sorry about missing happy hour, and today looked like a great beach day. Did we want to go? I wasn't sure Maria would be able to go after her mother's meltdown, but Maria texted, *Yes*. I was excited to go, too.

I saw the beach sign up ahead, and Fran got into line for the beach parking lot. After a few minutes we reached the gate.

"That'll be twenty-five dollars," said the parking attendant. I was stunned.

Fran pulled out twenty-five dollars in cash. When she headed toward a parking space, I asked, "Is it always that much?"

"Yep," said Fran. "You can get a beach pass for seventy-five, but I hardly ever go to the beach."

I reached into my tote bag and pulled out a twenty.

"Well, let me put in some money toward it," I said. "Maria brought lunch, and you're using gas—"

Fran waved it off. "You can get it next time."

As Fran drove through the parking lot, I marveled at this difference between Banyan Beach and Winslow beaches. In Winslow, we had no parking fees or permits.

Fran parked under a tree for shade, and Maria pulled her cooler out of the trunk. Fran and I grabbed beach chairs, each of us carrying our tote bags. We trudged along the path, and I looked longingly at the bathroom, but Fran and Maria moved quickly past it, so I followed them to the sand.

"Does this spot look okay?" Maria asked.

"Sure," Fran and I agreed.

After setting up our chairs and towels, Maria and I plopped down in our seats.

"I'm going to talk a walk along the beach," said Fran. "Sand-walking is great exercise."

"No wonder she stays so thin," Maria mumbled.

I figured that Fran wasn't a sun worshiper, either. She

was wearing a long-sleeved, high-necked shirt over her bathing suit, and a straw hat that covered her fair skin.

Maria took off her cover-up and started putting on sunscreen. When she handed it to me, my hands felt shaky. I was probably hungry, with the Florida sun fueling my appetite. When I looked at my watch, it said 10:30 a.m. Darn, too early for lunch.

Maria and I laid back on our lounges.

"How are you enjoying Palmetto Pointe so far?" Maria asked.

"Well, the inmates are definitely running the asylum." Maria laughed and nodded. "Speaking of—I had a crazy experience in the parking lot yesterday, but I'll wait until Fran gets back to tell you both."

Maria frowned. "I hate waiting. Can't you give me a hint?"

"Sure," I laughed. "It involves this old guy who sits on a piano stool."

"Oh, that's Stanley Stein," she chuckled. "But everyone calls him Mister Highpockets, because he wears his pants up to his armpits."

"Yes, I noticed that," I said, laughing with her. "Oh, and I have some questions—like who thought up the name 'Palmetto Pointe' with an *e* at the end, no less? I just learned that even though a palmetto is a little palm tree, when people use the word 'palmetto' in Florida, they mean a big cockroach."

Maria nodded. "You're right, but for some reason, people seem to like the word 'palmetto' here. Boca Raton has a Palmetto Parkway and a Palmetto Circle. Go figure."

"Maybe so, but up North, they'd never name a place

'Cockroach Pointe,' especially an Over-55 community," I said, and we had a fit of giggles.

"And Harriet Bertulli is my next question. Does everyone call her the 'Black Widow' because of what she wears? I have to admit, when I first met her, the song 'Don't Fear the Reaper' started playing in my head. Except that I did fear her."

Maria chuckled. "Well, I don't know if we should fear her, but all three of her husbands died in mysterious circumstances."

"Really?"

"Yep. The first one drowned, the second one choked on something, and the third one, 'Carmelo the Saint,' had a heart attack."

"Maybe she just had really bad luck."

"That's possible," said Maria. "But the first husband didn't know how to swim, and Harriet suggested they cool off in the ocean. She was the only one eating with her second husband when he choked and died, and she and Carmelo were alone when he had his fatal heart attack."

"How did you hear about all of this?"

"Joyce Davis," Maria replied.

Shaking my head, I said, "It's never a dull moment around here, unlike up north. Anyway, it's really hot out. Let's go in the water."

We walked in slowly. It was low tide, and the water was shallow. After walking out a good distance, Maria pointed straight ahead.

"Look at that guy," she said.

I turned to see a good-looking Black guy in his early twenties, holding hands and walking in the water with a girl. They were laughing and chatting.

"In my day, we would never have seen an interracial couple together," said Maria. "I'm kind of jealous of kids today. I had a crush on a boy in high school, but I would never have had the guts to go out with him."

I had a burning question, but I didn't know if it would shock Maria. But since she had brought up interracial dating, I thought she might be okay with it.

"Same here. But I also wondered if I would be comfortable going out with someone who might not be circumcised."

"You never had sex with someone uncircumcised?" Maria asked.

"Nope. I only dated Jewish guys, or my mom would have blown a gasket."

"Well," Maria said. "I've only slept with one man, my husband, Rafael. He was uncircumcised. And I loved sex." Sighing, she said, "I really miss it, too."

Maria had just scored higher on my friendship scale. If you can talk about sex and circumcision, you can talk about anything.

We turned to look at the couple again, and all of a sudden, Maria yelled, "You have the best body on the beach."

"Thank you so much," he responded, delighted.

"I can say that because I'm old enough to be your grandmother," Maria replied.

I was speechless. Maria shrugged. "Just because I'm old doesn't mean I can't look."

Nearby I heard laughing, and thought maybe someone had heard the conversation. But it was Fran, throwing a beach ball with some young children near the water. I waved, and Fran made her way over.

"Those kids are adorable," she said.

"If you love kids so much, feel free to take my grandchildren to the beach when they visit," said Maria, laughing.

"I'd love to," said Fran, and Maria and I looked at her, surprised.

Out of the corner of my eye, I saw a man, to our right. He was wearing huge headphones that covered his ears. We could only see the top half of him walking slowly through the water. It looked like he was wearing a safari vest.

"What's he doing?" I asked.

"It looks like he's using a metal detector," said Fran.

As he got closer, I asked him. Sure enough, that's what he was doing.

In the many years I had spent time at the beach, I'd never encountered someone using a metal detector in the water. I was full of questions.

"Have you ever found jewelry?" I asked.

"I find so many rings," he said.

"Wedding rings?" I asked.

"Yep. Every single time I come out here, I find a man's wedding ring in the water."

"Wow Do you ever find engagement rings with diamonds?"

"Yep."

"So do you sell them, or—"

"Nah. I do this for fun, not for the money. I keep all the rings in a jar."

"Hmmm, interesting."

He moved past us and I whispered to the girls, "If anyone is looking for a sugar daddy, I think he's a good candidate."

Maria and Fran burst out laughing. Then my stomach growled.

"Is anyone ready for lunch?" I asked, hopefully.

"Sure," said Maria. We headed back toward our chairs.

Fran stopped abruptly, and pointed to the right.

We noticed an older man, probably in his eighties, with a middle-aged woman who might have been his aide, walking into the water. The man was wearing a snorkel mask and carrying what seemed like a huge net.

"What the heck does he need that net for?" Fran huffed. "I hope it's not to catch these tiny fish that we keep seeing. They'll probably be traumatized. These fools don't realize that we're visitors in the ocean. We need to respect the creatures that call it home."

"Uh, Fran, I didn't know you were so passionate about ocean conservation," I said.

"I've been into it ever since I started teaching," she said. "Teaching kids about the ocean and food chains opened my eyes. And don't get me started on littering."

Wow, I thought. You just never know about people.

Fran kept her eyes on the man. Apparently when she was championing ocean creatures, she became fearless. "Sir, I'm just wondering—what are you planning to do with that net?"

I braced myself for his reaction.

"I use it to see the little fishies that nip at my feet," he said, pleased with himself.

"Why do you do that?"

"Because it gives me something to do," he answered.

"Do you know you're probably traumatizing those fish?" Fran continued.

"What?" asked the man, confused. The aide just looked worried. Fran looked fierce.

"They're just tiny fish. When you catch them in a net, they don't know what's happening. Why are you catching them in a net when you can see them using your snorkel?"

"That's ridiculous," the man protested. "I'm just having a little fun."

"Oh—so it's all about you?" asked Fran.

"Yes," he yelled. "It's all about me."

With that, his aide pulled him aside and they wandered farther down the beach, presumably so he could catch his fish without Fran's commentary.

"What a *schmuck*," I said, shaking my head. "Maria, you probably know that *schmuck* means a jerk, but the actual Yiddish translation is penis."

For once, Maria was speechless. Fran just looked confused and started turning red. She hadn't been part of our earlier conversation. It was time to change the subject. Plus, my bladder was about to burst.

I took Fran and Maria aside and whispered, "Fran, since you know about ocean stuff, is it okay if I pee in the ocean? I don't want to ruin the ecological balance in the ocean or whatever, but I really have to go."

"Sure," said Fran. "Fish pee and poop in the ocean, too."

"Uh—TMI," I said. "But I'll move far away so I won't get any on you two."

"TMI," said Maria. "We can head back to the chairs and I'll start putting out lunch."

Ahhh. Relief. Now all I felt in my stomach was a giddy feeling. I had successfully broached the subjects of sex and peeing with Maria and Fran. Maria seemed better with conversations about sex, and Fran was more comfortable with peeing. Either way, they weren't the kind of conversations I would have with acquaintances. These friends were keepers.

LUNCH WAS WORTH THE WAIT. MARIA HAD MADE HOMEMADE fried chicken, potato salad, and lemon bars.

"You know you can buy fried chicken already made at Publix, right," said Fran, her mouth full.

Maria rolled her eyes. "Yes, but it's not the same."

"Well, Maria, you will never have any competition from me in the cooking department," I said. "I wouldn't even know how to start making fried chicken."

"It's actually easy," she said. "You just—"

"No," I interrupted. "I don't want to know. That way I can be blissfully ignorant if the time ever comes when someone asks me to make it. Besides, yours is so delicious."

As I grabbed a second lemon bar, Maria asked, "How the heck do you have such a big appetite and stay so slim?"

"I have no idea," I said. "My appetite started increasing right before I came down to Florida, but I've been losing weight. Maybe I need more food to have the energy to live my best life." I laughed, but the truth is I'd started to wonder about my increased appetite and need to visit the bathroom more often.

"You need to have that checked out, Debbie. Did you find a primary care doctor yet?" Maria asked. "It's a must down here. Otherwise, if you get sick, you're up you-know-where."

Both she and Fran belonged to MediSource, the HMO

of choice in Palmetto Pointe. I had never belonged to an HMO before, but when in Palmetto Pointe, do as the Palmetto Pointees do.

"As a matter of fact, yes." I had signed up with MediSource and selected Banyan Beach Medical Associates as my primary care group (because their ads in the newspaper were the biggest). And I chose Warren Ross, M.D. as my doctor because he was the one who had the earliest available appointment.

"My appointment is in a couple weeks."

"Good," said Maria. "I'm sure you have nothing to worry about."

I'm glad she was sure, because I wasn't. Something felt off, but I didn't know what.

~

Back at home, I called Lori.

"That kind of stuff never happened at beaches here," Lori agreed. "Those sound like *Huffington Post Weird News* stories."

"In Florida, truth can be stranger than fiction," I said.

"Do you remember when we'd get French fries with malt vinegar at the beach?" Lori asked.

I did. "Oh, yeah. That makes me hungry. I could go for some fish and chips. They use a local fish called mahi-mahi for fish and chips here a lot, but I prefer cod or flounder."

"Same here. And Delaware doesn't really have any good fish-and-chips places. That's something I miss, too," Lori said.

"Well, at least we both have beaches. I couldn't live without them, could you?" I asked.

"No," she said. "Remember when you would pack fruit..."

Memories began flooding in. Good ones. Making sandcastles on the beach when Lori was little. Going to the beach with Roz when Lori was in high school and didn't want to hang out with me. Taking a walk along the beach on a summer morning.

My life up north hadn't been all bad, I reminded myself. I had found moments of joy. I just wanted more of them, that's all.

CHAPTER 10

"Might as well share, might as well smile. Life goes on for a little bitty while…"

With my car radio at full volume, I sang along as I drove to Applebee's. I loved country music so much Roz called me a "Jewish redneck."

I had to drive around for a few minutes until I could find a space.

Wednesday night was Ladies' Night at Applebee's, with discounted drinks and appetizers. When I walked in, it was packed with women, mostly over sixty, in groups of two or three, chatting and standing in the bar area with a glass of wine in their hands.

"I guess the third time is the charm," I said to Fran and Maria. "I'm glad we finally made it."

They smiled and Maria said, "Let me put our names in so we can get a table." She walked up to the hostess stand, which had a long line.

While we were waiting for Maria, I looked around and learned about casual Florida mature-lady fashion—bright shirts and capri pants, with open-toed sandals and wedges. Lots of deep tans, of course, which set off silver and gold jewelry, and coral or pink manicures and pedicures.

Apparently, Maria got the memo. She was wearing black capri pants and a bright yellow shirt, with black sandals. Fran, however, was wearing a long blue polyester skirt, a light blue button-down Oxford shirt, and loafers. My outfit fell somewhere in the middle. I wore black pants and a khaki-colored blouse that Lori said brought out my hazel eyes, and pumps, since I was always the shortest person in any group. Based on what I saw tonight, I made a mental note to add capri pants and sandals to my wardrobe. And some bright shirts, too. Again, I thought, a part-time job would really come in handy.

"All these tropical colors are giving me a headache," said Fran.

"The women here sure dress differently than what I wore in Winslow," I said.

"Same here. I don't really care about fashion, anyway," said Fran. "I just wear what I wore when I was teaching."

"So what do you wear for casual events, like a BBQ or volunteering?"

"Like I said, I just wear my teaching clothes. Unless I go to the gym or play sports. Then I wear my workout clothes."

"Huh," I said. Meaning—that's crazy.

"Well, I guess you save a lot of money that way," I said.

"That's not why I do it. I just don't care, and I don't want to waste my time on shopping."

Just then Maria walked back to us, frowning. "We have a thirty-minute wait for a table. Is that okay?" Maria asked.

"Okay by me," I said.

"Same here," said Fran.

Maria looked at her watch. "It's okay with me, too, as long as I'm home by nine to check in on Mom."

"Doesn't she have your cell phone number?" I asked.

"Yes, but she gets confused a lot and forgets how to use the phone."

Wow, I thought. That's gotta put a damper on your social life. Poor Maria.

"Okay then, since we're on a schedule, let's get started with our wine while we're waiting for a table," said Fran. Waving down the bartender, she asked, "What do you girls want?"

"I'll have a cabernet," I said. "Me, too," said Maria. "That's three cabernets," Fran told the bartender. We all laughed.

"What are the chances that we all chose cabernet?" said Fran.

"I don't know," I said. "But if we keep hanging out together, we could call ourselves 'The Cabernet Club.'"

Fran clapped her hands. "That's perfect. I really love my cabernet."

"Same here," said Maria. "And this round's on me," she said, handing the bartender a twenty.

When we got our drinks, I raised my glass. "To The Cabernet Club." Maria and Fran raised their glasses and clinked mine. I took a big swig of wine, already starting to feel relaxed.

"By the way, Maria, I love your outfit. The yellow makes your face glow. And those sandals look so comfortable."

"Thank you, Debbie," Maria smiled. "Everyone has these Clark's sandals, but I found them in black patent leather at Beall's. A couple of times a year they have a buy one, get one fifty percent off sale."

"Please let me know when the next one is," I said. "I definitely need to get a Florida wardrobe. Oh—and does anyone wear jeans here? I was the only one wearing them at the dance, so maybe the Black Widow had a point."

"The dances tend to be dressier," said Maria. "I keep gaining weight, and I wanted to wear a skirt, and my denim one was the only one that fit me. But for every day, if I had a figure like you or Fran, I'd wear jeans. Or shorts, if I didn't have spider veins."

"I don't care how I look in shorts. I'd rather be comfortable," said Fran.

I nodded. "Oh, and I need to get some bathing suits, too. Speaking of bathing suits—Fran, we missed you at the pool on Monday."

"Yeah, sometimes I get called in to cover a shift at We Care."

"Right. What exactly does We Care do? Other than care, of course?"

Fran explained that We Care volunteers drove Palmetto Pointe residents to doctor appointments, free of charge. "I usually answer the phone and schedule appointments."

"That's really nice of you, Fran," said Maria. "Were you always into volunteering?"

"Not when George was alive," she said. "I was a third-grade teacher, and I never seemed to have any extra time to volunteer before I retired."

"Wow, a teacher. You must love kids," I said.

"I do," said Fran.

"So how many kids do you have?" I asked.

Fran looked down and said softly. "None. George didn't want any."

Oops, I thought. Sometimes, in my eagerness to learn about people, I didn't think about how some questions might be hurtful.

"But luckily I got to spend time around kids for my job," Fran continued. "And I have my doll collection." She sighed. "Actually, I wanted to foster a child."

Maria and I did a double take.

"My best friend as a kid was a foster child, and I've always wanted to do it," Fran continued. "But we're not allowed to have kids at Palmetto Pointe. I was looking for something to do, and a lady I know from the gym mentioned We Care."

"Right, the gym," Maria said, obviously trying to change the subject. "Do you like to work out?"

"Yes." said Fran, her eyes lighting up. "George and I met playing in a coed basketball league. My basketball-playing days are over, but I love going to the gym, and I've started playing pickleball."

"I've heard about pickleball," I said. "I might want to try it sometime. How about you, Maria?"

"I wish," she said. "I need a knee replacement first. But I don't know when I'll be able to schedule it, because someone will need to take care of Mom, and take care of me."

Maria's cellphone beeped, signaling that our table was ready. We made our way to the table and ordered another round of drinks and some appetizers.

"Debbie, you always ask us so many questions, but you never talk about yourself," said Fran.

It's true, I didn't. I was more interested in learning about other people.

"Tell us about your family," said Fran.

"Not much to tell. It's just me and Lori."

"So—you were an only child? Fran asked.

My heart started pounding. After a few seconds, I replied.

"I had a brother, but he passed away years ago," I said.

"Oh gosh, Debbie, I'm so sorry," said Maria.

"I really don't like talking about it," I said, because I didn't. Especially because sometimes I started tearing up, like I did now.

"Excuse me, girls, but I need to use the restroom," I said.

"I'll go, too," said Maria.

In the restroom, Maria tried to console me, but I told her I was okay, and I'd rather just try and have a nice time tonight.

When we got back, Fran was laughing at her phone.

"What's so funny?" Maria asked.

"I just love these *Truckin' Cats* videos," she chuckled. When we looked confused, Fran turned the phone toward us.

We watched a video showing a guy in a long-haul truck, with a cat on his shoulder. Then the same cat was rolling around on the dashboard. Maria and I laughed along with Fran.

"I love cats, too," I said. "When I was growing up, we had an orange-and-white cat. He always slept with me, and then one day he got out of the house and ran away."

"We had a bunch of cats in the house, too," said Maria. "They helped keep down the mouse population."

The server came with our food and another round of cabernets for the table. I dug into the tacos, boneless chicken wings, and cheesy spinach and artichoke dip with chips that we had ordered for the table. Maria took a tiny bit of dip with a chip, a wing, and a taco. Fran had more than Maria, but less than me. Maria looked longingly at the food and just shook her head.

After we had eaten, I looked at my phone. "I should probably get going. I have an interview at City Hall tomorrow."

"You're getting a job?" Fran asked.

I caught her up on the discussion Maria and I had had at the pool. And Joyce had come through with more information, that the job paid eighteen dollars an hour for twelve hours a week at the Recreation Office. That wouldn't have been my first choice of offices to work at, since I wasn't really sporty, but the low number of hours and the fact that it was an office job were appealing.

"Let's get together soon," said Maria. She looked thoughtful. "Actually, how about coming to my house for dinner a week from Saturday?"

"That would be great," I said, and Fran agreed. "It can be our first official meeting of The Cabernet Club."

"What should we do at our meeting?" Fran asked.

"I for one hope it doesn't become a 'Weeping Widows Club,'" Maria said. "Fran and I went through that at the Palmetto Pointe Bereavement Group." She quickly added, "And of course you were divorced, Deb. Wait—no offense."

"No worries," I chuckled. "I've been divorced since Lori was three years old."

"Was there anyone special in your life since then?" asked Fran.

I had tried to bury those memories, but they were still there. Sam. With his blue eyes and booming laugh. We met at a writers' group. He always complimented my writing and told me that I had the most beautiful smile. Sam was separated, but we didn't go out together in public, since he wasn't officially divorced. Lori was only five at the time. Usually he would leave in the early-morning hours, but one time he overslept, and Lori found us together in my bed. I was horrified and broke it off with him. I never went back to the writers' group, either.

"It was difficult dating, since there weren't many single moms at that time. And I always put Lori first. But still, I've had some relationships, but no one that I ever wanted to spend the rest of my life with," I shared. "In fact, I'd rather be alone than stuck with an awful man, or, God forbid, be a nursemaid."

Maria and Fran nodded.

"My mother used to say, 'there's plenty of fish in the sea,'" said Maria.

"Yeah, but I'm still floundering around trying to find the right one," I said. Maria and Fran laughed.

"So you're open to finding a guy here?" Maria asked.

"Sure. And I'm also interested in exploring my other passions. Like writing. I've always loved to write. In fact, I'm going to the first meeting of the Palmetto Pointe Creative Writing Group this Saturday."

"Do you want to write a novel?" Fran chimed in. "I read all the *New York Times* bestsellers."

"No, I like writing nonfiction. Personal essays. But I love to read fiction, too." Fran was really starting to grow on me. "I need to get a library card."

Fran told me that the county library system also had a

great selection of eBooks that could be downloaded. Winslow had one small library, and no electronic book option, so I was excited.

"What kind of books do you like to read, Maria?"

Maria frowned and took a second to answer. "I don't really like reading books, except for cookbooks. I'm not brainy like the two of you."

I smiled and shook my head. "Maria, you are the most amazing cook and a terrific conversationalist. The only thing I like better than a great book is a great meal."

We all laughed.

I realized I hadn't had this much fun in a long time. On the way home, buckled in my seat belt, I had this warm, happy feeling—the kind I had back in fifth grade when I met some new kids and realized they were going to be my friends. My first friends in Florida, and we even have a club. Maybe I really do belong here.

CHAPTER 11

After changing outfits three times, I settled on a black skirt with a light blue, short-sleeved silky looking blouse with two ties that I turned into a bow, and my black pumps. I figured since it was the Recreation Department, I could get away with not wearing a suit for my interview.

I left early, and I'm glad I did, because even with the GPS on my phone, I got lost. I had always been directionally challenged.

Five minutes before the interview, I approached the front desk.

"I have an interview with Ursula Redmond."

The woman at the front desk nodded. "That's me." She pulled out a clipboard. "Go ahead and fill this out, and then we can talk."

Looking at the form, I said, "I already submitted my resume and job application online. It looks like these are the same questions."

Ursula frowned. "I know, but I like to have a paper copy of everything."

"Can't you just print it out?"

She gave me a withering look. "Listen, do you want to interview for this job or not?"

"I do," I said, and filled out the form. A few minutes later I turned it in, and Ursula spent a few minutes looking at it then opened the door to the office. "Come on in."

I was shocked to see Ursula wearing gym clothes and sneakers. She was probably in her early fifties, with dyed blonde hair and a tall, heavy build. When we walked to the conference room, I saw a few other employees, also wearing workout gear.

After sitting down, Ursula looked me over. "So, do you play any sports?"

"Ummm." I'd never been asked that question before during an interview.

Before I could answer, she said, "Because most of the people here are into sports. I played volleyball and softball in college."

I decided to try some humor. "If typing was an Olympic sport, I'd win the gold medal."

Ursula frowned. I guess the joke fell flat.

"So why do you want to work at the Recreation Office?" she asked.

I didn't want to tell her the real reasons. Good hourly pay, short hours, and a job where I didn't have to stand all the time. But based on her first question, I guessed that an interest in fitness would be a good answer.

"I like to work out," I said. That was somewhat true. I had been a member of a gym up north, but hadn't joined one in Florida yet. "And I'm thinking of trying pickleball, too."

That got a nod out of Ursula. "We're thinking of opening up some of our basketball courts for pickleball play in the morning. A group of seniors petitioned the city, and it's a great way for us to get new members. Speaking of seniors, how old are you?"

"What—um—" Seriously? Didn't she know that question was illegal? I was about to tell her so, but she interrupted me.

"Never mind. I can tell by your outfit."

Okayyyy—

"Anyway, let's talk about your typing skills. How fast can you type?"

"About ninety words per minute."

"Huh," she said. "That's fast. I guess you don't have arthritis in your hands or anything, right?" She laughed. I didn't.

"We mostly need help with typing and paperwork, which is not my strong suit. I usually work the front desk, but you'll need to cover for me at lunch or when I go out."

"That should be fine," I said. "I was an office manager and legal secretary, and I often had to cover the front desk."

"And the dress code is workout gear. You can wear any type of workout pants or capris, a shirt with sleeves, and sneakers."

"Sounds good," I said, thinking I'd need to make a quick trip to Target or Walmart.

"Okay. It pays eighteen dollars an hour, and the hours are Monday, Wednesday, and Friday, from eight to four."

I did a quick calculation in my head. The job ad said it was only twelve hours a week, but this would be twenty-four hours. It was more than I wanted, but maybe it would be good for me to earn some more money.

"Oh, and once you've been working here for fifty hours, you get a free beach pass."

"That would be great," I said. "I can't believe how expensive parking is—"

"Okay, so do you want the job?"

"Oh—yes—sure. When did you want me to start?"

"Monday would be good. Let me get someone from HR to get you some more paperwork to fill out, and you should be all set."

When I got home, I thought about the interview. Ursula didn't seem very nice, and she was kind of condescending, but did that really matter? This was a part-time job that paid well and seemed low-key—unlike working in a legal office, where we were constantly dealing with deadlines and urgent issues.

The only urgent issue now was finding some nice workout clothes on clearance. I called Maria and set up a shopping date.

CHAPTER 12

The sign on the door said "PPCWG Meeting." I guess it was easier than writing out the full name of the Palmetto Pointe Creative Writing Group.

It was ten on Saturday morning, and the group met weekly in the main clubhouse. This particular room's ambiance left much to be desired. It was small and windowless, with bare walls. Today, five "creative" writers were sitting on very uncomfortable chairs at a long table that reminded me of The Last Supper.

Most of the people seemed to know each other, which made me feel shy and out of place. They were talking together, and I sat uncomfortably, with a notebook and pen in hand. Then a silver-haired man stood up.

"Good morning. I'm Norman, your group leader. Everyone, please introduce yourselves. Let's start with our new guest," he said, looking at me.

"Um, I'm Debbie Gordon."

"Welcome, Debbie. Normally we have a larger group,

but some of our members are seasonal. What made you decide to join our group?"

"I've always liked to write." Duh—so did everyone here. Was that really the best answer I could come up with? God, I wish I didn't have stage fright. When I was writing, the words flowed smoothly, but in a group, I often got tongue-tied.

"What do you like to write?" asked a short, grey-haired, pointy-eared man, who looked like an elderly elf.

"Mostly essays and nostalgia pieces," I said. "Years ago I joined a writers' group, but—"

"We're never going to get to share our writing at this rate," a woman interrupted. She was skinny and wearing tight ripped denim capri pants and a form-fitting sleeveless coral tank top, with gold wedge sandals. I guessed she was in her seventies, but it seemed like she was determined to look young forever. She had long blonde hair á la Goldie Hawn, bangs that fell into her eyes, and a face as tight as a fitted sheet. "The rest of us can just tell our names. My name's Eunice." She looked to her left.

"I'm Howie," said the guy who looked like an elderly elf.

"I'm Astrid," said a woman wearing a flowy dress, who looked to be in her sixties, with long, brown hair.

"Consuela," said a woman in her thirties, with a heavy Spanish accent.

"Okay, everybody, let's get those creative juices flowing this morning. For the first half hour, we're going to do an exercise. Think of it as freestyle writing. Don't edit; just write as much as you can, as fast as you can, okay? And don't worry if you can't find the right word. Just keep on writing. That's the whole point."

"I bet he'll have us write some kind of description," whispered Astrid, who was sitting next to me. "It's Norman's favorite part of writing. Whenever he reads from his novel in progress, he has so many detailed descriptions of people, places, and weather that none of us can remember what the story was about." We both chuckled.

"This exercise will be challenging," Norman told the class. "Write a description of yourself."

Along with the moans and groans and good-natured laughter, I heard an "I told you so" from Astrid, under her breath. "It's not easy to describe yourself," protested Howie, the letter-writer.

Consuela raised her hand, "Norman," she said in her thick accent, "what do joo mean—deck-strip-son?" She tripped over the word, and Eunice snickered.

"Write about yourself," Norman said in a kind, patient way. "What you look like, where you come from, how you think, what you feel, who you are, what you hope for. Do you understand?"

"Jes, I theenk so." Consuela sounded doubtful. Eunice rolled her eyes.

Everyone began scribbling furiously; everyone except me. I had become so accustomed to typing on a keyboard that writing in longhand was slow and laborious. Also, I wasn't sure how to begin. After a couple of minutes, I started writing.

As the song goes, I've grown accustomed to my face. When I was young, like every girl, I wanted to be beautiful, but I had to settle for "cute." I see myself as pleasant-looking, and that's fine. I think if you're pleasant-looking, people like you.

That sounded kind of dumb, but I kept on, *I have hazel*

eyes and my natural hair color is dark brown. I color my hair a light golden brown because you're supposed to lighten your hair as you get older.

Ugh. I crossed out that whole paragraph and continued writing. *I'm renting right now in Palmetto Pointe and hope to buy a condo when my lease is up.*

That was nobody's business, I decided, and put a big "X" on it.

I've been divorced a long time and brought up my daughter as a single parent. People think being a single parent is difficult, but to me, being married can be more difficult.

Nuh-uh. This is a description, not a confession. *I'm pretty shy in new situations but once I get to know someone, I have a wicked sense of humor.*

Um, no. Bragging is off-limits. *I lived most of my life in Winslow, Massachusetts except for the year I lived in New York City. That was the best year of my life.*

Reading over what I had written, I thought: This is such crap. Really—who would want to hear this stuff? I wanted to write what I wanted to write (although I wasn't sure what that was).

Maybe I don't belong in this group. Maybe I won't come back.

"Okay, people, time's up," Norman told the group. "Who wants to read first?" Only one hand shot up. It belonged to Eunice. Norman ignored her.

"What about you, Debbie? Do you want to share what you wrote? We'd like to hear what you have to say."

I shook my head.

"No? Maybe next time. What about you, Astrid?"

As it turned out, Astrid was an amateur astrologist who

charted zodiac signs, and what she had just written proved to be quite interesting. Her forte, she told the group, was astrological romances. "Ah, a new genre," Howie said.

Meanwhile, Eunice kept waving her hand close to Norman's nose. The class gave a collective sigh as Norman said, "Eunice, would you like to read?"

"Me?" Eunice feigned surprise. "Oh, well, all right."

"How can I describe myself?" Eunice began, smiling daintily as she read. "Growing up, I always got lots of compliments and always had a lot of boyfriends. I took dancing, singing and elocution lessons *blah blah blah* I won my first beauty contest at age two. When I met my husband, Mo, he said it was love at first sight because *blah blah blah* People cannot believe I am a grandmother and *blah blah blah...*"

As Eunice droned on and on, I wondered why some people—especially when they get older—needed to constantly be in the limelight. You would think a lifetime would be enough attention.

After what seemed like forever, Eunice finished reading.

"Thank you, Eunice," Norman said. "Does anyone have any comments or thoughts?"

Nobody spoke. Finally Consuela raised her hand. "Joonice," she said slowly, "joo are like the parrot—talk, talk." For emphasis, she opened and closed her fingers. "Joo are—how do you say it?" she looked at Astrid to supply the right words, "too much filled of jourself."

"She means you're full of yourself," Astrid translated.

Eunice jumped up. "I certainly am not. I'm just telling the truth. And you," she pointed a threatening finger at Consuela, "do not belong in this group. This is not English as a Second Language. The way you talk—like Carmen Miranda."

Consuela jumped up, too, eyes flashing. "Carmen Miranda," she cried, rolling the *r*s, "did no speak Spanish. Carmen Miranda spoke Portuguese. Carmen Miranda was Brazilian, stupido."

"Did she just call me stupid?" Eunice demanded.

"Sounded like that to me," Howie said.

With that, a screaming match began between Eunice and Consuela as the group erupted in laughter.

Norman tried to quiet the uproar. "Ladies, please. That's enough. Let's move on."

"Stop jelling at me," Consuela hollered.

"I am not jelling—I mean yelling," Eunice hollered back, and even Norman couldn't keep a straight face.

Howie stood up, waving sheets of paper. "I've got something to read."

"I hope you did the description exercise," Norman told him. "Not another letter to the *New York Times*."

"No," said Howie. "This is a letter to the *Palm Beach Post*."

For some reason, that got everyone laughing hysterically. Eunice tittered, and even Consuela cracked a smile.

I was enthralled. How could I have ever thought of quitting the PPCWG?

Yes, it was chaotic and crazy, but it was also entertaining. What was going to happen at the next week's reading and the week after that? I felt addicted to this group already, eager for the stories to unfurl. Would the Pisces protagonist in Astrid's astrological romance find true love with a Sagittarius? Would Eunice confide in her ongoing memoir that she didn't win every beauty pageant she entered? Would Howie finally get one of his letters published?

The Palmetto Pointe Creative Writing Group was the best show in town.

And, like all my favorite things in life, it was free.

CHAPTER 13

It was after work on Monday night, and I was on my way to meet Maria and Fran for dinner. Fran had gotten a mailer about new summer early-bird specials, and we decided to go for a quick, inexpensive meal.

I was in a great mood. The weather was beautiful, and I had some fun stories to share with my friends about my new job and the writers' group. I had also forgotten to tell them about Elliott and Freda, and the pilfered parking space. But most of all, about that really cool mystery woman who pretended to be the condo director. Damn, she was good. During my drive, I rehearsed the story in my head so I wouldn't forget any of the details.

And before I knew it, I had arrived at the restaurant.

A reed-thin man pounced on me the minute I walked in. He had blonde Shirley Temple curls that cascaded down his back.

"Oh, I'll bet you're the charming lady they're waiting

for," he chirped. "Your friends are already seated. Allow me to escort you to them. My name is Randy."

He grabbed my elbow and led me to a table in the back of a dimly lit room. Maria and Fran jumped up to greet and hug me.

"We had to order something so we could get the early-bird special in time," Fran explained, pointing to the three glasses of wine on the table. "I come here sometimes for lunch with the people from We Care. It's not fancy but it's fun."

"Oh, Debbie, I invited—" Maria started to say when Randy's high-pitched voice broke in. "And what is your pleasure, princessa?" he asked me. "I'm thinking Riesling or maybe you're a sangria."

"I already have my drink," I pointed to the glass of wine. "My friends were nice enough to order my cabernet."

"That's not cabernet, sweetie, it's pinot noir," Randy corrected. "And it's not your drink. It's, well, whatever her name is."

"What are you talking about?" I asked, confused.

"Oh, my God, I can't remember her name, either." Maria smacked her head. "I'm getting as forgetful as my mother."

"I forgot her name, too," Fran said. "She's in the ladies' room."

"I didn't know anybody else was coming," I said.

Randy tapped his foot impatiently. "While I enjoy nothing more than standing around and listening to such stimulating conversation, I need to know what you," he pointed to me, "want to drink."

"I'll have a glass of cabernet, too." I was surprised that

Maria had invited somebody else along. After all, this was supposed to be just the three of us.

As if reading my mind, Maria gave a helpless shrug. "It was a spur of the moment thing. I've seen this gal around and we got to talking at the mailbox and she seemed—I can't explain it—kind of alone, you know? So I invited her to join us for dinner."

I had to smile. Kind and caring, that was such a Maria thing to do.

Randy had bolted off to greet a couple who had just come in. He made a big production of leading them to a cozy booth in the corner, where they snuggled up next to each other. The woman was dressed all in black, and even from a distance, you could hear her jewelry jangling as she played with the few strands of gray hair on the man's head.

"Oh, my God, look—that's Harriet Bertulli, our fearless condo director." I lowered my voice. "She's with Barry, the guy from the Temple Shalom dance."

Maria swiveled her head to get a better look at the couple, then turned back and stared at Fran and me. "Okay, kids, we need to talk. Randy has a boyfriend. The Black Widow has a boyfriend. Even my mother's friend who lives in assisted living has a boyfriend. What's wrong with this picture?"

"Boyfriends? We ain't got no stinkin' boyfriends," I joked.

"Seriously, why not? We're three eligible women, we're attractive, we're fun, but nothing's happening with us," Maria said. "Maybe we're not trying hard enough. What about you, Debbie? Is there anyone you're interested in romantically—besides Mister Highpockets, of course?"

"Actually, kind of," I admitted. "I was having a hard

time reaching some Cool Whip at Publix and he helped me. He told me he makes his own whipped cream and was kind of cute. But he's some kind of coach and had to go to work before I got his name. I hope I see him again. Anyhow, that's my story. What about you, Maria?"

"Well, I met this nice man, Peter, at church," Maria said slowly. "His wife is in the Alzheimer's unit where my mother's friend is. The other day he asked if I'd consider going out to dinner with him, not as a girlfriend, but just someone to talk with, you know? He doesn't have family down here and he's lonely."

"What'd you tell him?"

"I told him I understand what he's going through, but I'm not sure I feel right about it." She looked at Fran. "Hey—why are you blushing? Are you hiding something from us?"

"It's always the quiet ones," I gave Fran a tap on the arm. "Come on, tell us."

Fran blushed even more deeply and kept clearing her throat. "Well, um, the other day, I was emptying the trash, and this guy came out of nowhere and stood by the dumpster, watching me."

"Dumpster Guy?" Randy had materialized at our table, pen and pad in hand, ready to take our order. "How intriguing, Miss Fran. So then what happened?"

"I was upset because he's always lecturing me about the environment and saving the planet. I told him that I certainly know how to recycle properly."

"And then?" Randy prompted.

"And then he said, 'Oh, I know you do. Actually, I wanted to ask if you'd like to have dinner with me.'"

"Oh, my goodness, did he mean then and there?"

Randy delighted in his own line of questioning. "Dinner at the dumpster, or dinner from the dumpster?"

"No—of course not," Fran sputtered. "He meant—"

"Who knew that dumpsters are the nouvelle cuisine?" Randy clasped his hands. "Is it any wonder restaurants are hurting? Who can compete with such ambience? And on that note, ladies, I'll be back when you're ready to order. Toodle-oo."

"So, Fran, what did you say?" Maria moved her chair closer so as not to miss a word. "Are you going out with him?"

"I told him I'd think about it. I don't even know his name. For all I know, he could be an axe murderer."

"More likely just a lonely guy," I said. "I think you ought to give him a chance. Anybody who cares that much about the environment has to be pretty much okay."

"Hey, I know how to find out about him," Maria announced. "I'll ask Joyce Davis. Remember? She knows everything about everyone in Palmetto Pointe."

"But I don't want to go out with someone I met at a dumpster," Fran protested.

"Where you meet someone is ir-rel-e-vant." I was feeling quite relaxed from the cabernet and was almost tripping over my words. "Love is wherever you find it—at a dance or a deli or a dumpster."

"I'll drink to that," Maria said. We raised our glasses in yet another toast, and Randy materialized seemingly out of nowhere.

"And may I ask, is your friend still in the Ladies Lounge? Did she fall in? Should we contact the Coast Guard, do you think?"

Fran craned her neck. "I think I see her coming now."

"No, no," Randy admonished her, "please keep your eyes on the menu, my dear Fran. I realize it always takes you a while to make up your mind. And this is a major decision, not to be taken lightly. But you might want to consider the tilapia special." He gave a little wave and scampered off to another table.

I was about to ask Fran if she'd had the tilapia before when I noticed a woman approaching our table. Because of the lighting, it was hard to see but—

Omigod, what an amazing coincidence.

Of the thousands of people in Palmetto Pointe, what was the chance that the woman Maria had invited was, in fact, the blonde mystery woman herself? Tonight she was dressed more casually in white jeans and a black tunic. Her oversize sunglasses were perched on top of her head, and as she came nearer, I saw her face.

Oh, dear God—it couldn't be.

I hadn't recognized her with her sunglasses on, especially since the last place I would ever expect to see her would be at Palmetto Pointe.

But now, I saw her clearly. The cheekbones, the green-gray eyes, the blonde hair—shorter now, but still thick and shiny. Even though it was a lifetime away from Winslow, Massachusetts, it was as if time stood still.

"I know you," I blurted out. "You're Kay Caldwell. I remember you from high school."

"What? You two know each other from *high school*?" Maria's jaw dropped. "I can't believe it. What a small world."

"You were the senior prom queen," I rattled on. "You married Rick Jason—Jackrabbit Jason. Everyone had a crush on him."

"Jackrabbit," Kay repeated in that husky voice of hers. "I haven't heard that name in years." She didn't seem to recognize me, and she didn't even bother to ask my name.

"I'm Debbie Gordon. My maiden name was Debbie Shapiro," I said slowly, waiting for a reaction.

Kay didn't have any reaction. Instead, she gave a slight nod and picked up her menu.

"So Kay, how do you like living in Florida?" Maria asked, politely.

"Oh, I don't live here. I still have my house near Boston. I'm building a place in Banyan Falls so I come down once in a while to check on the progress."

Maria whistled. "Those homes go for over a million dollars."

Kay looked embarrassed. "I've made some good real-estate investments."

"So, how come you're staying in Palmetto Pointe? Why not rent somewhere nicer?" Maria and Fran caught my snarky tone and looked at me curiously.

Kay just shrugged. "It's my friend's place, so I can stay here for free."

I just shook my head. Of course Kay would have somewhere to stay for free. She's building a mansion, and she doesn't even have to pay to rent a place. She's still living the perfect life, while the rest of us are struggling.

"Oh, ladies, I'm b-a-a-c-k," Randy announced. He looked Kay up and down. "Well, you were certainly worth waiting for. Did I tell you that I'm Randy?"

"Oh, I bet you are," Kay drawled, and Fran and Maria laughed. Finally, we gave our dinner choices and he flounced off, crying "Hallelujah."

"Well," Maria said, "Randy certainly does make a statement."

Maria and Fran did most of the talking. Kay volunteered little about herself, except that her husband had worked for Coca-Cola and they had moved all over the country. They had a son, Mitchell, who lived in Colorado.

I knew Maria wanted to bring me into the conversation. "Oh, Debbie, you never told us that funny story about someone taking your parking space."

"I don't even remember," I forced a laugh. "Senior moment."

Kay didn't say a word.

My happy mood was gone and my mind was whirling. It was surreal, one crazy coincidence after another. Meeting the mystery woman who had helped me on Saturday afternoon, and now realizing she was the very person who had affected my life so much.

And yet we had never said a word to each other until now.

I picked at my food, lost in thought, hardly realizing that Randy was clearing the table and announcing choices for dessert. "Attention, my lovelies, dessert comes with dinner. We have raspberry marble cake, sugar-free ice cream, chocolate pudding, whatever. And," he said pertly, "your choice of coffee, tea, or me."

"You," said Kay, "are worth the price of admission."

Everybody opted for the raspberry marble cake. Fran ordered regular coffee and Maria, Kay, and I ordered decaf.

When Randy brought the coffee, he winked and said to Fran, "Now, Madame Frances, you wanted regular coffee to keep you regular, correct? Metamucil not working lately?

And you asked for cream on the side, correct? Ah, but which side—right or left?"

"I—uh—the left side," Fran giggled and blushed. "You always tease me whenever I come here."

"That's because I love to see you blush. I mean, who blushes anymore?"

Kay looked up at him. "You ought to blush, Randy. You know damn well this is not decaf. I don't want to be up all night because of the caffeine."

Maria took a sip, then put her cup down. "I wondered why this decaf tasted so good. That's because it's not decaf, it's regular coffee. I've heard restaurants do that a lot."

I had to agree. "You guys are right. Decaf has a different taste, and it's usually lukewarm because it's been sitting around. This is hot and it tastes good. You gave us regular coffee," I told Randy, who kept insisting that it was, indeed, decaf.

Kay pushed her cup away. "Listen, mister, my nose knows. You need to take these away and put on a fresh new pot of decaffeinated coffee. Now. While we're young."

"Well, aren't we the dominatrix," Randy sniffed.

All that wine at dinner had given Fran a sense of bravado. "You know, Randy, we could report you to the manager."

"The manager? Get real. I'm the big kahuna here, I own the place," he said, chuckling. "You think anybody would hire someone like me?"

"Enough of this bullshit. Move your ass," Kay demanded in the imperious tone I remembered from all those years ago back in high school. "Otherwise, we'll go back to Palmetto Pointe and tell everyone this restaurant has an 'R' rating."

"What's an 'R' rating?"

"You know, Rats. Roaches. Really crappy food."

"What a huffy muffy you are." Randy stared at Kay with grudging admiration. "I bet you were something in your day. I bet you had all the boys creaming in their jeans."

"Randy," Kay said with a wicked grin, "if you'd known me back then, I guarantee you'd be straight today."

CHAPTER 14

I could hardly wait to tell Roz.

As soon as we left the restaurant, I hurried to my car and took out my cell phone.

Before Roz could even say hello, I yelled, "You will never, in a million years, guess who I bumped into. Somebody from Winslow High."

"How come you're calling so late?" Roz grumbled.

"Late? It's only eight o'clock."

"Well, you usually call around quarter of seven, right before *Wheel of Fortune*. And how come you're yelling?"

"Because I'm calling from my car."

"What's so important you have to call me from your car?" Roz demanded. "I was just about to give Cy his ice cream." Cy was her boyfriend. To Roz, he was the winning lottery ticket. To me, he was so old, he farted sawdust.

"So, wait till you hear who I just met. Are you sitting down?"

"Don't drag it out. Tell me already. Who did you meet?"

I paused for dramatic effect. "Kay Caldwell Jason."

"What?" Roz gasped. "Where? How?"

"At dinner tonight. My neighbor invited her. It's a long story. I'll tell you the details later. But get this, Kay Caldwell Jason is staying here. In Palmetto Pointe."

Another gasp. "In Palmetto Pointe? I can't believe it. What the hell is someone like her doing there?"

That was the kind of reaction I wanted. Sometimes it took a longtime friend with a shared history to really understand.

Roz whistled. "Wow. You must have shit a brick when you recognized her. Did she remember you?"

"Yeah, right. About as much as she did in high school. I told her who I was but she didn't blink an eye."

"I still can't believe it. Kay Caldwell. It's crazy. So, what does she look like after all these years?"

"Blonde hair, great figure, expensive clothes. Still a knockout," I said begrudgingly.

"She probably had plenty of work done on her face," Roz declared.

"Well, I have to admit Kay is a sport," I said. "She picked up the whole tab for all of us, dinner and drinks."

"Big friggin' deal," Roz snorted. "I'm sure she can afford it. She came from plenty of money."

"And from things she said, I think her husband did very well, too," I said. "Jackrabbit was a big shot with Coca-Cola."

"I was just going to ask you about him. Oh, my God, Jackrabbit Jason. He was so cute." Roz was gushing like a teenager. "I had such a crush on him. I can picture him in those tight little running shorts. Remember how we used to go watch him at track meets?"

I cleared my throat. "I hate to break this to you, but Kay wasn't wearing a wedding band and she didn't talk about him in the present tense. Not to sound cruel, but I believe Jackrabbit Jason is no longer racin' if you get my drift."

"You mean, he—he died?" Roz began to wail, even though she hadn't set eyes on Rick Jason since high school graduation. In the background Cy was yelling something to her.

"It's nobody you know and the goddamn ice cream can wait," Roz yelled back. She stopped sniffling and asked, "Do you think you'll be seeing Kay again?"

"Not if I can help it. Anyhow, she's not here permanently. Somebody she knows is letting her use their condo. Everything always came easy to her," I added bitterly.

Cy was hollering again. "You forgot to buy Cool Whip."

"Oh, my God, I've got to go. But listen, Debs, don't let all this get to you," Roz's voice softened. "It's water under the bridge. Let bygones be bygones. You're making a new life there. Don't let Kay ruin it. And she's only there temporarily, right?"

"You're right. It's just that—" my voice trailed off.

"You know," Roz said, "ever since you moved to that crazy Palmetto Pointe, your life has been like a soap opera —*The Young and the Restless*."

"More like *The Old and the Listless,*" I said, and we both laughed.

THAT NIGHT, UNABLE TO FALL ASLEEP, I GOT UP, HAD SOME ice cream, and watched TV. Still wide awake, I decided to work on an assignment for the upcoming creative writers' group to describe a memorable day in your life using as much sensory description as possible.

The words practically flew off the computer keyboard.

Ever since I could remember, my favorite downtown store in Winslow, Massachusetts was Kresge's Five and Ten.

It was always bustling—the ring of cash registers, the smell of fresh coffee from the lunch counter, and a colorful jumble of everything I loved: candy, games, and Nancy Drew mysteries.

That Saturday in December, my aunt Evvie took me there as a special treat. She was my father's kid sister, just eleven years older than me, and living with us at the time. "Your brother gets all the attention, Debbie," she said. "It's about time someone paid attention to you."

We started with the early movie, then went shopping for my special gift. I picked out two Nancy Drew books and a bottle of Jean Naté perfume.

"Where do you want to eat?" Aunt Evvie asked. "The Waldorf Cafeteria? Chinese?"

"I'd rather have a hot dog here," I said. Nothing, to me, tasted better than a Kresge hot dog with mustard and relish, washed down with a frosty glass of root beer at the lunch counter.

After lunch, we lingered to window-shop. When we missed our bus, we decided to walk home along North Avenue, the tree-lined boulevard in the ritziest part of town. We joked about which of the big, imposing houses we'd buy if we ever struck it rich.

Then we came to the house I'll never forget—a big white one with gray shutters, a wraparound porch, and a circular drive. Snow blanketed the yard, turning it into a Christmas card scene. Just as we passed, a black sedan pulled in. A red-faced, heavyset man climbed out, followed by a pretty blonde girl in white boots and a camel-hair coat. She flipped her hair from under her collar like the rich girl in the movie we'd just seen.

"That's Mr. Caldwell," Aunt Evvie told me. "Preston Caldwell. Big shot at the gas company. A real anti-Semite. I aced the typing test for a job there, but they never hire Jews. The Society Page always has his family's pictures. That girl's Kay, the younger daughter. The older one's about to be a debutante."

She went on to say that Mr. Caldwell's wife, Bootsie—a wealthy socialite—had drunk herself to death when Kay was about four. That was something I loved about my aunt: she knew everything that went on in town.

I can still see it as clearly as a photograph: the navy pea coat I wore, handed down from a cousin; Aunt Evvie's pink angora hat pulled over her dark curls, her cheeks red from the cold.

And that blonde girl—her hair catching the sunlight—walking so confidently into that big white house.

I didn't know then that the Caldwells would change my life—or that, not long after, my beloved Aunt Evvie would be gone.

But those, as they say, are stories for another day.

I printed it out, looked over what I had written and knew I could never read it aloud at the writers' group. Or anywhere, for that matter.

I crumpled the pages and threw them away.

CHAPTER 15

"May I speak with Deborah Gordon?" the male voice was deep, with a strong New England accent.

Another overeager telemarketer, I thought in exasperation.

I had thought up a clever response whenever a strange voice called, asking for Deborah Gordon. "This is her home health aide," I would say in a singsong voice. "Miss Deborah, she has Alzheimer's. Would you like to speak to her?" The telemarketers hung up every time.

For some reason, I didn't use that response this time. Instead, I said, somewhat reluctantly, "Speaking."

The caller cleared his throat. "Hello, Deborah. My name is Jim Tierney. My friend, Cy, up in Massachusetts, gave me your number. He said you're new down here and he thought we should get together."

"Oh, right, yes." I stumbled over my words. "Cy's high school friend. Yes, I heard about you." A week or so ago, Roz called to say that her boyfriend, Cy, was going to fix me up with his high school friend in Boca Raton, a recent widower. I had forgotten about it. After all, how many times did someone say they were going to introduce you to someone, and it never panned out?

But here was Jim Tierney from Boca Raton with the deep, wonderful voice, calling to ask me out for Saturday. And here I was, giggling like a teenager as we chatted.

"Well, all right then, Debbie. I'm looking forward to meeting you," he said.

When I hung up the phone, I didn't know who to call first—my daughter or Roz to say "Guess what? I've got a date!"

I couldn't remember the last time I had said that.

Lori's reaction was annoying. She started to chant, "Mom and Jim, sitting in a tree, K-I-S-S-I-N-G …"

"I hate when you do that. Stop it," I told her.

Lori was contrite. "Sorry. Mom, I'm just so glad for you."

"It's only a blind date, for God's sake. You're carrying on like it's the love story of the ages."

"Are you buying a new outfit for your date?"

"No," I said. "I had to buy some workout clothing for my job, so that isn't in the budget."

"Mom, if you need some money, I have no problem giving you—"

"I'm fine, Lori."

"Hey, remember my high school awards ceremony, when you didn't have enough money to buy me an outfit, and I had to wear one of your dresses?"

"Uh, is that supposed to make me feel better, Lori?"

"No, I mean, we're past that. I can help you, now."

"Drop it, Lori. I don't want your money." I had never taken money from anyone, and I wasn't about to start now.

Roz was just as annoying. All of a sudden, she had become Dear Abby, dispensing wisdom and giving dating advice. "Now don't be Miss Independent," she cautioned. "A man wants a woman to take care of him. If he asks you out again, invite him over for a home-cooked meal."

"Wow, Roz," I said, dripping with sarcasm, "that's so cutting edge. You're way ahead of your time. And remember? I'm a terrible cook."

Maria and Fran were happy for me and even came over to help me decide what to wear. The purple top with black pants was Maria's choice. Fran, who mostly wore skirts, thought a dress would be better. As it turned out, I chose an entirely different outfit at the last minute.

And all of a sudden, it was four-thirty on Saturday and Jim Tierney was banging on my door.

The picture I had in my mind—someone tall, dark, and handsome to go along with that deep voice—did not turn out to be accurate.

Jim Tierney had a deep voice, it's true, but he was maybe five feet four inches, a little taller than me, with skinny legs and a big belly. He was wearing shorts and a red polo shirt that barely covered his middle. And he wore black socks that almost came up to his knees, with ugly black shoes.

"Well you sure are a sight for sore eyes," he said. "Good thing I wore my new polo shirt. Let's get going. I don't want to miss the early-bird special."

"O-kay," I stammered, grabbing my purse. I hadn't planned on rushing out. In fact, I had bought a couple of different wines and put together a cheese tray, so that we could have some wine and cheese before dinner. I thought he might want to have a glass of wine before heading out, so we could get to know each other. Oh well, I guess the drink and chat would just happen at the restaurant.

Jim scored some points by opening and closing the car door for me. As soon as I was seated, however, my heel turned on something. "Ow."

"What's wrong?" Jim asked.

I looked down, and saw that it was an empty water bottle. "Oh, yeah, I didn't have time to clean up the car," he said. "Be careful. I think there's a couple of candy bar wrappers, too."

Ew. There goes a point.

"But I like your shoes," he said. "It's nice when a woman dresses up," he said. "Especially one who wears heels, and is still shorter than me." He laughed and continued. "I have to wear special shoes and socks, no heels for me," he laughed.

That reminded me. "You know, I've seen a lot of men wearing that combination of socks and shoes. Why are they special?" I asked.

"The compression socks help my circulation, and the shoes have special orthotic inserts to help with my back and leg problems."

"Ah, that makes sense—"

"All those years of installing toilets and cleaning out drain pipes really did a number on me."

"Oh, that's right, you were a plumber—"

"Yeah, up north. If only I had moved down here when I was younger, I would have made a killing. You can't find a decent service guy anywhere around here."

I listened to him drone on and on, mostly because I was

tired of getting interrupted. Was interrupting a Florida thing? Or did I also accidentally get a tattoo on my forehead that said, "Please Talk Over Me"?

Finally, we pulled up to the Italian restaurant Jim said was one of his favorites. "They have the best garlic rolls," he said, before opening my door for me. Well, at least I knew we wouldn't be kissing tonight, thank goodness.

We walked in, and it was pretty empty.

"Huh," he said, frowning. "It's usually busier during the early-bird special. Oh well, we'll just get better service."

"Just take any seat you like," said the server, in her twenties, and dressed all in black, which seemed to be the style for all Florida servers. Harriet Bertulli would fit right in.

We took a seat and she put down menus. Jim's eyes followed her as she walked away.

When he saw me noticing him noticing her, he said "She reminds me of my granddaughter," he said. Yeah, right.

I ignored his comment and opened the menu. "I'm starving," I said, and I really was. I had been too nervous earlier to eat much earlier.

"Hey. They forgot to give us the early-bird special menus," Jim said. He called out to the server. "Miss, we need the early-birds."

She came over to our table. "We don't have early-bird specials on Saturday nights."

"What? Since when?" His tone was panicky.

"Since the beginning of the month. The owner said we were losing too much money on Saturday nights. But don't worry, the meals are only a little bit more expensive."

"I can't believe this. You know what? I think I should be

grandfathered into the early-bird special prices since I've been a loyal customer."

"I'll go talk to the manager," said the server, rolling her eyes.

I felt myself blushing, which was a rarity for me. This was embarrassing. The prices here weren't that bad, even without the early-bird specials.

After a few awkwardly quiet minutes pretending to scan the menu while this man privately fumed, the server came back with the manager.

"Thank you for being a loyal customer," said the manager. "As Emma explained to you, unfortunately we can't offer the early-bird specials to anyone on Saturday night. But as a one-time favor, we will provide a free glass of our house Chianti for both of you with your meal this evening."

I could see Jim getting more and more angry, so now I took it upon myself to be the interrupter. "That's very generous of you." I said. "Thank you."

"I don't even like wine," Jim grumbled.

"I'll take your glass, then," I said. Two drinks would definitely help get me through this date.

"No, I'll drink it," said Jim.

When they walked away, I continued, "I think I'm going to have the chicken parmesan. What are you going to have?"

"I always get the shrimp fra diavolo," said Jim.

"Oh, I've never heard of that. What is it?" I actually knew what it was, but I wanted to redirect Jim from his early-bird outrage.

He proceeded to explain it to me in overly thorough detail until Emma took our orders.

After we placed our orders, Jim said, "I want to know more about you."

Okay, one point restored. That's a good sign. Someone who actually wants to learn about what's important to me. I opened my mouth—

"So—do you like the Red Sox or the Marlins?"

"What?" Was this what he meant when he said he wanted to know more about me?

"Umm, I'm not really a baseball fan."

"Not a baseball fan? But Cy and I talk about baseball all the time. I figured he'd want to set me up with someone who liked baseball. I'm kind of disappointed."

I stayed silent, because how was I supposed to respond to that?

"Anyway, maybe you just don't know much about baseball. Let me tell you what's happening with the teams."

Jim chattered away, while we were served our salads and dinners. At first I tried to bring up other topics of conversation, but he kept interrupting me, so I just ate my food and zoned out, thinking about topics I could write about for the next writers' group meeting—possibly even this date I was (barely) living through.

After we had cleaned our plates, Jim said, "Wow, I've never seen such a small woman pack it away like you do."

"Flattery will get you everywhere," I said.

Emma came over to clear the table.

"Would you like dessert?"

Finally, my favorite part of any meal. "Yes," I started to say, but Jim shook his head. "Dessert only comes with the early-bird specials."

"But the chocolate cake looks really good—"

"Can you wrap up some garlic rolls for me?" he asked.

Emma sighed and nodded.

After Emma brought a bag of rolls to the table, Jim waited until she had turned away and grabbed some of the leftover butter pats and sugar packets. "Since they're being so stingy with early-bird specials on Saturdays, I'll just take a couple of these things," he whispered.

Jim signaled for the bill. When he got it, he scratched his head. "I can never figure out how to do the tip."

"Just take the first number and multiply it by two. So if it's forty dollars multiply four by two or eight dollars."

"Why do you multiply it by two?"

"For a twenty percent tip."

"What? That snippy waitress getting twenty percent? Hell no. I'll give her ten percent and she's lucky to get it."

He put four dollar bills on the table and got up to leave. I reached into my purse and grabbed another five dollars and put it on the table when he started walking to the door.

Unsurprisingly, Jim talked more about the game on the way home. When we got to my condo, he parked in a guest space. "I'd walk you in, but I don't want to miss any of the game."

"That's okay," I said, relieved our date was ending.

He reached over, and I smelled the garlic on his breath. I quickly turned my cheek to receive his kiss, so he missed my mouth, thank goodness.

"Let's get together again soon," he said.

"I'm really busy, but I'll try," I said.

Before he had a chance to open my door, I opened it, shut it, and almost ran back to my place.

~

THE PHONE RANG AT 7:30 A.M. "SO HOW DID IT GO?" MY daughter asked. "What was Jim like?"

How to describe Jim Tierney? I couldn't put it into words. Finally I said, "Lori, he's the kind of man who takes home the rolls."

"He drives a Rolls?"

"No—the garlic rolls," I said. "Jim asked the server for extra rolls and he took all of them home. Every single one, and he didn't even ask if I wanted any. Oh, and he took the pats of butter and sugar packets, too. It's a wonder he didn't take the salt and pepper shakers or the tablecloth."

"Well, maybe he just—" Lori's voice trailed off.

"Oh, come on," I said. "That's what goofy old people do on those senior citizen bus trips. They take everything from the table, and they even take toilet paper from the rest rooms."

Lori chuckled. "Sounds like he needs someone like you to teach him the right things."

"Oh, sure. You know what they say about old dogs and new tricks."

"Well, I'm relieved," Lori said.

"What do you mean?"

"If you liked him, you might want to stay in Florida."

"Oh, I thought you'd forgotten about wanting me to move to Delaware," I said.

"Ha ha," said Lori.

The call waiting beeped. "Uh-oh, gotta go, that's Maria on the other line. Love ya. Bye."

I clicked over to the other line. "Debbie, we're dying to hear how the date went. Fran's here with me. I'll put it on speakerphone."

The girls laughed nonstop as I told them about my date with Jim.

Fifteen minutes into my tale I got another call beeping in.

"It's my friend from back home, Roz. Her boyfriend set up this blind date. I need to talk to her."

"Okay, see you soon," said Maria, "Yes, see you soon," said Fran.

Roz sounded unusually pleasant. "So, how did you like Jim?"

"Oh, Jim is—um—a very nice man."

"What does he look like?"

"All old guys down here look pretty much the same," I replied, stifling a yawn.

"Uh-huh. And what did the two of you talk about?"

Where was this going, I wondered. "Well, actually, Jim did most of the talking. About baseball."

"Well, that's the way it's supposed to be," Roz said as if she were talking to a child. "A man likes a woman who listens."

And listens and listens and listens, I wanted to say but kept my mouth shut.

"And he took you out for a nice dinner, did he?"

"Yes, he did," I said cautiously." I didn't get into the fact that he had argued about the early-bird pricing.

Just like that, Roz's pleasant tone changed. "So, if Jim Tierney is so nice, and he took you out for a nice dinner, how come you turned him down when he asked to see you again, huh? You said you were busy. What are you so busy with, Miss Bachelorette?"

In the background, Cy bellowed, "Who does she think she is, Miss America?"

"Look, I can explain—"

"What is your problem?" Roz sounded furious. "Jim Tierney is a lonely widower. He's looking for a nice woman. And I understand he has a beautiful home in Boca Raton."

"Oh, please. He has a one-bedroom condo in Sundown Village," I corrected her. "Which is only a step above Palmetto Pointe. Or maybe a step down because those condos don't have washer-and-dryer hookups. I'm sorry to say that he's a *shtik fleysh mit oygn*." That had been one of my grandmother's favorite Yiddish put-downs.

"Really? A piece of meat with eyes? Roz demanded.

"Give me a break," I said. "This guy was such a dud. I can't believe Cy had the nerve to fix me up with him."

"When did you get such a smart mouth?" Roz demanded. "This is all very disrespectful to Cy."

Roz slammed down the phone. It was something she had done numerous times over the years, and after a brief cooling-off period, she would call me and resume our friendship as if nothing had happened.

But a week passed. Then two. And Roz still had not called.

I called her, but the conversation was brief and chilly. "I meant what I said," Roz told me bluntly. "Are you going to apologize to Cy?"

"Seriously?"

Silence.

"Okay," I groaned. "Hand him the phone."

I apologized to Cy, but apparently I wasn't too convincing, because he hung up on me when we were done.

Oh well, I'm sure it'll eventually blow over, I thought. I'll give it more time.

CHAPTER 16

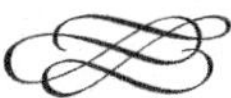

I had to force myself to sit down at the computer and work on something for the writers' group. At the last meeting, Norman reminded me that I had not yet shared my writing with the group, and I had promised to bring something to read.

Trouble was, I just couldn't get started, so I called my daughter. "I've got writer's block, Lori. I thought maybe you could give me some inspiration."

"Inspiration? Well, why don't you write about some of the crazy things that go on at Palmetto Pointe?"

"Nah. I like more serious stuff—personal stories, nostalgia, you know?"

"Nostalgia? Since when? You never even talk about what it was like growing up."

"Well, I was too busy working and raising you to get stuck talking about the past."

Lori must have heard something in my voice. "Mom, that sounds ominous. Is something bothering you? You know you can always talk to me. Or if something's bothering you, maybe writing about it would be good therapy."

"You're good therapy," I told her. "Nothing's bothering me. I just felt like talking with you, that's all."

But something was bothering me.

I had started to dream about Danny again. I'm sure seeing Kay triggered it.

In the dream, Danny was sitting at a small bistro table with a girl. She had her back to me so I couldn't see her face. I hurried over and said to Danny, "We were so worried about you. Are you all right?"

"I'm fine," Danny assured me. "At the last minute, I decided to stay home."

"Oh, I'm so glad. So then you'll be going to college after all?"

"You bet." Danny stood up and grabbed the girl's hand. "But first we want to dance."

In the background, a voice called out, "Jump, jump, jump."

Suddenly, the music changed. Now the song they were playing was *Danny Boy*. "This is too hard to dance to," he said and led the girl off the floor. The music swelled.

"And I'll be there in sunlight or in sorrow, Oh, Danny boy, oh Danny boy, I love you so."

When I woke up, my face was soaked with tears.

I couldn't get the dream out of my mind. And now here it was, nine o'clock on Friday night, and I still hadn't come up with anything to read for tomorrow. Once again, I glanced at the list of topics Norman had suggested, and one leaped out at me: Write about the person who most influenced your life.

It was as if I had been waiting all these years for the assignment to write the words.

Whenever I think of Danny, I see him as he was in his high-school yearbook photo. Even now, all these years later, his face still pulls at your heart—the crew cut, the crinkly dark eyes, the easy smile, his head tilted slightly as if nothing bad could ever happen.

Daniel Jay Shapiro—D.J. to everyone—was good-looking, smart, and popular. Senior-class president, straight-A student, all-around athlete with scholarship offers from top colleges. My big brother.

The summer he graduated, Danny fell in love with a girl named Caroline. He told me about her but made me promise to keep it from our parents. Caroline's family belonged to the Winslow Beach Club—"restricted," meaning No Jews Allowed. She used to sneak Danny in as a guest under a fake name.

Only later did I realize she was Caroline Caldwell—the older blonde debutante from that big white house on North Avenue, the one whose pictures always filled the Society Page.

I can still hear my mother's scream that Sunday afternoon. The club manager called to say Danny had been in a freak accident—he'd dived into water that was too shallow. His neck was broken; he was paralyzed. He died a few weeks later.

The grief was unbearable—and the gossip made it worse. Caroline's father, Preston Caldwell—a known bigot—was said to have sneered, "He didn't belong here. That's what happens when you show off."

Worse still was what one of our cousins said: "That's what comes of going with a shiksa."

Later we heard Caroline had been whisked off to California. We never heard from her again. No call, no note, nothing from her family.

Then, in my junior year at Winslow High, everyone buzzed about the new girl—rich, beautiful, and rumored to have been kicked out of two private schools. Overnight, she ruled the school—cheerleader, prom queen, the girl every guy wanted.

She was Kay Caldwell, Caroline's younger sister. Every day I had to see her—and be reminded of what happened to Danny. She never spoke to me or even looked my way—and I never said a word to her. Rumor had it Kay was there that day—urging my brother to dive into the shallow water, shouting, "Jump, jump, jump."

I stopped typing. Well, this was therapy all right. But certainly not something I would ever read at the writers' group. I decided to save it and maybe share it someday with my daughter. I had never told Lori much about Danny, the uncle she would never meet.

But in the meantime, what was I going to bring to the writers' group tomorrow?

The answer was simple—nothing.

For once, I'd skip the writers' group. I'd sleep late and then head to the Banyan Beach mall. For lunch, I'd treat myself to bourbon chicken and lo mein at the Food Court, and maybe I'd find a cute hat to wear to the pool.

Because sometimes the best therapy is retail therapy.

CHAPTER 17

Maria opened the door, smiling broadly. "Welcome to the first official meeting of The Cabernet Club of Palmetto Pointe." She ushered us into the living room. "Sit down and get comfy." We heard a cellphone ringtone. "Let me just see who that is," Maria said.

It was my first time in Maria's condo, and the first thing I noticed were the photos. They were everywhere. I plopped down on an overstuffed chair and immediately felt more relaxed. The blue-and-green color motif and knick-knacks made the place feel warm and cozy, like Maria herself.

Someday soon I hoped I'd have a comfortable place of my own.

"Bobby, I told you I'll send you the money at the beginning of the month, when my Social Security check comes in. Yes, okay, listen, I have some ladies over for dinner, I'll call you back tomorrow."

Maria came out from the kitchen looking flustered. "Sorry about that, girls."

"Your loan shark?" I asked, joking.

Silence. Again, one of my jokes fell flat.

"That was my son. He's always asking for money."

Thank God I didn't have to worry about that with Lori. I tried to model living frugally and saving when Lori was growing up. She had taken those lessons to heart, and, as an accountant, now regularly schooled me on budgeting and financial ideas. Sometimes it was annoying, but hearing about a grown child asking for money made me realize that actually I was pretty lucky.

"Are these your grandkids?" Fran asked, pointing to a photo of a group of three kids laughing with a beach in the background.

"Yes, that's Christina, Oliver, and Lucas, at our annual beach picnic. I was in charge of the food, especially the clam boil," said Maria.

"And that's a picture of you and Rafael on your wedding day, of course," said Fran, gesturing toward a picture in a silver frame.

"Yes, when I was slimmer and before I had my white hair," Maria laughed.

"He was very handsome," I said.

"Yes," she said. "We met at a dance. I was a senior in high school and Rafael had already graduated and was working."

"OK, so you met Rafael. What happened then?" I asked.

"Well, that was it," Maria smiled, remembering. "He was the one. My girlfriends thought he was cute and I did, too. On our third date, he asked me to go steady. We went out for two years and then on my birthday, he gave me my ring. We married a year later."

"Did you want to go to college?" Fran asked.

"Are you kidding? I was lucky my parents didn't yank me out of school when I was sixteen to go work in the mills," Maria said. "So I did what every Portuguese girl around me did. I got married and had a family."

"Yeah, Fran was the only one of us who got to go to college. But Maria, just the fact that you like to cook and clean is pretty amazing to me."

"It's how I grew up," said Maria. "I was the only daughter in a hard-working Portuguese-American family, and I learned at an early age that girls were expected to do a lot of chores around the house. Both of my parents worked in the mills, and my grandmother taught me to clean and cook and iron my brothers' shirts."

"Rafael used to brag about it," Maria continued. "He'd say, 'My wife didn't need on-the-job training. She was already broken in when I married her.'"

Fran and I were silent. That sounded pretty obnoxious to me, but Maria kept talking.

"From the day we came home from our honeymoon in the Poconos, I kept the house clean and had a hot meal on the table every night. On Sundays, after church, Rafael's widowed mother and aunt, along with some other relatives, would come over for dinner, served promptly at one o'clock. Over time, our house became the center for all holiday gatherings."

"It sounds exhausting."

"I was used to it. And when Rafael retired, we planned

to do some traveling," Maria said. "But just a few months later he got sick with a stubborn cough that turned out to be lung cancer. I took care of him for two years until he passed away."

"That's so sad," Fran said. "But at least you made it down to Florida to enjoy your retirement, right?"

"Well, yes," said Maria, "except that my mom takes up a lot of my time."

"Speaking of your mom," I said, "where is she?"

"She goes to sleep at seven which is why I decided to have our meeting at seven thirty."

"That makes sense. But did your mom ever consider living in an assisted living place? Some of them are super fancy, I've heard."

"Her best friend is in one of them, but they cost a lot of money."

"Yeah," I agreed. "But at least you were able to buy a place to live. I wish I had owned a home, so I could have at least sold it and used some of the money to buy a place here."

"Yes, Rafael and I owned a nice colonial back home," said Maria. "But I gave it to my son Bobby and Pam, his second wife. They were living in a cramped apartment with a young child and couldn't afford to buy a decent place. And Bobby doesn't want me to spend much of our savings. He says it's a parent's obligation to provide a good inheritance."

"What?" I almost screamed the words. "I'd say it's about time you had some fun and spent some of that money on yourself."

"Maybe," said Maria, speaking more softly. "But more

importantly, I'm so glad the three of us found each other. I haven't spent time with friends in ages." She thought for a moment. "This sounds so pitiful, but I don't think I really had any friends down here before the two of you."

Fran nodded. "I don't like playing card games or going to shows," she said. "I've been out with some of the other volunteers from We Care a couple of times, but mostly I just go to the gym."

"Whenever I go out, it's either with my mother or my kids or grandkids whenever they're down here," said Maria. "It was so much easier to spend time with friends when we were younger, wasn't it?" Maria asked, and we nodded.

"I remember spending so much time with my cousin Isabel and lots of friends. We all used to go ice skating, shopping, and dancing. On summer nights before I met Rafael, we would go strolling past the group of boys lounging in front of Costa's Drugstore. I wonder what happened to those girls? How could everything change so much?"

"What changed were your priorities," I said, firmly. "When you got married, your family came first."

Maria nodded. "My cousin Isabel recently gave me some advice," she said. 'It's enough with the family,' Isabel told me on the way to the airport. 'I can see what's happening. You took care of your husband and kids, and now you're taking care of your mother.' Isabel, one of the strongest people I know, even had tears in her eyes. 'I just want you to do something for yourself, OK? Get a life, cuz. It's your turn now.'"

I nodded. "It *is* your turn now, Maria," I said. "In fact, it's time for all of us to do what we want."

Maria looked like she had some tears in her eyes, too. She stood up.

"Let me finish getting everything ready," she said, heading to the kitchen. "You two can go ahead and get the meeting started." She noticed me fanning myself with a napkin.

"Debbie, do you want me to lower the AC?"

"Yes, please."

Fran looked at me expectantly. "Okay, what do we do now?"

We just looked at each other.

"I'm not sure," I said slowly. "I never started a club before. Maybe we could start with a statement of purpose or something?"

Fran thought for a second and smiled. "Well, since this is The Cabernet Club, I think we need to start the meeting with a glass of cabernet."

"Now that," I said with a smile, "is what I call an excellent statement of purpose. I second the motion."

Fran jumped up and headed to the kitchen with the bottle of cabernet sauvignon she had brought. After she asked Maria for a wine opener, both women came out of the kitchen a minute later, and Fran deftly poured wine into each of the crystal wine glasses set out on coasters on the coffee table.

"A toast to our new club." I lifted my glass. "And to new adventures."

"To new adventures," Maria echoed.

"Um—what kind of adventures?" Fran asked in a hesitant voice.

"I'm thinking maybe an orgy," I deadpanned. "Or we

could pose naked for a Palmetto Pointe calendar featuring mature ladies with droopy boobs."

"Wow," Maria commented. "I was thinking along the lines of visiting a museum or a boat ride, but the orgy thing sounds more sociable."

We talked and laughed and finished our wine in short order.

"I'm glad I brought two bottles," said Fran. "And the best part is we don't have to worry about driving home," Fran was gleeful. "We can just walk back to our condos."

"All well and good, but we're getting off the subject of the club itself," I pointed out. "What do we want this club to be?"

"I would love to share some of the funny things we've heard and experienced at Palmetto Pointe," said Maria. "I make a motion that we always share funny stuff at our meetings. Does anyone have anything funny to share?"

"Actually, yes," I said. "A funny thing happened on the way to the mailbox."

"Mister Highpockets," Maria and Fran said together.

"Actually, it was his sister, Freda. She was sitting outside on her brother's piano stool, and as I walked by, she grabbed my arm and said, 'I need to talk to you.'"

"What about?" Maria asked, and Fran leaned forward expectantly.

"Freda is worried about Stanley. She says he's lonely and she thinks he and I should get together. She even gave me some coupons for Burger King."

"And you said what?"

"I said, 'Freda, these coupons already expired, and besides, I am not interested in going out with your brother.'"

"And Freda pipes up, 'Yes, my brother is very interesting.' Apparently, she's as deaf as he is."

"Oh, I almost forgot," Maria said. "I have some news. Harriet Bertulli is now selling Avon. You should have seen her. She was wearing a long black caftan, and she looked like she'd just come from a coven meeting. And she even had the nerve to try and sell me some Avon stuff."

"Just hearing her name can drive me to drink," I said, getting up and pouring myself some more wine. "I don't want anything to do with her."

We went back to the subject of The Cabernet Club. Should we have an election of officers? No, because we only had three members. What about rules? Only one: What happens in The Cabernet Club stays in The Cabernet Club.

"I have an idea, based on our earlier discussion," I said.

"Which part?" asked Fran.

"When we were talking about the fact that it's finally our turn to live the lives we want to live."

Maria and Fran nodded.

"Except that it's hard to do that on our own, so maybe we can help each other?" I said.

"That sounds like a great idea!" Maria exclaimed, smiling.

"And I need help, fast," I said.

Fran and Maria looked confused.

"I only have a lease until the end of November," I said.

"That's such a short amount of time," said Fran.

"Exactly," I said. "Palmetto Pointe, as wacky as it is, already feels like home to me. Plus, it's the most affordable place in the area. And I've never owned a home and was hoping I could buy here. I could use your help finding a place."

"I'm happy to help," said Fran. "I could use some help from The Cabernet Club, too. But I have different issues. I really want to help out kids, and I wouldn't mind a boyfriend, but I'm not sure what I'm looking for."

"I want a boyfriend, too," Maria said. "And I want to get my mom into an assisted living facility somehow, so I can have free time."

My mind was moving fast. "I've got it," I said proudly, standing up.

"Got what?" Maria asked.

"The motto for The Cabernet Club. It's 'Why can't the rest of your life be the best of your life?'"

Fran nodded slowly.

"Well put," said Fran. "You have a way with words, Debbie—have you considered writing?"

We all laughed.

Finally, Maria stood up and announced, "We have a lot of work to do. And it's easier to come up with great ideas on a full stomach. I make a motion we adjourn for dinner."

We brought our wine glasses to the table. Everything was delicious—the roast beef with mushrooms, the romaine salad with raspberries and goat cheese, the rice pilaf.

"You're such a good cook, Maria," Fran took a second helping. "I'm terrible. George used to do all the cooking. When it's my turn to host the club, I'll probably do takeout."

"Whatever—that's fine," Maria told her. "You could always get takeout from The Rendezvous. Like Randy told us, the food isn't great but there's a lot of it."

"We ought to go back to Randy's again," Fran

suggested. "It was fun. And I still can't get over the fact that Kay and Debbie were in high school together. By the way, has anyone seen Kay lately?"

Maria shook her head. "No, and I haven't seen her car around. Anyhow, let's sit a while and discuss how we can get started on getting a life before we have dessert and coffee."

Just then we heard a loud knock at the door. "Who the heck can that be?" asked Maria. She went to the door.

"Sorry to bother you," said a familiar husky voice, "but I just got back, and I saw a notice from Fed Ex that they left a package with you."

I felt my stomach lurch.

Maria opened the door. "Oh, Kay, hello. Yes, I've got your package. I almost forgot about it. Come on in."

"Sorry. I didn't know you had company. I can come back." As always, Kay was beautifully dressed, now in a long white skirt and blouse with turquoise jewelry, her hair and makeup perfect.

"No, no. It's only Fran and Debbie. We were just having dessert. Sit down. Please."

Maria bustled around, cutting slices of cake and pouring coffee. "Come on, join us."

"I really can't—"

"We were just talking about you a little while ago," Fran babbled. "We haven't seen you in a while. Where have you been?"

"I was away," Kay said, noncommittal as always.

"Have some coffee with us. I promise it'll be decaf. "

"Nothing for me, thanks. So, Maria, if you'll get me my package, I'll say good night. I'm beat."

"You do look tired." Maria went to her bedroom and returned with a manila shipping envelope.

Kay grabbed it. "That's my lucky rabbit's foot. I'd forgotten to bring it down here."

"Well, I'm glad I'm not superstitious, knock on wood," Maria joked and everyone chuckled.

After Kay left, we were silent for a few minutes.

A rabbit's foot, I brooded. Why the hell does she need a rabbit's foot? She's got all the luck in the world. She always did.

A memory came back to me then. Junior year at Winslow High School. Everyone is buzzing about the new student, a rich, beautiful girl whose photos often appear in the *Society Page* of the local paper. According to gossip, she had been kicked out of a ritzy private school for letting a boy climb up to her room.

That first day she strolls into Miss Dugan's homeroom, wearing a blue babydoll dress. All the guys are ogling her blondness and her boobs.

A joke goes around the school. "Did you hear that Kay Caldwell has T.B.?"

"Oh, my God, she does?"

"Yeah, she's got T.B., all right. Two beauts."

Fran's giggle broke into my thoughts. "Hey, look. I still remember how to make a pin curl." She twisted a piece of hair around her finger.

I had never seen Fran so animated. She started to reminisce about a host of things—TV shows, games kids used to play, old advertising jingles.

I willed myself to focus on the lighthearted banter, but once again, my happy mood had dampened when I saw Kay.

Luckily nobody noticed. The otherwise wonderful evening came to its end and we made plans for the next meeting.

As I walked unsteadily into my condo, all I could think of was Kay Caldwell. It may have been a lifetime away from Winslow High, but once again Kay had managed to spoil things—even the first official meeting of The Cabernet Club of Palmetto Pointe.

CHAPTER 18

When I picked up my mail, I saw a 9 x 12 envelope postmarked Winslow, Massachusetts, with no return address. I recognized the big, loopy handwriting of my friend, Roz, or maybe I should say my former friend. We had not been in touch for nearly three weeks, ever since the blind date incident.

Ripping open the envelope, I found obituary notices of two former classmates, neatly clipped from the *Winslow Dispatch*, with a terse yellow Post-it note that read, "They're dropping like flies."

Now, if there is one thing guaranteed to bring people together and reconcile hurt feelings, it is the mutual need to inform the estranged that somebody they both knew has passed away, and to discuss details of the death.

I grabbed the phone and called Roz.

It was as if we had never had a rift. "I'm stunned," I told Roz. "I can't believe Priscilla Benson died. She was the youngest one in our class. Oh, and Manny Lopes, too. He was so much fun. Remember how he always used to kid around?'

"Well, he's not kidding around this time," Roz said. "He's ten toes up, that's for sure."

"Oh, and you know what else, Roz? I got an email last night from the reunion committee that Richard LeClair passed."

"Passed what?" Roz asked.

"He passed, he died. What did you think I meant when I said he passed?"

"I thought you meant a kidney stone. My poor Cy passed a kidney stone last week. He was in such pain."

I gave a deep sigh. "Well, it looks like the circle is narrowing. We're in the first-row orchestra."

"Yeah," Roz agreed. "Life is short. That's why," she added pointedly, "you gotta be nice to people, especially old friends."

I got the message. "Hey, Rozzie, I'm looking at Priscilla's obituary. Wow, she even hyphenated her name—pretty fancy. Listen to this: "Mrs. Benson-Hewlitt was a graduate of Winslow High School and Bridgewater State College in Massachusetts. She married the love of her life, the late Carlton Hewlitt, M.D. She taught for many years in the Connecticut School system until her retirement, beloved by students and parents alike. She enjoyed music and the arts, and played a mean game of tennis. She was a member of Ladies Who Garden, the Maplewood Country Club, the Women's Auxiliary. She will be mourned greatly by her three loving children and seven grandchildren as well as her devoted longtime companion, Lawrence Moss. She had a smile that lit up every room and will be sorely missed by—"

"I think you have to pay for obituaries these days," Roz

broke in. "I'm not sure if it's a set fee or you pay by the number of words. Anyhow, why are you making such a big deal? You hardly knew Priscilla Benson."

"That's not the point," I said. "Her obituary sounds so interesting. She belonged to the Country Club, she was a teacher, and she had a devoted boyfriend after her husband died."

"That Priscilla Benson—she was no American beauty, let her rest in peace," Roz said. "I don't know how she snagged a doctor as a boyfriend."

"Never mind her, what about my obituary?" I felt suddenly depressed. "What the heck can they write about me? Nothing interesting. I worked as a secretary, whoop-de-doo. What organizations did I belong to? The Cabernet Club and my Writers' Group? My life is deadly dull, no pun intended. Seriously, Roz, what can they write about me?"

"What do you care what they write? You won't be around to read it."

I had to laugh. "That sounds like something your dad would say. He was so funny. I remember whenever people asked what somebody died of, he would always say 'shortness of breath.'"

"He was a gas, all right," Roz said softly. "You're one of the few people left who remembers my father and mother."

"You and I go back a long time," I agreed. "We have a shared history."

"Those new friends of yours in Florida—they don't have that," Roz said, a note of jealousy in her tone. "You know that old saying, 'Make new friends but keep the old; one is silver and the other is gold.'"

"Okay, Golden Girl, you made your point," I said. "But

getting back to the obituary stuff, it's like my life is so small. I wish my obituary would sound a little more substantial."

"So go write it yourself. My son keeps telling me to get my obituary ready and send it to him. Otherwise he says he wouldn't know what to put in the paper."

"Kids are so thoughtful these days," I murmured.

"I've got an idea. Maybe you and I can get together and write our obituaries when I'm in Florida," Roz suggested. "Cy and I want to come down in December."

"I hope I have my new place by then, because that's what I call a real fun Girls' Night Out." I said. "Hey, we could always make up a bunch of lies and have everybody confused. Might as well go out in a blaze of bullshit."

"Leave it to you to think of something like that," Roz chuckled. "You're even crazier since you've been living in Palmetto Pointe."

That gave me an idea. I grabbed the free local paper from my counter, *The Banyan Beach Times,* and started to read the obituary page to Roz. Of course we didn't know any of these people, but it'd still be fun. Just about everyone who died here had been born somewhere else. Made sense.

I didn't read the obituaries for men, only women, and only those whose photos looked interesting and not too elderly. This would become a ritual. First the *Living* section, then the *News* section, and then the *Local* section which contained the "Death Notices." I preferred the classic term "Obituaries" but oh well.

I read about Eileen Murphy Scarpone (who had five sons and learned Italian cooking from her mother-in-law), and Charlotte Levine Glassman who, at age fifty, with a sick husband and children in college, went back to school and earned a nursing degree.

They were interesting, but nobody was as memorable as Loretta Barr Winograd, whose obituary read: "Our beautiful mother graced this earth for ninety years," and told about a woman placed in an orphanage at a young age, who went on to carve out a career in fashion, marry a philanthropist, raise five children, and launch a dynasty of successful kids and grandchildren.

"It takes my breath away," I told Roz. "I mean, it reads like a novel. I almost feel like sending Loretta's family a letter to say this is the most beautiful tribute I've ever read, but I'm not sure who to send it to."

"I think you've got too much time on your hands," Roz said. "You'd be better off learning to play mahjongg."

"Oh, did I tell you I have an appointment with this pre-needs planning guy to see about cremation?"

"Cremation?" Roz sounded stunned. "What do you mean? You've got a cemetery plot up here, right near mine, and you can't get your money back."

"I know, but things have changed. My daughter's in Delaware now and she'll probably never go back to Winslow. And so what if I don't get my money back. I don't care. Besides, I don't want to be in the ground. I'm claustrophobic. I'd rather be cremated."

"You'll be just as claustrophobic stuffed in an urn or a pill box or whatever the hell they put your ashes in." Roz was shouting now. "And your cemetery plot is right near mine. I won't even know who's going to be buried near me."

"For God's sake, Roz, it's not as if we're going to have conversations or coffee klatches down there. And almost everyone I know in Florida is planning to be cremated.

Maria signed up with Leon Leiberman and I think Fran will, too."

Roz was silent for a moment. "Oh, I see—it's your friends. They've brainwashed you. Next thing you know, you'll want one of those ha-ha fun funeral services where everybody has a good time and they talk about celebrating life and all that crap."

"Hell, no," I said. "I don't want them having fun at my funeral. I want loud crying and hysterical sobbing. And maybe some gospel music. I saw this video on YouTube of the Mormon Tabernacle Choir, and this Black guy with a beautiful voice singing, "Going Home." It's a real tear-jerker. You know that one, don't you?"

I started to sing: "Going home, going home, I'm just going home—"

I was halfway through the song before I realized Roz had hung up.

CHAPTER 19

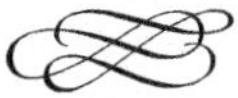

"Hi, Mom."

"Listen, Lori, can I talk to you later? It's raining, and I need to concentrate on the road."

"Of course. Please be safe."

"You, too. Love you."

"Love you."

I ended up driving really slowly. The rain was coming down hard.

When I made it safely to the parking lot, I grabbed my umbrella and walked carefully to the city offices, trying to avoid the puddles.

Inside, I shook out my umbrella and moved quickly to the Recreation Office.

Ursula was waiting for me. She looked pointedly at the clock on the wall.

"I see you're five minutes late," she said.

"Sorry, yes, it took me longer because of the rain."

"Didn't you have rain, and even snow, where you came from before you got to Florida?"

"Yes, but—"

"And didn't you have to leave extra time for bad weather to get to work on time?"

"Yes, but—"

"Exactly." She smiled meanly. "Don't be late again."

I nodded and went to my desk. This was typical of Ursula. For some reason, she had it out for me and seemed to look for ways to make me seem incompetent. Mostly I tried to ignore it, but it was starting to bug me.

"We need this to go to the printer on Friday," said Ursula. "So you need to get everything typed up today." I had been about to get a cup of coffee, but I guess Ursula wanted to make sure I wasn't taking any extra time in addition to the five minutes that I was late.

I took a look at the forms Ursula handed me.

"Why don't the instructors just enter their information online and then we could pull it together into the course booklet?" I asked. "It would save so much time."

Ursula looked at me like I was speaking in tongues. "I know you were an office manager before you retired, and your fancy law office had all kinds of technology, but this is the way we do things here," she shot back.

"It's not difficult at all," I said. "I can explain to the instructors how to do it."

Ursula glared at me.

I sighed. "Okay. I'll get these papers together and start typing everything out."

I worked nonstop, not even bothering to go to the bathroom. That seemed to satisfy Ursula; she gave me a left-handed compliment. "Who would think somebody your age could type so fast?"

"Um—thanks, I think."

"Oh, and how are you liking the pickleball at Palmetto Pointe?" Ursula asked, making conversation now that I had finished my assignment quickly.

"Well, I haven't started it yet, but I plan to go soon," I said. Ursula frowned.

I was saved from more pickleball questions when another employee, Charmaine, waltzed in. Literally. She was always doing some kind of dance; she would tango on her way to the copy machine and samba as she waited for the copies.

That, among other things, drove Ursula nuts. When Charmaine came to work, Ursula acted nice enough. Or at least as nice as Ursula could. As soon as Charmaine left, however, Ursula's demeanor changed. The first time it happened, Ursula explained:

"I've been working here for over twenty years, and she got a job here because her husband helped the mayor get elected." Ursula frowned. "I never would have hired that useless dumbass."

Charmaine was a chirpy-voiced, dishwater blonde with a wide grin and a "What, Me Worry?" attitude. I got a kick out of Charmaine, who didn't have the greatest work ethic but was good-natured and fun.

Ursula's greeting to Charmaine was, "Oh, so you're finally back from that bloodsucking dentist of yours. How much did he soak you?"

"My dentist believes in saving teeth, not yanking them all out like your redneck dentist did," Charmaine replied.

"Well, I had soft teeth, so he had to pull them all out

when I was nineteen." Ursula tapped her dentures proudly. "I bet you spent more on one tooth than I did for all these choppers."

I was amazed. "You had all your teeth out when you were nineteen?"

Ursula shrugged as if to say, "Doesn't everyone?" She looked at the clock. "I'm taking the afternoon off. Mr. Oppenshaw says I have to use up my vacation days."

Charmaine and I exchanged glances. Ursula always seemed to be taking time off, a day here, half a day there. Having worked at the city offices for over twenty years, she had accumulated what seemed like a staggering number of vacation and sick days.

Charmaine asked, "So where are you off to today?"

"Wendell and I are going to a seminar," Ursula said loftily as she grabbed her purse and marched out of the office.

I shook my head. "How does she have so many sick days and vacation time coming to her?"

"Well, for one thing, she's never out sick," Charmaine said with her tinkly laugh. "Her cheapskate husband, Wendell, won't let her. And they never go away on vacation except maybe to visit relatives. Those two have never traveled anywhere."

"Really?"

Charmaine nodded. "Yeah, they hate to spend a dime. They go to Costco for the free food samples for lunch or dinner on the weekends."

"You're kidding."

"It's true. Today they're going to one of those fancy financial seminars where they give you a free gourmet lunch," Charmaine rattled on. "You've seen those ads for Wealth Preservation."

"What—they're wealthy?"

"Hell, no. They don't have a pot to piss in," Charmaine hooted. "Wendell hasn't worked in years, and he spends a fortune on cigarettes and big-ass crappy old cars. I don't know how they keep getting into those seminars. I mean, wouldn't you think the seminar people would catch on after a while?"

"Huh. There's a whole world out there I never knew about," I mused, and resumed typing.

The afternoon went by quickly, and suddenly it was almost time to go home. Charmaine had returned from yet another jaunt to the ladies' room and reported that it looked as if it were going to rain again. I sighed as I put on my combination windbreaker/rain jacket and grabbed my purse and umbrella.

What a crazy day it had been weather-wise. "I hope it doesn't rain too hard," I remarked to Charmaine as we walked out the door.

Rain? What rain? The sun was dazzling, the skies were blue, and the parking lot was dry.

"Look at that," Charmaine marveled. "If you don't like Florida weather, wait a minute. Florida weather is crazy."

"Florida weather isn't just crazy," I declared, "it's positively schizophrenic."

When I got to my car, I called Lori on speaker.

"Hi, honey," I said. "Can you believe that it's now sunny out?"

"Sure," she said. "It's beautiful here today. Sunny, only eighty degrees, and no humidity."

I knew what she was trying to say. If I had been in

Delaware, it would be sunny, less hot, and with no humidity. But I wouldn't take the bait.

"So how's work?" I said.

"Good. And much slower than tax season, thank God. Oh, and Greg can't take any vacation time yet, but I'm going to take a week off at the end of July. The kids and I would love you to come visit us. We can hang out, go to the beach, and spend time together. We miss you."

I smiled. "I miss you guys, too. But I can't take time off from my job until I've been there three months. I'm so sorry."

Silence.

"Seriously? It's a part-time job, Ma. You can't take a week off, in the summer, in Florida? That's ridiculous."

"It's actually a really busy time at the Recreation Office," I explained. "Summer camp, and they're getting ready to launch pickleball—"

"Really? Well then why don't you just quit? You don't really like it anyway, right? I'm sure you could get another part-time job."

"I could, but I don't want to be on my feet, working in food service or retail."

"Oh for crying out loud, I'm sure you could find another part-time administrative job, Ma. Don't you want to see us?"

"Yes, and I'll definitely see you and the kids at Thanksgiving. I can't wait."

"Obviously, you can. I'll talk to you later, Ma." And Lori hung up.

CHAPTER 20

By the time I got to the pool on Sunday morning, Fran was already standing by the lounge chairs.

"Maria can't make it. Something to do with her mom, but she said she'll definitely be at our dinner tonight. Oh, and is that a new bathing suit? That color looks great on you."

"Thanks," I preened. "It was on sale for $25 at Macy's. Oh—and fun fact—did you know that aqua is one of the colors that looks great on everyone?"

"Really? No. What's the other one?"

"Coral," I said.

"You're always full of interesting information, Debbie," Fran said.

"Yeah, it really helps me have conversations with strangers," I said, and we laughed.

I laid out my towel on the lounge chair next to Fran, and started rummaging around in my tote for my sunblock.

Just then, who should rush over but The Black Widow,

Harriet Bertulli. She wore a black sarong and an armful of bracelets and waved colorful flyers at us.

"Look, I've got some Avon specials you're gonna love." She took off her sunglasses and stared at Fran, who was wearing her usual long-sleeved, high-necked shirt over her bathing suit, and a straw hat covering her face.

"My God, you look like you belong in a rice paddy," Harriet said. "Avon has a special on sunblock that would be perfect for you."

"Thanks, but I already have a good sunblock. My dermatologist recommended it."

"Then how about a bronzer? You could use some color," Harriet observed. "You're pale like a corpse." Fran shook her head "no," but the Black Widow persisted. "Well, Avon has some very nice jewelry, see?" She jangled the bracelets. "The two of you could use some spiffing up."

I was trying to think of a snappy comeback when Harriet hissed, "Oh, my God, look who's going into the pool. You see him?" She pointed to a good-looking older man with silver hair and a toned body. "What a waste."

"What do you mean?"

"He's—you know." Harriet tapped a finger to her head. "I call him Nut Job. Look how he's carrying on."

The Water Aerobics Class was in the midst of doing their twenty-five jumping jacks. "Apart, together, apart in front, apart together, apart in back," the group chanted. Maxine, the instructor, was keeping count as they jumped and splashed and waved their arms. "Eleven," she called out.

"Thirteen," Nut Job yelled and blew her a kiss.

"Twelve," Maxine shouted, trying to ignore him.

"Fourteen."

By now, the class was confused. "What number are we up to?" somebody asked.

"Please, Glenn, don't interrupt the class," Maxine pleaded.

A young woman hurried into the pool and grabbed his arm. "Come on, Dad, you're bothering the ladies." He followed her out meekly.

Harriet snorted. "Now do you see what I mean? He's out of it. They shouldn't let him in the pool."

"Why not?" Fran said. "He's not hurting anyone."

"Yeah," I agreed. "Guys just want to have fun."

"Oh, give me a break," Harriet huffed. "Let me tell you what happened. I met him a couple weeks ago, and I wasted nearly an hour on him. At first, I'm thinking, wow, this guy's a catch, then I realize he's repeating himself and asking me the same things, over and over. The porch light's on but nobody's home, ya know?"

"What a bummer," I said. "I mean, wasting your time and all."

"You got that right," Harriet nodded, and looked over my shoulder. "Oh, I see some of the girls from pickleball. I'm gonna love ya and leave ya." She gave one last look at Nut Job, who was sunning himself on a lounge, next to his daughter.

Harriet sighed. "I could have gone for him if it wasn't for the dementia."

"Oh, well," I said, "nobody's perfect."

Soon Harriet was talking up her Avon products to a group of ladies on the other side of the pool area.

"Speaking of pickleball, I have a favor to ask you," I told Fran. "Can you teach me how to play? I want to start playing, plus my boss at the Rec Office keeps asking me about it."

"Actually, Palmetto Pointe has a really great beginner's clinic—the one where Harriet dumped me and flirted with the coach," said Fran. "The Friday morning clinics are for new players, so you can learn how to play the game. But I know you work on Fridays, and I think they have a clinic on Wednesday nights, too. I'll check and let you know."

"That would be great," I said, grabbing some cookies and a bottle of water from my tote.

Fran got up and I saw her move to pick up a beach ball that had gotten thrown out of the pool. She walked over to a group of laughing kids in the guest pool, and started talking with them.

After a few minutes, she came back, smiling.

"Those kids were having so much fun."

Fran looked at them wistfully.

"You really love kids, don't you?"

"Yeah, and I really miss being around them."

"So have you thought about doing some volunteer work with kids?"

"Not really. I kind of shut down when I learned I couldn't have a foster child."

I looked at Fran. "You said your childhood best friend was a foster child, right?"

Fran nodded. "Yes, Patsy. Patsy O'Keefe." She looked out at the distance and continued. "I'm not even sure she was officially a foster kid. She was taken in by our landlady, Mrs. Gunkel, who lived upstairs. Patsy's mother was supposedly 'working things out' and in exchange for staying with her, Patsy had to do a lot of chores for Mrs. Gunkel."

"It sounds like a hard childhood," I said.

Fran shook her head, then smiled. "But Patsy was always cheerful, even though kids without family support had a tough time in those days."

"Huh," I said. Then I had a thought.

"Fran, there are all kinds of programs to help kids these days. We could brainstorm some ways that you could volunteer with them."

"Hmm," she said, taking a moment. Then she smiled. "That's a good idea. When do you want to do it?"

I pulled out my notebook and pen. "How about now? Luckily, I always have a pen and paper, so I'll write down the ideas, and I can email them to you later."

"Okay," said Fran, sitting up straighter. Then she slumped down. "But my mind is blank."

"I'll get us started," I said.

After twenty minutes or so, Fran and I had come up with a list that included everything from volunteering as a tutor at an elementary school, to helping kids at an after-school program, to becoming a Guardian Ad Litem for a foster child.

Fran had never heard of the Guardian Ad Litem program, so I had been especially proud to contribute that idea. Over the years, several lawyers in my office had worked with the Guardian Ad Litem program. When I told them I was retiring to Florida, one of the attorneys said he had heard there was a thriving Guardian Ad Litem program there, and suggested that I consider volunteering for it. But I thought Fran was a perfect fit.

"You're basically an advocate for a foster child," I explained. "The court might ask you to check out a foster child's living situation, interview friends and teachers, review school reports, attend court sessions—whatever is needed to make sure that a foster child is taken care of."

"So you don't need to be a lawyer?"

"Nope, they train you."

Fran's eyes lit up. "That sounds amazing I love the idea of helping foster kids have a great life. Patsy could have used something like that."

"I'm sure they have information about it online," I said. "And you can check out the tutoring and afterschool volunteering options, too."

"Perfect." said Fran. "Thanks, Debbie. You have such great ideas."

I smiled, and thought of those funny Someecards, "I've received too many compliments, said nobody, ever."

CHAPTER 21

"I've been thinking about boyfriends," I told the girls at the first Cabernet Club dinner I hosted. Maria, bless her heart, as they say in the South, had helped me deep clean my condo and buy some inexpensive placements, tablecloths, and other tchotchkes to make the place feel homier. And since the exterminator had been coming, I hadn't seen a palmetto, thank god.

We all three Cabernet Clubbers wanted a boyfriend, so I thought it was time to take some action.

"This should be interesting," said Maria, from the kitchen. "Let me bring in this artichoke dip while it's warm. Fran, you already have the cabernet out, right?"

Fran nodded. "Make sure to take the glass with your special wine glass charm," I said.

"Oh that's what those little things are," said Fran. "And I love sea turtles. I hope mine is the green one?"

"Yep, since it's your favorite color," I said. "Maria's is purple, and mine is blue. I got them at HomeGoods. I just love that place. We had a HomeGoods about thirty minutes away from us in Winslow, but I never went there."

Fran nodded. "I got the cutest crib for one of my dolls there."

"Hey, have any of you seen Kay around?" asked Maria. "I haven't seen her in a few weeks."

Fran and I shook our heads. "Maybe she's traveling," I said. And maybe she'll never come back, I hoped. I was still having haunting dreams about Danny.

"Okay, girls, grab some chips and dip and wine, and let's start talking," said Maria, putting the steaming bowl on the table.

"Oh, before we get started, I want to thank Maria for using the oven," I said. "I've never turned it on, so it's nice to know that if I ever need it, it works."

We all laughed. "Okay, Debbie, what's this about boyfriends?" said Fran, taking a sip of cabernet.

"So," I said, "the other day when Fran mentioned she wasn't sure what she was looking for in a boyfriend, it reminded me of high school. Remember when we made those lists about what we wanted in our husbands?" They nodded. "Well, I think we should make a list of what we'd like to see in a boyfriend. It will definitely be different now that we're older and in a different life stage, but it might help us attract what we're looking for."

"I'm not sure about that," said Maria, "but it still sounds fun."

"And we can each create our own list, and compare it."

Fran clapped her hands together. "Great. When do we get started?"

"Right now," I said, grabbing some notebooks and

pens. "Let's spend fifteen minutes writing down the top five things we want in a boyfriend."

"That's not very much time," said Maria.

"Well, we always have a short timeframe for writing in the writers' group," I said. "Is thirty minutes better?"

"Yes," Maria and Fran answered.

"Alexa, set a thirty-minute timer," I said.

When Alexa charmingly told us the time was up, I was so glad. I had finished my list in five minutes, and spent the next twenty-five minutes eating too many chips with dip, drinking two glasses of cabernet, and watching Maria and Fran slowly write out their lists.

"Okay girls, let's share what we've got," I said.

"Why don't you go first, Debbie?" said Maria.

"Sure," I said. "In no particular order, here are the five things I'd like in a boyfriend, 1, Likes to try new activities; 2, Respects me; 3, Has a good sense of humor; 4, Isn't clingy; 5, Drives at night."

Maria and Fran were silent. Then a few seconds later, Maria said, "Could you explain each of those a little more?"

"Okay," I said. "So the first one is about trying new things. I mean, I love my books and Netflix, but I don't just want to sit around and do that every night. I like to go out, too, and I like to try out new 'cool' things. Like axe throwing. Lori told me she went out with some people from work and had a blast."

"Huh," said Maria, not sounding too convinced. "How about the other ones?"

"Well, the second one is based on my time with my husband," I said. "He used to put me down because I didn't go to college, even though he barely squeaked by. Whenever we would go out with friends, and I would try and talk about current events, he'd say, 'Oh, the high school graduate has some important opinions.'"

"That's awful!" Fran exclaimed.

"Sometimes my husband would embarrass me, too," said Maria. "I was always a little chubby, and when we had family dinners, if I went to get seconds of something, or had more than a small piece of cake, he'd say, 'Do you really need to eat that?'"

"Wow," I breathed. "That sucks."

"Yeah," said Maria, looking down at the table.

"Well," I said, to shift the conversation, "I can tell you that I've dated respectful men, but they didn't have the other important qualities. Like the third one, 'has a good sense of humor,' which is self-explanatory."

"Of course, since you're so funny," said Fran, smiling.

"Thanks." I smiled, too. "The 'Isn't clingy' quality means that I don't have to spend every minute of every day with him. I like my space, and I also want to hang out with my own friends, namely, you two."

"That's so true," said Fran. "Last year, I went out with one of the We Care volunteers, and he wanted to spend all his time with me. I felt like I was suffocating."

"Exactly," I said. "And last, but certainly not least, driving at night is my final important quality. I don't like driving, especially at night, so I want someone to be able to do that, so we can go out."

Maria and Fran laughed.

"I have that on my list, too," said Maria.

"Me, too," said Fran.

I joined in. "Well, I think every single woman in Palmetto Pointe would probably have that on their list."

"So, who wants to go next?" I asked.

Silence.

"I guess I'll go next," said Fran. "But my list isn't like yours, except for the driving at night."

"That's okay," I said. "I might even revise my list based on some of your thoughts. Or add to mine."

"Okay, so here it is," Fran said, and cleared her throat, "1, Loves animals and children; 2, Cares about others; 3, Interested in fitness; 4, Likes takeout; 5, Drives at night."

Maria and I looked at each other, confused.

"You're probably wondering why I included 'loves animals and children,' when I don't have any, and Palmetto Pointe doesn't allow any either."

We nodded.

"I love animals," said Fran. "Even if I can't have them here, I want to be able to laugh about my Facebook *Truckin' Cat* videos, or watch *Animal Planet* together," Fran explained. "Every time I had on an animal program, George always changed the channel to sports. Debbie and I came up with some ways I can volunteer with kids, and I'd like to be able to talk about that with a boyfriend, too."

"That makes sense," said Maria. "Same with caring about others."

"Yes, and 'likes takeout' goes without saying," I said, and we laughed.

"And I know we don't talk about exercise much, but it's an important part of my life," said Fran.

"Well, we know you go to the gym and play pickleball," said Maria.

"And I played a lot of basketball in high school and college," said Fran.

"That's right," I nodded. "Were you a star?" I joked.

"Actually, I got a basketball scholarship, and we were the champions in my junior and senior years of college," said Fran, shyly.

"Wow," said Maria. "How come you don't play anymore?"

"This body can't handle all of that jumping around anymore," said Fran. "But I still like to watch a great game."

"That is just amazing," I said. "I love learning all these interesting things about you, Fran." I turned to Maria. "And now it's your turn to share your fascinating list with us."

"It's actually pretty boring, compared to the two of you," said Maria. "I haven't dated anyone since Rafael died, and I'm not as creative as the two of you."

"Don't worry, Maria, you're not getting graded," said Fran, gently. "Let's just hear your list."

"Okay," she said, and shared it with us, "1, Handsome; 2, Christian; 3, Appreciative; 4, Sexy; 5, Drives at night."

"Great list," I said. "But of course I have to ask you about number four."

Maria giggled. "I don't know if that's the right word, but I want someone who's interested in sex. Rafael and I always had a good sex life, and I miss it."

"Well, that's not really that important to me. I never understood what the big deal was about," said Fran.

"Uh, I'll keep that part of my life private," I said.

"Now say more on *appreciative*," said Fran.

"The two of you inspired that idea," said Maria. "You're always complimenting me on my cooking and cleaning, and I like it. It makes me feel good, and I'd like a boyfriend to be the same way."

"That makes so much sense," said Fran. "I'm adding it to my list. Obviously, I won't get much appreciation for my cooking, which is nonexistent, but maybe I'll get some appreciation for my volunteer activities and amazing doll collection."

"Not to mention their chic HomeGoods cribs," I chimed in.

Maria and I giggled along with Fran.

"Oh, and no offense to you, Debbie, but being Christian is important to me because I really like my church, and it's always been an important part of my life," said Maria.

"No offense taken," I said. "And handsome, of course, would be great. But I'd settle for a full head of hair."

"Cheers to that," said Maria, and we clinked our glasses.

CHAPTER 22

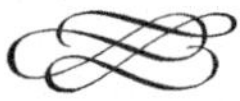

Now that we had our trusty boyfriend lists, I had another list to tend to. It was time to check an item off my to-dos. I couldn't wait to tell Ursula about it. Maybe she'd even offer me a smile.

Plus, the Wednesday night pickleball clinic was the best bargain in town.

For five dollars, we got a ninety-minute group lesson and the use of pickleball paddles and balls. Two courts were set up for our beginner lessons, and the other two courts were busy with residents playing games.

I was wearing some gym shorts, a t-shirt, and sneakers, and I felt a little underdressed. Most of the women had on tennis skirts, matching tank tops, and court shoes. Even Fran wore a tennis skirt.

The coach was a gray-haired man in his early seventies, wearing a backward-facing blue cap, grey gym shorts, and a light blue t-shirt, which was already pretty sweaty. He was wearing braces that covered his knees and legs.

"Fran," I whispered, nudging her elbow. "That's the coach I told you about. The one who helped me out at Publix."

He whistled to get everyone's attention. "I'm Coach Joe," he said. "The first thing people notice about me is that I have on these long leg braces." We all nodded. "I'm here to tell you that almost anyone can play pickleball, even people with bad knees, like me. But—and this is critical—it's incredibly important to warm up and warm down. And if something starts hurting, take a break. Let's get started with some dynamic stretching."

I had no idea what that was, but I followed along as we did something called high knee marches. Then I heard a familiar voice from the reserved courts.

"And I told her that everyone knows Skin So Soft prevents mosquito bites in addition to moisturizing."

Harriet Bertulli, aka the Black Widow, aka the Avon Lady, was, well—holding court—on the pickleball courts. I looked over, and sure enough, she was talking loudly and dressed in all black, including sequined court shoes and a glittery cap. It felt like it was a hundred degrees with a hundred percent humidity, but she didn't even seem to be sweating.

"Debbie," Fran whispered, "We're doing arm circles now."

I brought my attention back to the warm-up exercises.

Soon we were on the courts, and learning about "dinks," and "the kitchen." I didn't quite get the hang of the scoring, but Coach said that most people learn it after playing a few times.

By the end of the clinic, we were all sweating and

drinking water. We started chatting with each other, and I started to understand why people enjoyed pickleball so much. It seemed like a great way to socialize.

"Yoohoo, Coach Joe," I heard that familiar voice again.

"Yes, Harriet?" he said, with what sounded like a sigh.

"Maybe you'd be interested in a home-cooked meal," she said, in a flirty tone. "And you could give me a one-on-one lesson in return," she said, emphasizing the "one-on-one."

"I actually love cooking," he said, "but I'd be happy to trade a couple of lessons if you can help me transfer files from my PC to my new Mac."

"Your what to what?" Harriet asked, dumbfounded.

The group looked around at each other, confused.

Although it wasn't like me, I spoke up. "Uh—I'd be happy to help you with that," I said.

"Really?" said Coach Joe. He took a closer look. "Wait—aren't you the lady I helped out at Publix? I didn't recognize you in your workout clothes."

"Yes. I'm Debbie," I nodded, pleased that he remembered. "And I've transferred files to new computers many times."

"That would be a lifesaver," he said.

"Ugh—that techie stuff—I hate it," said Harriet, trying to bring the conversation back to her.

"Debbie loves it," said Fran. "Maria calls her 'Debbie the Digital Diva.' She set up Maria's iPad and Amazon Echo, and she removed some viruses from Maria's computer."

Harriet look confused, while Joe and I exchanged numbers and made plans for me to go to his house on Tuesday afternoon.

On the way home, Fran said, smirking, "Good job putting the boyfriend list into practice."

"Who, me?" I said, batting my eyelashes. "I was just offering to help. And I have no idea if he has any of those qualities."

But I couldn't wait to find out.

CHAPTER 23

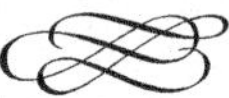

The smell of something delicious greeted me when pickleball coach Joe Moretti opened the door. I guess some people actually do cook in Florida.

"What are you cooking?"

"It's Tuscan chicken, with capers and artichokes in a balsamic sauce. Family recipe."

My stomach rumbled with involuntary gusto. "Well, I'll try and focus on transferring those files to your new computer, but I might have to have a taste," I quipped.

"Of course," said Joe.

I didn't tell him I was joking, because maybe I wasn't. I was pretty hungry…

"Great, but let me start working first."

I was delighted to find his condo refreshingly cool. Even though it had been years since I'd gone through "the change," I found myself sweating more and more. Maybe I just needed to get used to the Florida heat.

He showed me to his computer and about an hour and a half later, I finished my work.

"I can't believe how fast you got that done," Joe marveled.

"I've had a lot of practice," I said. "A few years ago the law office I worked for switched to Macs, and I had to move all the files from our PCs. And some of those files were shared throughout the office, so I had to set up—"

I stopped talking when I realized that Joe was no longer standing next to me.

"Oops, I have that effect on people when I start talking about computers," I started saying.

"No, no, I just had to check on the chicken," he said. "It's almost ready. Will you help me put everything on the table?"

"Oh," I said, surprised. "I was just kidding. You don't need to give me dinner."

"I want to," he said. "I have a feeling you're an appreciative guest." We laughed, and I went into the kitchen.

"Actually, first, why don't you pick a wine from the wine rack?"

I saw an impressive selection of wines, a bona fide bounty of colors and types of grapes.

"Uh, I'm not exactly sure what wine goes with Tuscan chicken."

"Oh, don't worry about that. Just pick something you like."

I hadn't heard of any of them, so they were probably pricey. I had no idea what to choose so naturally I chose a cabernet. The bottle said *Quilt.*

After I brought the bottle to Joe, he opened it expertly.

"Actually, cabernet is a big part of my life now," I said.

"Really?" Joe asked.

"Yes." I told him all about The Cabernet Club as he

put the chicken on the table, along with a Caesar salad and bread.

"Dig in," he said.

We ate for a couple of minutes without talking.

"Well, what do you think?" he asked.

"It's all so delicious," I said, not wanting to stop eating. "I love the chicken, and where did you get this Caesar dressing?"

"I made it," Joe said.

"Wow. And this focaccia bread just melts in my mouth. Did you get it at The Fresh Market?"

"Nope. I made that, too," he said.

"What?" I was amazed. "I don't know anyone who makes their own bread anymore."

"I learned how during the pandemic," he said. "But back to your Cabernet Club. You know, I envy women, especially as I've gotten older," he said. "Women are great at conversations and helping each other. I can't imagine finding a group of guys and creating a Merlot Club."

I chuckled. "Maybe so. But playing pickleball is a great way to make friends, right?" I asked.

"You'd think so, but I never get asked to go anywhere. Maybe they're intimidated because I'm 'Robocop.'"

I almost choked on a piece of bread. "Robocop?"

Joe chuckled. "Yeah, someone saw me playing with my leg braces and said I looked like Robocop, from the movie. I guess I'm kind of scary."

Laughing, I said, "Yeah, that's pretty badass. But the fact that you sweat in a heart shape should let them know you have a sensitive side."

"Oh, you noticed that," Joe said hesitantly, and I could

swear that he was blushing. "Me and my hairy chest. Not exactly dinner conversation."

I laughed again. "Okay, but back to the idea of making friends. Let me tell you a secret."

Joe sat up straighter.

"When I was about ten or so, I told my mom I was bored. She told me I could do some household chores, or I could find something to do. More importantly, she said, 'If you want to do something fun, sometimes you have to be the ringleader.' When I asked her what a ringleader was, she told me it was someone who came up with a good idea and made it happen."

Joe looked thoughtful. "Huh. That makes sense," he said.

"I never forgot that lesson," I said. "Not only has it helped me have amazing experiences, but I used the 'household chores' option with my daughter, who never said she was bored after the first time."

We both chuckled.

"I also have a daughter and a son," said Joe. "And four grandkids. You?"

"A daughter, son-in-law, and two grandkids," I said. "They moved away from our hometown near Boston recently, to Delaware. I didn't have any reason to stay, and I always wanted to live somewhere warm, so I came to Florida."

"I've been here three years now," said Joe. "I retired from the school system, and I was tired of the cold, too."

"Oh, so you were a teacher. What did you teach?" I asked.

"I was actually a gym teacher at Bronx High School for forty-five years."

My heart sank. What were the chances that I, not into sports, went on a blind date, then met another guy, and they both turned out to be sports nuts? I was definitely not going to be playing the lottery anytime soon.

"I don't think I've ever met a gym teacher before. So you must love sports?"

"My knees aren't great anymore, so I took up pickleball. But honestly, I'd rather cook, or read a good book, or watch a thriller series on Netflix. And I never liked watching sports."

Hallelujah.

"Other than the cooking part," I said, "we have a lot in common. I love a great book and a good thriller series, too."

Ugh—a lot in common? How stupid. It sounded like I was trying to suck up to him.

Joe asked a question and I missed it while I was analyzing my conversational deficiencies.

"What's that?"

"I was asking—were you always into technology?"

"In the last fifteen or twenty years, all of my office jobs required me to learn technology. I like learning new things, and I seemed to have a knack for it. But if I had gone to college, I probably would have been a journalist."

I congratulated myself for bringing up the "no college" part. I was pretty sure that I was still traumatized, all these years later, by my ex-husband's put-downs about it. And I had no room in my life for anyone else like that. Oops—but this wasn't a date. I kept forgetting.

"I barely squeaked by in college, but it was a good time to be a PE teacher. That was when the President's Council on Youth Fitness was created, and there was a big demand for gym teachers. But being a gym teacher wasn't my dream."

"Really? What was your dream?" I asked.

"I wanted to be a chef."

"Well, judging from my experience tonight, you would have been a great one. So what happened?"

"In my family, I was the only son, with four daughters. The women did the cooking, and my dad always wanted me to play sports. He loved watching my games. Whenever I tried making something in the kitchen, my mother would shoo me away, and my father would tell me that that was women's work."

"Hmm, wow. That's so different than my family," I said. "I hated cooking, and I was terrible at it. One time I needed to boil water for broccoli, and I let it boil too long, and all the water had evaporated. The pan was burnt, and we had to throw out the pot. For years, my mom told everyone, 'she's so bad at cooking she can't even boil water.'" We both chuckled.

"Well, that's what makes the world go round," said Joe. "I'm just glad that one of my family members is working on becoming a chef—my grandson, Joey."

"That's wonderful," I said. "Do you do video calls where you cook together?"

Joe looked thoughtful. "You know, we never have. But that's a great idea. I have to see if I remember how to do video calls. I wonder if I know anyone who can help me set that up?"

I laughed. "I might know someone."

"I hope you saved room for dessert," said Joe.

I pretended to groan, but who was I kidding? Dessert was my favorite part of any meal.

Joe brought a bowl of mixed berries to the table, along with what looked like freshly whipped cream. Aha. He really did make his own whipped cream.

As he spooned everything onto dessert plates, I asked, "Are you a widower? Maria and Fran are."

Joe shook his head. "I've been divorced for twenty years," he said. "Right after my wife turned fifty, she decided she liked women."

"Really? I've seen that happen, but only on TV or in movies," I said.

"Oh, it happens all right," he said.

"I've been divorced longer than you, and I've probably gotten too comfortable being on my own." Not sure why I shared that, but he was easy to talk to.

"But since you're a great cook and a pickleball coach, I'm sure you have a lot of admirers, including Harriet Bertulli," I said.

He coughed. "Well, Harriet does give me a lot of attention. But I'm not interested. I don't like women who seem desperate for a man. I'm pretty independent."

"That's refreshing," I said. "It seems like a lot of older men are looking for women to be with them all the time and take care of them."

"Who you calling old?" Joe laughed. "Oops, careful."

My hand shook just as I picked up my wine glass, and it almost spilled over.

"So tell me more about what you like to cook," I said. "And do you ever make tiramisu?" I asked slyly. "It's my favorite. Plus, it fixes most ailments."

"I certainly do," Joe said. "In fact, the next time we have dinner, I'll make it."

"You've got a deal," I said.

CHAPTER 24

I was still on a high from my unexpected dinner with Joe yesterday. When I talked to Fran and Maria about it, they said he definitely sounded interested. Although we had made no plans, he did mention that there would be a next time for dinner. So I'd play the waiting game as millions of women have done throughout history, hoping to get a visit from his carrier pigeon.

But in the meantime, I had to get to work. My euphoria quickly faded when I almost hit a car that stopped short at a light as soon as it turned yellow. Thankfully, I made it to work without any other incidents, and I was even a few minutes early.

Ursula was already at the front desk, of course.

"Don't forget, Charmaine is on vacation, and I need you to cover for me for a couple of hours at the front desk," she said.

"I remember," I said. "A lunch seminar?"

"It's really none of your business," she said.

I ignored her. Boy, was she a piece of work. Anyway, I

was happy to have a few hours without her breathing down my neck.

A few minutes before noon, she left, and I took over at the front desk. I enjoyed being able to help people of all ages, asking questions about upcoming events, or even just where the restrooms were. It was a nice break from typing.

"Excuse me, is this where I get a beach pass?" said a young woman, holding a toddler's pudgy little hand.

"It sure is," I said.

After she gave me her license and filled out the information, I said, "That'll be seventy-five dollars."

"What?"

"I said it's seventy-five dollars," I repeated.

"Isn't that for the whole season?" she asked, her voice rising.

"Yes."

"But the season ends on September thirtieth. So I should only have to pay for two months."

"I couldn't agree with you more," I said. "But the rules state that you have to pay seventy-five dollars no matter when you buy the pass."

"That is so stupid," she stomped her foot, and her daughter started to cry. "Now look, you made my daughter cry."

"Well, actually—I'm really sorry, but—"

"You know what? Let me speak to the manager," she said, loudly.

"She's out for a couple of hours. I can have her call you when she gets back."

"Not acceptable." By now a crowd had started gathering and were listening in on the conversation. "I'll pay for two months, and not a penny more."

"Again, I'm not authorized to do that," I said.

"You know what? I think you just don't know how to charge me for only two months," she looked at me meanly. "At your age, you probably aren't up on technology."

"What?" I jumped up. "I probably know more about technology than you do, Missy. So f*ck off and get your nails done or something, or pay the seventy-five dollars if you want a beach pass."

A hush fell over the group. Oh no. I hadn't meant to swear at her.

"You cursed in front of my three-year-old, you old bat. I'll be calling the mayor about this." She walked off, and people continued staring, shaking their heads, and finally walking off too.

I was shaking and surprised. Even though the woman had pushed my buttons, I had always been the calmest person in my legal office, even with all of the drama. This was not like me. After a minutes and deep breaths, I felt myself calming down. But calling *the mayor?* Was that really necessary?

When Ursula returned, she stopped by the front desk. "I got a call from the mayor's office. I'll be back after I talk to them."

Omigod. I hadn't really thought the lady would go to the mayor's office.

Twenty minutes later or so, Ursula came storming over to me.

"Come with me," she hollered, and I followed her to the conference room.

"I understand you cursed at one of our residents," she started.

"Yes, and I'm so sorry, but I can explain—"

"Cursing is unacceptable," she said. "How could you do that, especially in front of her daughter?"

"Well, here's what happened—"

"I heard all about it. The mayor made me call the woman, and she told me the whole story."

"Okay, good, so you understand she put me down and was trying to get a beach pass at a lower rate—"

"Well now we have to give her a free beach pass, thanks to you. Apparently her husband is friendly with the mayor. They play golf together at the Banyan Resort."

"Umm, okay—"

"Listen, Debbie, this is a warning. It's going in your personnel file. You get one more warning, and then your employment is terminated. Do you understand?"

"Yes, but—" I tried to hold back, but tears were starting to fall.

"You will never do this again. In fact, I don't think you should be working the front desk at all. You're not good with the public. I have plenty of typing for you to do. Now go to the bathroom and get yourself together."

I went, sobbing all the way.

On the way home, I called Lori. I really needed some sympathy.

"That stinks, Mom," she said. "But I really can't believe you swore at her. When I would come to work with you on Saturdays, everyone at your office would say that you were the calmest person around."

"But it wasn't fair," I wailed.

"I know, but it's still not like you. Is everything okay?"

No, it obviously wasn't.

"And I hate to remind you, but you could have quit that job and gone to the shore with us last week."

"Seriously, Lori? Now is not the time to bring that up," I shot back.

"Well, maybe you should consider getting another job," she said.

"Listen, I'm home now, and I'm starving," I said. "I'll talk to you tomorrow."

CHAPTER 25

I couldn't believe Lori, I fumed, as I ate my Swanson's lasagna. All I wanted was sympathy, and she had to bring up the family "vacation" I had missed, which was, most likely, a veiled attempt for me to help her take care of the kids at the beach. Lori and I had always been so close, but since I had decided to move to Florida, it seemed like we were at each other's throats more often than not. I hoped we could eventually get our relationship back on track.

I was still bothered by the incident at work, but I was too embarrassed to tell Fran or Maria about it. I decided to distract myself after dinner by watching *Fauda* on Netflix.

A few minutes in, my cell phone rang. I did a double-take when I saw the caller ID. It was Joe Moretti. I hadn't expected him to call so soon.

My thoughts whipped around the roundabout, shifting quickly from Job Grievances to Joe Giddiness. I guess no matter how many times I had been disappointed, I still got excited when a guy called.

"Hello?"

"Hi, Debbie. It's Joe Moretti."

"Oh hi, Joe. It's nice to hear from you."

"Well it's been a while, so I figured I'd reach out," said Joe, and we both chuckled.

"Seriously, Debbie, I know it's probably not cool to call you so quickly, but I don't want to waste any time. Are you free for dinner Saturday night?"

"Let me check," I said. I knew I had no plans, but I didn't want to sound too eager.

"Yes, that would be great."

Just then I heard loud shouting from the TV and a burst of Hebrew. I had forgotten to lower the volume when Joe called.

"What's that? Joe asked.

"Oh, sorry about that. I was just watching a show."

"Which one?"

"It's called *Fauda*. It's this Israeli show about—"

"I've seen all the episodes. I love *Fauda*."

"Oh, well I just found out about it," I said. "I share a Netflix account with my daughter, and she suggested it to me. Sometimes I talk to her about the episodes."

"That sounds nice," said Joe. "I want to know what other shows you like. Maybe we can talk over dinner Saturday night? I should be able to get a reservation since it's the summer. I'll try for 7:00 p.m. if that's okay."

"Sure."

"Any preferences?"

"Not really. I don't know too many places around here, and I eat just about anything. Surprise me," I said.

"Sounds great. I'll confirm everything with you and pick you up around 6:45 p.m. on Saturday."

"Can't wait," I said.

"Me neither."

I also couldn't wait to tell Maria and Fran.

CHAPTER 26

When I woke up Thursday morning, I was sneezing and congested like I was starring in a Nasonex commercial. I assumed it was allergies, but I felt so sleepy I went back to bed after breakfast and could barely get up by midafternoon.

I had a snack and then took an antihistamine, hoping to sleep it off so I would be ready for battle, also known as work, tomorrow. But when Friday came, I was feeling worse. I called in sick, which Ursula probably didn't believe, and then went back to sleep.

Saturday morning came, and I still didn't feel better. It figures, I thought. I have my first doctor's appointment later in the week, but I can't wait until then to be seen. I got up and went to the nearest urgent care center. Turns out I had a sinus infection.

I felt like crap, and not just because I was sick. I would have to postpone my date with Joe.

Around noon, I called him.

"Joe, it's Debbie."

"Debbie, are you okay? You don't sound so good."

"Actually, I'm not. I just got back from the doctor, and I have a sinus infection. I've been resting but I still don't feel great. I'm so sorry, but I'm going to have to cancel our date."

"Oh, no. Well, I hope you feel better. Is there anything I can do?"

"Yep, heal me," I said.

"I'll do my best," he said.

I slept for the rest of the day, and woke up around six to the sound of a text message.

"I left something for you on your doorstep. Let me know if it helps."

I grabbed a robe and went to the door. Outside were two packages. One was hot, and one was cold.

When I brought them into the kitchen, I was stunned. The hot bag contained a steaming container of chicken soup, and the cold bag had a large square of tiramisu.

Inside the chicken soup bag was a note, "Hope these heal you. Joe."

~

AFTER FEASTING ON THE SOUP AND TIRAMISU, I DID FEEL better. Soothed, I called Joe.

"Joe, I can't thank you enough for your thoughtful medicine. The soup was delicious. Was it from the Pointe Deli?"

"I made it," he said. "I make a mean brisket, too. Did I tell you my ex-wife was Jewish?"

"No, you certainly did not," I said. Wow.

"And you mentioned on Tuesday that 'tiramisu fixes

most ailments,' so I figured I'd make some of that for you, too."

"Are you real?" I asked.

"Yes," he said, laughing. "Call me when you feel better and we'll reschedule our date."

"You have a deal," I said.

Joe Moretti seemed just too good to be true.

CHAPTER 27

I was feeling better on Monday, when I had my scheduled first doctor's appointment. The parking lot at Banyan Beach Medical Associates was full, and I had to drive around twice until I found a space.

The waiting room was filled, too, mainly with older people. They were mostly sitting, stretching, or limping.

I figured I was lucky to get the first appointment after lunch, but maybe not, I thought ruefully, looking around at all the people waiting.

I signed in on the sheet that said "Dr. Ross and Dr. Chowdhury." A moment later, the receptionist peered out of the little window and handed me some papers on a clipboard. "Fill out all the sheets on both sides and sign it wherever you see a checkmark," she said and promptly slid the window shut.

The Health History was quite detailed, asking a "Yes" or "No" to a dizzying list of medical conditions and diseases. Have you had any of the following: I checked "Yes" to migraines, although I wasn't sure that was correct, because I did have migraines at one time but not lately. "No" to heart disease and cancer (being superstitious, I added a "Thank G-d" next to them, leaving out the "o" for extra measure). What was the date of your last period? Who could remember? I would need a scientific calculator, for God's—er, G-d's— sake. I took a wild guess, signed the forms, and put the clipboard on the ledge of the window. A moment later, a hand reached out to get the clipboard, and the window closed.

Some of the people in the waiting room were intently reading books or tapping their phones or iPads, which was not a good sign, I decided, because it meant they knew it was going to be a long wait.

Looking for something to read, I picked up one of the few magazines lying around, a tattered issue of *People* I had read months before back in Massachusetts.

A tiny elderly lady with monkey-bright eyes was sitting nearby, watching me. "Would you like this *People* magazine?" she asked in a sweet little voice. I recognized the cover, which was easily a year old. "Oh, I already read that. But thank you anyhow."

In the midst of this ocean of senior citizens were two or three young people filling out forms and looking bewildered at seeing so many oldsters.

"Excuse me, do you have the time?" a worried-looking young man asked me. "My cell phone battery died."

I glanced at my watch. "It's 1:45 p.m."

"Wow—is it always this crowded?" he asked. "I have to get back to my job."

I shrugged. I was almost tempted to say, "If you're seeing Dr. Ross, you can go ahead of me." But so many people were waiting that it probably wouldn't help much.

To pass the time, I pulled out the current creative writing assignment I had been working on, inspired by my recent beach day with Fran and Maria. This one, at least, was something I could read to the group.

A Day at the Beach

Back in the time of baby oil and iodine, Roz and I were teenage girls scrunched up on damp, sand-crusted blankets as we baked ourselves at Larson's Beach in Winslow, Massachusetts. Before we ever heard the word "melanoma," the sun was our friend, and we only went into the water to cool off between bouts of relentless tanning.

Our main concern was the question we always asked on the way home from the beach, "Did I get any color?"

Sitting near us were two heavy-set older women, planted in their sand chairs, eating sandwiches and drinking coffee from a thermos. They wore sun visors and those dark bathing suits with skirts that are supposed to make you look thinner, and their pale, lumpy legs bulged with blue veins.

Roz sat up on her elbow and stared at the women. "Oh, my God," she whispered, "if I ever start to look like those two, please shoot me."

We laughed because it was just so ridiculous. That would never happen to us. We were young and firm with smooth skin and tanned legs.

Just then, I looked up to see two beautiful young women striding jauntily into the waiting room. They had name tags on their jackets and carried large black bags, obviously filled with samples and literature from the pharmaceutical companies they represented. They waved to the receptionist and managed to find seats, one offered by the worried young man who seemed dazzled by them.

All the while, the two chatted away blithely, not even so much as glancing at or acknowledging the old folks, their potential clientele.

I had never really been aware of pharmaceutical reps when I lived up North, but I couldn't help noticing these two, who looked obscenely young, healthy, and gorgeous in their expensive suits with short skirts that showed off long, tanned legs in impossibly high heels.

As if on cue, the inside door to the doctors' offices opened, and out walked a tall, pretty young woman and a good-looking guy, both wearing name tags and brandishing pharmaceutical sample bags. They looked as if they could have stepped off a wedding cake.

"Glad you liked the lunch," the guy called back over his shoulder.

"Next time we'll bring the lemon chicken. It's to die for," the girl sang out as they left.

The little old lady who had offered me the *People* magazine stared at them, too, and whispered something to her aide.

The waiting room was still full, and hardly any patients had been called. The two Barbie Doll drug reps were talking and laughing when the receptionist signaled them. Gathering up their bags, most likely filled with costly new pharmaceutical samples, they were buzzed into the inner sanctum. One of them carried a beautiful bamboo plant. "To enhance the feng shui," she told the receptionist.

The young man who needed to get back to his job went up to the window and asked how much longer he would have to wait.

I couldn't hear the response but noticed he went back to his seat looking dejected.

About ten minutes later, the inside door opened again, and the two Barbies pranced out. The one who had brought the bamboo plant gave a pretty salute to the assistant holding the door open. "Tell Dr. Ross he's very welcome. And you only have to water it once a week."

The inner door closed again. And still nobody had been summoned inside.

All of a sudden, I was in motion. I ran up to the reps and blocked their exit.

"Enough of that bullshit and the feng shui," I yelled. "We're sick of you and the bloodsucking drug companies you work for. Stop bribing the doctors with those lunches and gifts. You're taking time away from us patients, and we don't have all that much time left."

My voice became louder. "You want some feng shui? Take that bamboo plant and shove it up your ass. I guarantee it'll get watered regularly!"

As I took a breath, I realized all conversation had stopped.

Omigod, what have I done? I never liked to wait at doctors' offices, I mean who does, but my reaction was next-level.

Mortified, I slunk back to my seat. A moment later, I heard my name called. "Gordon—Deborah Gordon? Dr. Ross will see you now." A nervous-looking young assistant held the inner door open.

Well, that was certainly one way to move to the top of the waiting list.

I stood up and said in a shaky voice, "I'm Debbie Gordon. But this poor guy," I pointed to the young man, "needs to get back to his job, so let him go ahead of me."

I glanced around the waiting room. “Does anybody have a problem with that?”

Nobody said a word.

The little old lady, still clutching *People* magazine, grabbed her walker and hobbled over.

She held up a thin, blue-veined hand and gave me a high five.

CHAPTER 28

"By the way, Mom, how did the visit go yesterday with your new doctor?"

"Oh—uh—fine," I said carefully, not wanting to divulge more to Lori. Otherwise, she'd really make a case for me moving to Delaware. "Most of the exam was done by his Russian nurse practitioner, Ludmila. These days you don't get to see the doctor unless you're really sick."

Or really crazy. Embarrassment washed over me as I recalled the encounter with the two drug company reps at Banyan Beach Medical Associates. No need to mention that to my daughter. Or how Ludmila said, "You have anger, Deborah Gordon. You may need talking to someone. We can give referral." I had assured Ludmila that I was just fine, thank you, and not angry about anything. In my haste I forgot to tell her about my shakiness and increased appetite. Oh, brother, what an idiot, I thought.

"Anyway, I'm almost at the restaurant, so I'm going to let you go," I said.

"I'm glad everything's okay, Mom. Love you. Be safe."

"Love you. Be safe."

~

RANDY WAS NOWHERE TO BE SEEN AT THE RENDEZVOUS Restaurant. Instead, a tiny Asian waitress was scurrying around, clearing tables and taking orders.

We gave a collective sigh of disappointment. "Oh, darn." Maria said. "And I was so psyched to see Randy again."

"Me, too," Fran agreed. "We had so much fun that time with Kay, remember?"

"Well, we're already here so we might as well stay," I reasoned. I had been looking forward to a fun night out with the girls. I needed something fun, especially since my visit to Dr. Ross.

"This place just isn't the same without Randy," Maria declared.

"Hell-oo," a familiar voice called out. "Did somebody mention my name?"

"Randy," we cried in unison. "You're still here."

"Still here—and still—well, you know." He held a large menu over his face as if he were playing peek-a-boo. "Welcome back, ladies."

He lowered the menu slowly, and the three of us gasped. "What did you do to yourself?" Maria cried. "If it weren't for your voice, I'd never have recognized you."

I said, "Wow. You look so different."

"This is my new persona." He twirled around to give us a better view. Gone were his long, blonde Shirley Temple curls. His hair was now blue-black, worn in a bob with bangs. "So —how do you like it?"

"You look like Prince Valiant," Fran said.

"Prince Valiant—oh, I love that. He was so brave and manly. I followed him in the Sunday comics for years, although I never knew what he saw in that Aleta." Randy escorted us to a table by the window, pulled out chairs, and handed us menus. "Cabernet, if memory serves me right," and off he went.

No sooner had we gotten settled in, than he was back at our table, balancing a tray with a bottle of cabernet and four glasses. "Whoops. Somebody's missing tonight. Where's the blonde bitch goddess?"

"You mean Kay? We haven't seen her in a while," Maria said. "But you certainly have a good memory."

"Who could forget somebody like her? And besides—I was pleasantly surprised that she left me a very generous tip last time. So many people are such dreadful tippers, don't you agree, Miss Fran?" he added slyly.

"You remembered my name." She sounded thrilled.

"As if." He rolled his eyes.

I had been studying the menu and it surprised me. "Wow, Randy, these specials have really changed. Since when do you serve Asian food?"

"Since I met Sung." Randy tossed his shiny black bob. "Sung is my new Asian boyfriend and chef."

"What's his specialty?" I asked.

"Oh, you dirty girl."

I groaned, and Randy bolted off to greet a couple who had just come in.

"So Debbie, when are you going on your date with Joe?" asked Maria.

"I missed a small window, I guess. He's traveling and

playing in some tournaments for the next couple of weeks, and he said he'll be in touch when he gets back."

"That's okay," said Maria. "And does he match all the qualities on your boyfriend list?"

I hadn't even thought of that.

"I don't have my notebook with me, and I don't even remember what I had on the list."

"I do," said Fran. And she recited them, "1, Likes to try new activities; 2, Respects me; 3, Has a good sense of humor; 4, Isn't clingy; 5, Drives at night."

Maria and I nodded with appreciation. "I know, right?" said Fran. "I have a good memory."

As I thought through the list, I wasn't sure.

"I don't really know that much about him yet," I said. "Although he seems to be respectful, and has a good sense of humor. He said he liked independent women, so I don't think he's clingy. And he drives at night."

"And you got a bonus number six with the fact that he loves to cook," said Fran. "I'm jealous. Except that he's too short for me."

"Once in a while, being short has benefits," I chuckled.

We looked around. The restaurant had started to fill up. Randy was rushing around, assisted by the little Asian waitress.

Fran put on her glasses to read the menu. "I've never heard of these things—Taiwan tacos, Japanese pulled pork, Sung's surprise."

"Well, you know how creative Randy is when it comes to marketing," Maria said. "You've got to give him credit."

"Actually, I prefer cash, ladies." As if entering stage right, Randy had appeared. "Here I am, ready or not."

Fran pointed to an item on the menu. "What is Sung's surprise?"

"It's hamburger—surprise." He whispered, "A helpful restaurant tip—best not to order anything that has the word 'surprise.' I would suggest the stir-fry. My sweetie does that so well. I always say he knows how to stir-fry my veggies."

"TMI." Maria handed him the menus. We all ordered the stir-fry, and it was delicious.

"Changing the subject," I said, "I need some help from The Cabernet Club."

"Sure," said Maria, and Fran nodded.

"I'm ready to start looking for a condo."

"Of course," Maria smiled. "I'd be happy to check them out with you. I can work around Mom's schedule."

"And I'll help, too," said Fran. "Since you're working, do you want me to pull up some listings for you? Then set up some times to see them?"

"That would be terrific," I said, a little choked up. "I'd like to look at a two-bedroom on the first floor. And I'd like them to be renovated, not like the one I'm renting now."

"You got it. I can set up the appointments on your days off. Do you have anything scheduled next Tuesday?" Fran asked.

I pulled out my cellphone and took a look at my Google calendar. "Nope, that would be great."

"Since you're doing all the researching, I'll go with Debbie to the appointments," said Maria.

"Sounds like a great plan," I said. "Thank you both so much."

When Randy came to clear the dishes, he looked at the empty plates approvingly.

"What good little girls you are," he said with a wry

smile. "And dinner comes with the dessert of the day—pistachio ice cream. Actually, that's the dessert of the day every day. We got a good price on pistachio. Oh, and let me introduce you to my serving wench, Wei." He grabbed the arm of the little waitress. "She's Sung's niece." He trotted off with Wei behind him.

Maria leaned back contentedly. "I'm stuffed. But somehow I'll find room for ice cream."

I finished the last of my meal, feeling calm and relaxed. I smiled at Maria and Fran. "I'm so glad to have friends like you in my life. This has been so much fun. And I can't wait to start looking at condos."

Wei brought over a big pot of tea and our pistachio ice cream. "Oh, look, we've got fortune cookies." Maria broke her cookie in half and read the message, "A fool and his money are soon parted."

Fran's fortune cookie said, "New opportunities await you."

"Aha—that might have something to do with the Dumpster Guy," Maria decided. "What does yours say, Debbie?"

I read the fortune cookie message aloud, "It is never too late to be what you might have been."

CHAPTER 29

I couldn't get the fortune cookie message out of my head. "It is never too late to be what you might have been."

The words were a rebuke and a rallying cry. What might I have been? I wondered. If Danny hadn't died. If my father didn't have his stroke. If I hadn't rushed into a marriage so young, to get out of my house. If I hadn't ended up as a single parent with a deadbeat ex, taking secretarial jobs since ad agencies were few and far between in Winslow. If I hadn't quit the writers' group I joined when Lori was a child, so I could avoid seeing Sam. If only.

My mind raced with the possibilities of roads not taken—the "what ifs," the "if onlys." And, now, what can I be? Unable to sleep, I sat down at the computer and the words flowed.

On Saturday morning, I brought what I had written to the writers' group meeting, and when Norman asked, "Debbie, do you have something you want to share?" I finally said, "Yes, I do. It's called "The Year of Living Magically." I began to read.

A sudden gust of wind turned my umbrella inside out and propelled me up the steps and into the lobby of the East End Hotel for Women. My roommate, Marisol, from Colombia, always said this was the coldest, windiest part of Manhattan, because it was across from the East River.

I hardly noticed the weather—I was still starry-eyed, even after a year, in the most exciting city in the world. At twenty-one, I was a secretary at a small, up-and-coming ad agency, and my boss had just started letting me try my hand at copywriting. In fact, I had just registered for a writing course at City College, which the agency was paying for.

It was Friday night, and the smell of fried fish met me at the door. The food at the East End Hotel was one of the few things I didn't like about living here. Luckily, I didn't have to face the dining room tonight. I was meeting Eduardo, a friend of Marisol's from Bogotá, for dinner. It was our third date and I really liked him, even though she warned me, "Never fall in love with a Latin man. They make good boyfriends but bad husbands." Marisol's stated life goal was to marry an American.

"Louder," called Howie. "You need to speak louder."

I took a deep breath and continued in a louder voice:

As I hurried down the hall, I heard her phonograph blaring. Marisol played records constantly—always Latin music, always loud. It was her ritual. At nine, the music stopped in deference to the television, which stayed on until after the eleven-o'clock news.

Several girls from South America lived at the hotel and had formed a tight-knit group, sharing their music, parties, relatives, and visiting friends. As Marisol's roommate, I was automatically included.

"Tu boca, tu boca rica… Tu boca, tu boca linda…"

Wearing a peach-colored lace slip, her dark hair in curlers, Marisol sang as she danced. As always, her clothes were scattered across the bed, the chair—even the lamp. Her dresser was cluttered with bottles, jars, and a trail of Lady Esther face powder.

She smiled when I came in. "Ah, viejita, where have you been? I was worried."

"My boss gave me a last-minute rush letter that had to go out."

"Everything with your boss is always rush-rush. Look at your hair." She made a face. "Like a drowning rat. Hurry to fix yourself up. They will be here soon."

"Who's they? Who else is going?" I asked.

"You. Me. Eduardo. Soledad. Carlos." She waved vaguely. "Maybe a few others. Hurry and get ready."

I had to smile. I should've known I wouldn't be going out alone with Eduardo. It never failed to amaze me how Marisol and her friends did everything in groups. It was nothing to see six or seven of them out shopping together on a Saturday.

Not that I minded. I liked being with them. They were warm and good-hearted and had taken me under their collective wing. When they chattered away in Spanish, I picked up bits of the language—which they appreciated. They called me La Deborita—little Deborah—and I loved it.

Once again, I was interrupted reading my story, this time by a man looking for the Introduction to Computers Workshop. Norman shooed him off and motioned for me to finish reading.

I didn't have time for a shower, so I washed up quickly, set my hair in rollers, and sat under my new pink dryer for fifteen minutes. Then I slipped on my navy-blue sheath with its white piqué collar. I stepped into my navy Paradise Kitten pumps—the only heels that ever felt truly comfortable.

Marisol finished curling her lashes, then turned to survey me. "Ah, no. That's what you're wearing tonight? Why not something more fancier?"

"I don't have anything really dressy."

She shook her head. Like all the Latin American girls there, Marisol owned a wardrobe of elaborate cocktail dresses—mostly black, trimmed with rhinestones or sequins. Her shoes were just as ornate, with sparkly trim and little bows. "Why you never wear black dresses?"

"My mother doesn't like me to wear black."

Marisol put on a pair of sparkly rhinestone earrings, then sprayed herself with Amour-Amour, her favorite Jean Patou perfume. "You dress like a little girl," she said. "You should dress like a woman."

We were just heading out when the telephone rang.

I hadn't meant to read that last line. I didn't want to tell them about the phone call. It was from my mother's cousin back in Massachusetts, and she was crying. "Debbie, honey, your Dad had a stroke. You need to come home as soon as you can."

By the time I got to Massachusetts, it was too late. After the funeral, my mother had a complete breakdown and was hospitalized for severe depression. So I stayed on in Winslow to take care of her.

I never went back to New York City. Somebody—maybe Marisol—packed up my things and sent them to me.

The critiques from the group were positive. Almost everyone's hand shot up. "You gave a nice sense of time and place," said Howie. "I remember the East End Hotel. I dated a girl who lived there. Or maybe it was the Barbizon."

"Didn't they close down?" asked Annette, a new member. "Reason I ask is because—"

"That's not relevant to critiquing," Norman told her.

"But yes, both the Barbizon and East End Hotel closed down. Years ago, right?" He looked at me and I nodded. "You have a comment, Consuela?"

"Jes," she said. "I like thees vary munch. I like Marisol."

"Oh, sure, you like her because she's from Colombia," Eunice piped up. She and Consuela were still sniping at each other.

"Joo make me to laugh. Ha, ha, ha," Consuela sniffed.

"Now, now," Norman said, "let's stop this bickering. "Yes, Ralph?"

"Nicely written, Debbie. Are you going to tell us more about the phone call? I'm curious to know—is this a vignette, or part of a memoir, or a short story? Where are you going with this?"

"I'm really not sure." I put the typed sheets back in my three-ring binder.

"But what happen to Marisol? Did she get marry-ed to an American?" Consuela persisted as Eunice rolled her eyes.

Actually, I had no idea what ever happened to Marisol, Eduardo, or any of them. I had lost contact with everyone. But I knew what Consuela wanted to hear.

"Oh, yes," I said. "Marisol married a rich, handsome man from Texas."

"Ah, bueno." Consuela sat back in her chair, looking satisfied.

"Nice job, Debbie," Norman said. "We hope to hear more from you next time. But now we need to move along. "Do you have something you'd like to share with us, Eunice?"

"I certainly do," Eunice said as Consuela made a gagging sound.

"This is a true story about the time I was voted Sweetheart of Zeta Beta Tau, my husband's fraternity." Eunice smiled demurely as she read all of her ten typed pages.

Well, things were back to normal, I decided. Or abnormal, as it so often happened at the PPCWG.

CHAPTER 30

"Oh, my God," Maria gasped as she opened the door. "Fran, look at Debbie. Her face is as red as a beet and her hair is dripping wet."

"Water. I need water," I croaked.

Maria hurried to the refrigerator and took out an ice-cold bottle of spring water. I opened it hurriedly, gulped it down, then grabbed a sheet of paper towel to blot the sweat that was dripping into my eyes.

"Where've you been? We were wondering why you were late," Fran said.

Maria had invited us over for leftovers from food she had made for her church supper. And since her leftovers were better than anything Fran or I would ever make, we were delighted.

I slumped down at the table and Fran joined me.

Maria turned down the air conditioner and I smiled gratefully. She knew me well. Then she walked to the guest bedroom. "*Mãe*, it's time for dinner."

A small, thin woman with short grey hair slowly walked down the hallway using a walker, Maria following behind.

"Ana, it's nice to finally meet you," I said, standing up.

Ana smiled and sat down at the end of the table, putting her walker to the side.

"I'm glad to meet you too," she said, with a heavy accent. "This is the first time one of your dinners was before my bedtime. It's almost like she doesn't want me around," she said, cutting her eyes to Maria.

"Um, Mom has been wanting to meet you girls, so I thought it would be fun to have a casual dinner," Maria said nervously. "Just serve yourself, girls. I have one thing I need to get from the oven."

I placed generous helpings of Maria's fried chicken and various pasta salads on my plate. I started eating immediately and took a break when Maria sat down a few minutes later.

"Maria, everything is so delicious. Thanks for this."

"Yes, Maria," said Fran.

Ana said nothing. Huh. Maybe she took Maria's cooking for granted. Or maybe they didn't say "thank you" in their family.

"You're welcome. I do love an appreciative audience," she said, turning toward Ana and raising an eyebrow.

But Ana said nothing.

Maria sighed, and turned to Fran.

"*Mãe*, Fran is the lady I told you about who volunteers for We Care."

"Luckily, I don't need them," said Ana proudly. "I have you to take me around everywhere."

Maria looked like she was suppressing a sigh and leaned toward me.

"And *Mãe*, Debbie is the writer I told you about. She just moved to Palmetto Pointe."

Ana looked me over. "Why are you sweating so much?"

"We were wondering the same thing," said Fran.

"Well," I started, "I just had a preview of hell. A place so brutally hot and humid that you cannot catch your breath, where the air conditioner has not been used in decades, and even the green shag carpet was sweating."

"Aha, I know," Maria said. "Hot with green shag carpet," Maria said. "You had to be in Joyce Davis's condo. I didn't know you knew Joyce."

"I don't. Just as I was leaving to come here, she called to say she had a piece of mail addressed to me and that I should come to her place and pick it up. I've never spoken with her before, and somehow she got my phone number."

"Joyce Davis is like the CIA of Palmetto Pointe," Maria said. "She—

"I know, I know," I interrupted. "She knows everything about everyone."

I told them how she made me stay and talk to her before she let me have my mail.

"I thought I would collapse from heat prostration. It's ninety-four degrees out today, but Joyce was wearing a sweater, can you believe it? Her place is like a sauna, but she insists air conditioning *isn't healthy*. She's got a little table fan that just blows the hot air around. And she was making soup! Of all things!"

"They did a story about Joyce a while back in *News and Schmooze*," Fran offered. "She was the first Black resident here. They mentioned her age but I forgot."

"I figure she must be about a thousand. Or maybe that's the temperature in her condo," I said, fanning myself with the envelope Joyce had given me, which turned out to be a piece of junk mail offering special rates on air duct cleaning.

"It's funny—when you go up to see Joyce, it's as if you're going up the mountain to see a guru," Maria said. "Joyce Davis—sees all, knows all. Never leaves the house. She has a young girl who comes to clean and do grocery shopping. It might be her great-granddaughter."

"She never leaves the house?" Fran asked. "What about doctor's appointments?"

"Joyce doesn't believe in doctors. Or air conditioners, evidently."

I shook my head in disbelief. "We're in the middle of a heat wave and Joyce is at the stove making soup. I don't get it. The woman doesn't go anywhere, doesn't socialize. But somehow she knew all about Harriet Bertulli ditching me at the Temple dance and Mister Highpockets hitting on me."

"Oh, that reminds me." Maria snapped her fingers. "I keep forgetting to call and ask Joyce about the Dumpster Guy. He invited Fran out again, and she doesn't know what to tell him."

"Well, Joyce is way ahead of you. As I was leaving, she said, 'Tell your friend Fran that Ira Miller took care of his wife to the very end. He's a nice man and she could do a lot worse.'"

Fran's mouth dropped open. "I can't believe it. Either Joyce uses phone taps or she's a witch."

"In Palmetto Pointe, anything is possible," I said.

CHAPTER 31

Fran came through and set up three condo viewings on Tuesday.

Maria picked me up, and drove to the first place, a ground floor, two-bedroom condo on Agave Way. The realtor was waiting for us out front. In her fifties, she had tastefully dyed red hair, and was wearing a sundress and platform sandals.

"I'm Tamara. Nice to meet you both," she said, shaking our hands. "This place is owned by Matt Schuller," said the realtor. "His wife died last year, and he's planning to move in with his kids up north."

She opened the door and I was greeted with a blast of cold air, a good sign.

We walked in and I couldn't believe it. This place looked so similar to the photos I had seen online before I rented my place. Everything was light and bright. Instead of beige carpeting, the floors seemed to be made of a light wood.

The realtor saw me looking, and said, "That's actually tile. Much easier to take care of."

An off-white couch and two matching loveseats faced a wall-mounted TV. The kitchen was spotless, with all stainless-steel appliances. And no palmettos.

The master bedroom had all white, modern furniture, and a queen-sized bed. The second bedroom had light wood furniture and a pull-out couch, along with a wall-mounted TV. Both bathrooms had granite counters and stone tiles.

"Nice, huh?" the realtor said, after a few minutes.

Maria and I both nodded.

"His wife was a decorator."

Ah. That explained it.

"This place is move-in ready, and it's a steal at $289K," said the realtor.

I had been looking at the master bedroom's walk-in closets and not paying attention.

"What's that?" I asked.

"I said, Matt really wants to move, so this is a steal at $289,000."

I blinked.

"What—"

"I said," the realtor said loudly, "Matt really—"

"Sorry to interrupt, but did you say $289,000?"

"Yes."

My jaw dropped and my brain froze.

"I remember reading an article about the low prices of condos here, during the pandemic," I whispered. "Someone was quoted saying you could get a two-bedroom condo for $80,000."

She nodded. "That's right. But real estate has

skyrocketed since then. So has the monthly maintenance fee."

"And what's the monthly maintenance?" I asked, nervously.

"It's $900 a month."

My throat felt like it had something stuck in it, a wad of accidentally, painfully swallowed Bazooka gum.

"But the article said maintenance was $500 per month—"

She nodded again. "True. And that has gone up, too." Then the realtor looked at me curiously. "Didn't you see the price when you looked up the listing?"

Maria answered for me, which was a good thing, because I was on the verge of tears. "Our friend set up the appointments, so we didn't look at the listings."

The realtor shook her head, clearly annoyed. "Well, next time, you should really pay attention to the prices. I don't like people wasting my time. And I have three other buyers interested in this place, so I hope we're finished here."

We made it back to Maria's car, and as soon as the air conditioning went on, the tears came.

"What the hell am I going to do?" I wailed. "I don't have $289,000. Not even close. And the maintenance fee—"

Maria patted my hand. "First of all, that was probably the nicest condo I've ever seen in Palmetto Pointe. And it's on the first floor, which makes it more expensive, because that's what people prefer. And it's a two-bedroom. Plus, that realtor was so mean. Let's check out the other two places before you get all wound up."

CHAPTER 32

"So what's so important that you had to talk to me?" Roz asked. She had called me back after I left her a message to call me as soon as possible.

I started sniffling, and Roz heard me.

"What—don't you like Florida anymore?"

"Of course I do," I answered, with a little sob. "But I feel like such an idiot."

"Well spit it out," Roz sighed. "What's wrong?"

"Okay," I said. "I don't know if I can afford to buy a place here."

I heard silence on the phone line. And then...

"But you read that article about those cheap Florida condos."

"Yeah, that was a while ago. Prices have jumped so much, they might be unaffordable for me. Maria and I looked at condos the other day and they were all over $250,000."

"What!" Roz exclaimed.

"Yeah, and then the monthly maintenance fees are $900," I said.

"What?" Roz yelled, again. And then, "How did this happen? You're so good about researching things."

I sighed. "I know. But the condo I'm renting is inexpensive, and I guess I didn't really want to think about how prices have been going up. But I was fooling myself. Apparently this rental is so cheap because it's really crummy and it's the off-season. And buying here, or anywhere around here, has gotten much more expensive."

Roz was unusually silent. "I'm really sorry, Debbie. You've worked so hard, and you're always trying to find ways to save money. This really stinks."

I started crying again. "That's why I wanted to talk to you," I told Roz, between my tears. "You know me better than anyone. I knew you would understand."

"Yeah," said Roz. "I remember in high school when your parents sold the house and you moved into that apartment on Winslow Road."

After Danny died, my parents were deeply depressed. How could they not be? My mom stopped socializing and stayed at home most of the time, and my father lost his furniture business. We ended up selling our house and renting a small apartment, and my father became a salesman for a furniture chain store.

"And then you couldn't afford college, so you went to secretarial school," said Roz.

Yes, I thought, I had really wanted to be a journalist.

"And then that deadbeat ex-husband of yours didn't ever give you child support or—"

"Okay," I interrupted. "This little trip down memory lane is getting me even more depressed."

"Well, okay, but why don't you just ask Lori for some money? You helped her out with college, instead of putting that in your retirement account. Maybe it's time she paid you back."

"No way." I cried. "First of all, I only had to contribute a little, since she got a scholarship from Boston College. Besides, I could never ask my daughter for money. I'd sooner jump off a cliff."

"Well," Roz said sheepishly, "I'd help you out if I could."

"My god, no," I said. "I wasn't trying to ask you for money. I'm really just venting."

"I understand," said Roz.

"But I'm going with Maria to look at one-bedroom places later this week. Maybe I'll have more luck."

CHAPTER 33

"I can't talk too long," I told Lori. "I'm on my way to Fran's. We're helping her decide what to wear on her date with Ira—you know, the guy we used to call the Dumpster Guy."

"Oh, so he went from the D-List to the A-list?" she asked.

"Ha. That's right, ever since Joyce Davis gave him the Good Housekeeping Seal of Approval. Apparently, Ira Miller is one of the 'Good Guys.'"

"Wow, Mom, when I ask you what's new, I sure don't expect these crazy stories."

"Well, this is a crazy place," I said.

"So what about your love life? Anything happening with Joe?"

"Nope. We haven't even had a real date yet. He's still away at his tournaments."

"Oh, by the way, Zack got your birthday check, Mom. He says thank you. But you know how boys are. They never write thank-you notes."

"That's okay. Tell him Mimi loves him and misses him. Love you all."

I was grateful for the diversion with Fran. Maria and I were going to look at condos next week, and I didn't want to spend all my time worrying.

~

WE HAD NEVER BEEN TO FRAN'S CONDO BEFORE AND KNEW she collected dolls, but we weren't prepared for what we saw. Dolls. Everywhere. Probably over a hundred of them.

When Fran gave us the grand tour of her place, we saw Raggedy Anne and Andy nestled in a rocking chair. A life-sized baby doll lay on a satin pillow in a miniature crib. Dozens of other dolls were dressed in bridal gowns, ball dresses, and colorful costumes. I had never seen so many dolls in my life.

All I could manage to say was, "Wow, Fran, this—um—this is something."

What I actually meant was, "Wow, Fran, this is something weird."

Fran beamed with pride. "I've been collecting dolls for years. They're my babies. I love them."

"That one on the middle shelf—is that a Princess Di doll?" asked Maria.

"Yes, it is. And the one above her is Jackie Kennedy. Come and see all the dolls in my bedroom. Whenever George and I traveled, we'd bring home a doll as a souvenir."

We kept oohing and aahing, although the sight of all these dolls staring back at me with their vacant black eyes was definitely creeping me out.

The microwave beeped and I smelled something yummy.

"Let me set the table," Maria offered.

When Fran brought the takeout containers to the table, I must have frowned.

"I thought you liked Chinese food," Fran said.

I do, but looking at the China Palace containers reminded me of the parking space incident with Kay. It seemed like Kay was always in my thoughts.

"I love Chinese food," I smiled. "I was just wondering if I'd have to fight Maria for the fried rice."

We laughed. Maria always took the smallest portion of food, since she was usually on some kind of diet.

"I'm limiting my carbs right now, Debbie, so you're in luck," said Maria.

After dinner, we cleared the table and I started doing the dishes.

"Just leave those, Debbie," Fran said.

"I may not be a good cook, but I'm great at washing dishes," I said, over the running water. Fran had said her dishwasher wasn't working. "Besides, I need to keep up my skills. Maria is great at cooking, you're wonderful with kids, and I have to be able to do something to contribute to the community during the zombie apocalypse."

Fran just shook her head and Maria laughed.

Then Fran clapped her hands, like I'm sure she did thousands of times to get the attention of her students.

"Okay, girls. Let's talk about my outfit." Fran didn't want to look too dressed up, but she didn't want to look too casual either, she said, wringing her hands.

"Look," I said, "this guy has only seen you in whatever

you wear to the dumpster, so anything is bound to be an improvement." Maria chuckled, but Fran frowned.

"Let me show you what I'm thinking about wearing. And I want your honest opinion." Fran hurried into the bedroom and emerged a few minutes later, wearing a gray skirt with a matching jacket, a grey print blouse, and black medium-heel pumps.

"So—how do I look?" she asked.

"Like you're going on a job interview," I told her.

"Helloo—this is Florida," Maria clucked. "That looks like an outfit you would wear in New Hampshire."

Fran looked crestfallen. "I did. But I have a green outfit that might work better." Once again she went into her bedroom, carefully shutting the door. Maria shook her head. "That woman is such a prude. God forbid we should see her in her underwear."

"Maria," I whispered, "Didn't I ever tell you about Fran's wardrobe? It's her old teaching clothing or gym clothing, that's it." Maria looked stunned. "That explains so much," she whispered back.

"Do you like this one better?" Fran came out wearing hunter green slacks, a coordinated green-and-white top, and a jacket.

I sat up. "This is just like the gray outfit except it has pants instead of a skirt. And that shade of green is too wintery looking."

"Let's see what's in your closet," Maria suggested. She marched into the bedroom and exclaimed, "My God, Fran, do you own stock in Alfred Dunner? I'm counting at least half a dozen outfits and they all look alike. Don't you have anything more—you know—a pretty top or a cute dress or—"

"And as long as we're at it, those shoes need to go, too," I said. "You could get some nice wedge sandals, or even some of the more fashionable Clark's sandals…?"

Maria and I decided that Fran should get some dressy black pants and a couple of soft, pretty tops. "No blouses or shirts with collars," Maria told her. "Something flowy and feminine."

"That's right," I agreed. "Remember, you're going on a date, not an interview."

Fran bit her lip. "I don't know. This is a lot to think about."

"Emergency meeting of The Cabernet Club," Maria announced and pointed to the kitchen. "We need a glass of wine. You know the drill, Fran."

As we sat and sipped, everything seemed to fall into place. Fran became more agreeable to our wardrobe advice and even decided to get her hair colored at Happy Hairstyles Beauty Salon in the main clubhouse instead of doing it herself.

"Maybe I ought to get a trim as long as I'm there," Fran said. It was more like a question than a statement.

"Another glass of wine and you'll be going for a boob job and a butt lift," I said.

"I'll drink to that," Maria said, raising her plastic cup.

"And to finding great friends in the autumn of your life," I toasted.

"The autumn of your life," Maria repeated. "I like that. I bet you're a good writer, Debs. Someday you've got to show us your stuff."

"Someday. Maybe. Meantime, Fran, let's get you a new outfit."

CHAPTER 34

"Maria, these are still way out of my budget," I whined, as we drove to the first listing.

"Well, you never know," she said. "They might be desperate, they might like you, you might just get lucky. I learned this stuff in realtor school. Did I tell you I got my realtor's license in Rhode Island? I always loved real estate."

"Really?" I asked, my curiosity edging out my worry. "Did you ever sell real estate?"

"I was hoping to do that part-time when we moved to Florida," Maria said. "I didn't count on Frank dying and my mom needing so much help."

"Huh," I said.

"Well, here's the first one," said Maria, pulling into a guest spot.

We walked up the short concrete path and the door was immediately on the right. We saw a lock on the door, and the realtor was nowhere to be found.

Just then, Maria got a text. "He's running ten minutes late."

Ugh, great, I thought. By the time he gets here, I'll be a puddle of sweat in front of the door. Then I remembered that Maria had to wait, too.

"I'm sorry you have to wait, Maria," I said, proud that I had remembered to have some empathy while being worried sick about this situation.

"No problem," said Maria. "I'm glad to get out of the house, and out of the kitchen. All I've been doing is cooking since the kids arrived."

"So does that mean you won't be able to go with us to happy hour tomorrow night?"

"Hell no," said Maria. "I can't wait to hear about Fran's date."

Just then the realtor came running up. He looked to be about eighteen years old, wearing a wrinkled polo and khaki pants that were too long.

"Hi ladies, I'm Robbie. Sorry again for being late. I overslept."

Maria and I looked at each other. "Um, it's 2:00 p.m.," I said.

"Yeah, late night," he said.

"How old are you?" Maria asked. "Oh, sorry, that's rude," she said.

He smiled. "Well, I'm old enough to own this unit," he said. "My grandmother left it to me in her will. And I studied finance and real estate in college, so this is a great start."

Maria looked at me quickly and winked. I knew what she was thinking—this might be the lucky deal we were waiting for, with a newbie seller.

"It's hot out, so let's go in," he said.

This condo was the same size as my one-bedroom rental but looked bigger, since it had no furniture.

"My family cleared everything out when my grandma passed away," said Robbie. "But, as you can see, we have newer appliances, tile floors, and updated counters in the kitchen and bathroom. That's what they say to focus on in real estate, right," said Robbie, winking at us. I guess we weren't going to put anything over on this kid.

"Do you have any flexibility on the price?" Maria asked.

Robbie shook his head. "It's priced to sell, at $209,900."

I wanted to cry again. Even this condo was out of my budget.

As were the other two listings.

In the car, I was about to start crying again.

"I should have known that owning a condo was a pipe dream," I wailed.

"Hang on a minute," said Maria. "I know it's not exactly what you're looking for, but maybe you should see if the Altmans would be willing to sell the condo to you."

I took a second and smiled.

"That's a great idea, Maria. And I'm already living there, so it would be easy." And even though it didn't have the "light and bright" feel I was looking for, I could change that. For the first time in weeks, I finally felt like I could breathe. "I'm going to call them when I get home."

CHAPTER 35

"Ira was actually very nice," Fran reported the next morning when the three of us got together for what I called a "Special Meeting of The Cabernet Club Without the Cabernet." Maria was exhausted from a full weekend of cooking for her son Bobby's visit, and I was tired from all the shopping Fran and I did, but the morning meeting was a must.

As we sipped coffee at Maria's kitchen table, Fran told us about the date with Ira Miller aka Dumpster Guy. "We went to the Outback for dinner, and I was surprised that Ira ordered steak. I figured he'd be, you know, a vegetarian or really into health foods, but he's not. He said his daughter got him into the environmental thing because she thought he needed to get involved in something after his wife died."

"Did he talk a lot about his wife?" Maria asked.

"Not really. He did mention that his first love was a tall redhead," Fran said, blushing.

"So he has a thing for redheads. Excellent," I said.

"And he loves to watch basketball, too. He played when he was younger."

"You two seem to have a lot in common. Okay, we'll give you permission to have a boyfriend, but you have to keep some free time for The Cabernet Club and your good pals," Maria teased her.

"Of course I will," Fran said fervently. "I told Ira that my friends are the most important thing in my life."

"What did he say about that?"

"He said I'm lucky. Men don't have friendships like women do. Oh, and I told him that I'll be starting the Guardian ad Litem training in November, too. Thanks again for telling me about that, Debbie."

"What's this?" asked Maria. Fran explained the program.

"That sounds terrific," said Maria. "I wish I had something fun to share. My update is a little depressing, though, and it was a wake-up call for the kids, too. After dinner last night, we heard Mom talking to someone in her room. We all went to see what was happening. When we got to her room, she was standing in front of the mirror, gesturing and talking to herself. I said to her, 'Ma, what are you doing?' And she turned to me and said, 'It's rude to interrupt. Can't you see I'm talking to someone?'"

Maria forced a laugh but her eyes were bright with tears.

"Oh, God," I breathed. "That's awful."

"She needs a lot more help than I can give, and we really need to move her to assisted living. But I'm afraid to bring it up to Bobby. He hates it when I spend money from his 'inheritance.' He'll probably brush it off and say that I can take care of her, like I've always done for the family."

"That's nuts," I said. "There comes a time when everyone needs help, even you, Maria. And I'd be happy to tell him so," I joked.

Maria was silent and then she smiled, "Would you?"

"Would I what?

"Would you help me explain everything to him?"

"Oh, well, I was just joking. I don't want to get involved in your family affairs."

"The problem is, I get all tongue-tied around him, Debbie. You're so good at explaining things, and you're so assertive, that this should be a breeze."

"That's different—"

"Please, Debbie. Consider this an official request for help from The Cabernet Club. Why don't you come over for Sunday dinner tomorrow? I'm making chorizo."

"That's not fair," I whined. "You know I can't resist chorizo." My mouth was already watering thinking about the sausage.

"It's settled then. See you at 5:00 p.m. tomorrow."

CHAPTER 36

When I walked up to Maria's condo, I heard a lot of noise coming from her place—a young child's cry, a TV newscaster, and a man yelling. I hesitated before entering the frenzy, then knocked.

Maria answered almost immediately.

"Oh Debbie, it's so nice to see you." Maria looked spent. She was sweating and wearing an apron over her pants. She gestured to her family. "Debbie, this is my son Bobby, and his wife Pam. You know my mom, and that's my grandson Lucas."

Bobby and his wife waved to me but seemed distracted.

"*Vovó*," Bobby said loudly, "You can't just change the channel like that. Lucas was watching Baby Shark. Look, you made him cry."

The wailing got louder as Maria's mom held fast to the remote.

"I'm older, and I have less time left. So I'm watching the news," she said.

"Dinner should be ready in about twenty minutes,

Mãe," said Maria. "Can't you let Lucas watch his show for a little while?"

"No."

Maria looked like she was about to tear her hair out, so I intervened.

"Hey," I said. "Don't you have another TV in the house?"

"Yes," said Maria. "In my room."

"Ana," I said, "it would be much quieter in Maria's room. You could enjoy the news a lot more there."

Ana looked at me suspiciously.

"Who are you?"

I was surprised. I had just shared dinner with her at Maria's condo a few weeks ago.

"I'm Debbie, Maria's friend."

Maria hurried over and grabbed her mom's arm. "I'll set you up in my room, *Mãe*."

A few minutes later we heard the TV go on in Maria's room, and Maria came back to the living room.

"Debbie, let me get you a glass of wine," she said.

I followed her to the kitchen. "Thanks for saving me back there," she whispered. "I knew it was a good idea to invite you tonight."

"I didn't do much—just reminded you that you have another TV," I said.

"Right, but I just seem to stop thinking when all this drama happens. I don't like it when everyone's yelling, either."

"Maybe a glass of cabernet will help," I joked.

"I agree," said Maria. "I'm going to bring up the idea of assisted living, and if I start having trouble, help me out, okay?"

"Will do," I said.

A somewhat chaotic 30 minutes later we were finishing up dinner.

"Are we going to the pool again tomorrow with Fran?" Lucas piped up.

"We're going to the beach," said Pam.

"Can Fran come with us? She plays with me in the water."

"I'm sure Fran has other things to do," said Bobby. "It's family day."

"I only want to go with Fran," Lucas stood and stomped his feet.

"If you keep this up, we won't go at all," Bobby said, standing up too.

Lucas started crying, and Pam stood and took him by the hand. She set him up in front of the TV.

"I'm going back to watch TV, too," said Ana, walking to Maria's bedroom.

After she closed the bedroom door, Maria said, "I need to discuss something with all of you. Please sit down," she gestured to Bobby and Pam, her voice quivering.

Once they were seated, she continued.

"As you know, *Vovó* has been declining rapidly," she said.

"She's just a little forgetful—she's old," Bobby said.

"You saw her talking to herself the other day," Maria continued. "And last week I got the official diagnosis that she has Alzheimer's."

There was a stunned silence.

"I'm so sorry, Ma," said Pam. "That's terrible."

"I can't believe it. Poor *Vovó*. She was always on the go, doing things," said Bobby. With a glimmer of a smile on his face, he said, "And she did so much for me. Remember that time she made me a Batman costume for Halloween? And I won first prize?"

"What?" Maria stood up straighter. "*Vovó* didn't make you that costume. I did. *Vovó* couldn't thread a needle."

"No, *Vovó* made my costume," Bobby said stubbornly. "I remember."

"Maybe she helped you put the costume on," Maria insisted, "but I was the one who made it. *Vovó* is not the only one getting things mixed up."

"Whatever," Bobby said dismissively. "But when I think about *Vovó*, I remember all the family stuff, the big dinners, the singing, the fun."

I could almost see the steam coming out of Maria's ears. "I remember those big dinners too," she said, her voice unsteady. "I was the one who did most of the cooking, not *Vovó*. And most of the cleaning up too, so I don't remember all the fun."

Bobby shot her a quizzical look. "What's the matter with you, Ma? Why are you bad-mouthing *Vovó*?

"I'm not bad-mouthing her," Maria said, with new confidence in her voice. "She's my mother and I love her. But the fact is, *Vovó* was never the one who cooked or sewed or took care of the house."

"Whatever, Ma," Bobby said.

"And I'm still taking care of everybody." Now Maria had tears in her eyes. "I'm so tired, and *Vovó* needs more and more help. We need to start thinking about moving her to assisted living."

"Wait—what?" Bobby asked. "That's a big step. And it's expensive."

"It's not cheap," Maria agreed. "But that's what savings are for."

"Mom, this probably isn't a great time to mention it, but I was going to ask you for a loan to start my own plumbing business," said Bobby. "Pam and I have talked about it, and she agrees that after all this time it's important that I have my own business."

"Bobby, you already have the house," Maria said quietly. "Maybe you could get a home equity line or a second mortgage to fund your business."

Bobby stood up, his voice rising, too. "You get a nice chunk of change from Dad's social security, and I know you don't have a mortgage on this place. But you want me to get extra loans on my house?"

"Well, that's not how I meant it—"

"This is what Dad would have wanted, Ma," Bobby interrupted. "You know he always wanted to have his own business. You should respect that. Remember, you didn't earn any of that money. Dad did. You were just a stay-at-home mom."

I was embarrassed for Maria, but I was angry, too. I had to say something.

"Bobby, your family wouldn't have been able to have such a great life without your mom. Plus, the money your parents saved is hers. She can do what she wants with it."

His eyes turned to slits. "Lady, it's none of your business what my mom does with my inheritance."

"Bobby, that's so rude," Maria said.

"This whole conversation is stupid," Bobby pounded the table with his fist, and we all jumped. "For God's sake, Ma, *Vovó* isn't that bad. I had a customer whose mother had Alzheimer's for five years. You can take care of her until things really get bad, so I can get my business started."

Maria stood up and everyone stopped talking.

"Bobby, Alzheimer's symptoms can progress rapidly, even in a matter of months," she said.

"Oh, now you're a doctor?" he said, snickering.

"No, I'm not a doctor," said Maria. "But I've talked to the doctors, and I've done a lot of research. And you know *Vovó's* best friend Luisa is in the assisted living facility down here. She went from being diagnosed with Alzheimer's to not knowing where she was in three months' time. What if your *Vovó* walks out the door one day and accidentally walks into the street and gets hit by a car?"

Bobby was silent.

"We have to make sure she's safe," Maria continued, sounding stronger. "I can't be with her 24/7, and it actually costs more to have aides come to the house 24/7 than it does for her to live in a facility."

"Huh," he said, looking thoughtful.

Maria called me later that evening.

"I can't thank you enough for sticking up for me," she said. "That helped me get the courage to speak up to Bobby."

"You did great, Maria," I said. "I was so proud of you. And I never knew about the financial issues of Alzheimer's patients who stay at home. You are so smart."

She laughed. "Actually, I made that up. I'm not sure it costs less to have aides full-time at home. But I know that Bobby is all about the Benjamins."

"You are amazing," I marveled.

"That means a lot, coming from you," said Maria. "And I just realized that if my mom moves to an assisted living facility, it will be the first time in my life that I'll be living by myself."

"Does that make you nervous?"

"Heck no," she said. "Maybe I'll eat breakfast naked, watch TV all day, and make a microwave meal for dinner."

"Just like me. The microwave dinner part," I joked, and we laughed.

CHAPTER 37

“Say, don’t you people have your holidays this month?” asked Ursula.

“Yep. And they come early this year.”

“How many days are you taking off?”

“Just one day, Yom Kippur. Rosh Hashanah falls on the weekend this year.”

“Is that when you eat—what do you call it defiltered fish?” Ursula wanted to know.

“Gefilte fish,” I replied. “Sometimes we have it for the high holidays, but usually we just have it for Passover.”

“I tried that fish one time. I didn’t like it.”

“You have to develop a taste for it, I guess.”

“So when do you eat those big crackers?” Ursula hailed from a small town in Central Florida and had known very few Jewish people.

“Oh, you mean matzah? That’s for Passover, right before Easter.”

Ursula shook her head. “Wow. And you have your own Christmas, too.”

"We have Hanukkah. But anyhow, as I said, I'm only taking off one day, and it's without pay, and I'm giving you advance notice, so there's really no problem, right?"

"Still in all," Ursula pointed out, "you people sure do have a lot of holidays."

I had never been particularly religious, but I always managed to go to services on Yom Kippur to say Yiskor, a prayer to remember those who had passed on. And I had always fasted.

But now that I was in Florida, everything was different. I wasn't affiliated with any temple, and I didn't want to go to services alone. Maria was Catholic, and Fran was—actually, I wasn't sure if Fran practiced any religion. I decided I would say the prayers at home instead. And since I was feeling hungry all the time, fasting was out of the question.

On the day of Yom Kippur, I woke up in a strange mood. Instead of feeling a sense of forgiveness and new beginnings, I kept thinking about the comments Ursula had made at the office about the Jewish holidays. That led me to recall other incidents over the years. And then I mulled over the stories in the news about the rise in anti-Semitism lately.

I got so worked up that I made a wild decision.

Today on the holiest day on the Jewish calendar, when I should be in a synagogue or at home, fasting and praying, I would instead venture out to see for myself, once and for all, what was really happening in the rest of the world.

Wearing sunglasses and a big hat, I pushed my shopping cart slowly through every aisle of Publix, half-expecting the non-Jewish cashiers and customers to be celebrating and cheering loudly and wildly—maybe knocking down displays of Manischewitz soup and making derogatory comments.

I was almost disappointed to see it was like any other day. And it suddenly dawned on me that I was acting like a lunatic. What the hell was I doing?

Lost in thought, I walked through the frozen foods section and smacked into another shopper.

"Oh, I'm so sorry," I said and was stunned when I saw Kay. I almost didn't recognize her. She wasn't wearing much makeup and had dark circles under her eyes. And instead of her usual chic outfit, she was wearing sweatpants and a t-shirt.

"Did you just come from the gym?"

She shook her head. Then she asked, "Isn't this your Day of Atonement?"

So much for small talk.

"I'm not the one who has anything to atone for," I replied and immediately realized I sounded like a pompous ass.

Kay nodded. "I sure do have plenty to atone for. And I'm not Jewish, but I always thought that Yom Kippur made so much sense."

She had taken the wind out of my sails of anger with her response, and now I was curious.

"What do you know about Yom Kippur?"

"My sister converted to Judaism." Kay then proceeded to tell me that her sister had married a Jewish doctor from Boston. When she married, she got more involved at the temple, and now she was the president of the temple's sisterhood.

I stood there, not knowing what to say or do. My mind was racing. Never in a million years would I have expected to be discussing Yom Kippur with Kay Caldwell Jason. Maybe Kay had changed. Maybe she was sorry about what happened and didn't know what to say. Maybe I should say something. Yom Kippur is the time you're supposed to forgive people. But how could I forgive Kay?

We stood together awkwardly for a few seconds. "Well, Happy New Year," said Kay, and wheeled her cart away.

~

WHEN I GOT HOME, I SAID YISKOR, IN MEMORY OF MY parents and brother.

But that strange, jittery feeling that had motivated me to go to Publix on Yom Kippur gnawed at me.

I am not myself lately, I thought. Something just isn't right with me.

I called Banyan Beach Medical Associates and made an appointment to see Dr. Warren Ross.

CHAPTER 38

As I anxiously awaited a visit to my primary care doctor, I was once again seen by Nurse Practitioner Ludmila Petrofsky.

I only got to spend a minute or so with Dr. Ross, just long enough for him to give me a referral. To a shrink, of all people.

And it was all because of Ludmila Petrofsky's eyebrows.

During my brief exam, Ludmila pushed her glasses to the top of her head, and I noticed the woman's eyebrows for the first time. They looked like two dark, menacing caterpillars. Were they shaped that way naturally? Or did Ludmila draw them on with some strange kind of pencil? Or did she use a crayon?

I was mesmerized. Look—now they're frowning, now they're going up and down. Uh-oh, are they fighting with each other?

"Why do you stare at me so?" Ludmila demanded.

"Oh, um, s-sorry," I stammered. "Well, anyhow, as I

was saying, I haven't been feeling right lately. I'm kind of shaky and nervous and sometimes I fly off the handle."

But instead of making eye contact with Ludmila, I couldn't stop glancing up at those caterpillar brows. Would they turn into butterflies and fly away, or—

Ludmila pushed her glasses down. "You need speaking with someone," she said firmly. "I told you so first time I saw you."

"You mean a shrink? I don't need a shrink," I protested. "This is something physical, not mental. I mean, I just don't feel like myself these days." It was no use. Ludmila (and probably everyone at Banyan Beach Medical Associates) had pegged me as a crazy lady ever since my confrontation with the two snotty drug company reps in the waiting room.

Before I could say anything more, I was bustled into the office of Dr. Warren Ross, who patted my head, scribbled a referral, and told me, in a soft, soothing tone, that my symptoms would be greatly helped with talk time and medication.

A FEW DAYS LATER I WALKED INTO THE OFFICE OF DR. Marvin J. Lochner, listed every year as "Favorite Psychiatrist" by the Palmetto Pointe *News and Schmooze*, probably because (a) he was the only psychiatrist who advertised in the paper; (b) he had a full-page ad every month listing his specialty as "treating anxiety, stress, and depression in later life"; and (c) he was one of the few shrinks in the area who accepted MediSource, my low-cost HMO.

When I told Maria I had been referred to him, she said, "Oh, you mean 'Dr. Feelgood.' He loads patients up with medication and he gives them less than fifteen minutes talk time. That way, he can book more patients per day and he doesn't have to listen to long-winded, whiny old people."

According to Maria, just about everyone in Palmetto Pointe had been seen by Dr. Lochner at one time or another. "He's got a huge practice. I took my mother to him for an evaluation," she went on. "They say he's dying to retire, but his new trophy wife won't let him. She likes to keep redecorating his office, and she also likes that he's making a fortune."

It had to be the new trophy wife sitting at the reception desk, because no ordinary employee could afford such an expensive-looking outfit, not to mention the huge diamond she was absently polishing as she chatted away on her cell phone.

I handed her the referral slip and told her "I have a 3:20 p.m. appointment."

Mrs. Lochner looked annoyed at having her conversation interrupted. Without saying a word, she gave me a clipboard with some forms to fill out, took my credit card for copayment, and resumed her telephone diatribe against rude hairstylists.

You could tell that she was not a first wife, because she was too well-cared for, from her stylish ash-brown hair done in a Grecian knot, to her stunning silver outfit and stilettos that practically screamed, "These cost a fortune and I'm worth every penny."

A couple of other people were sitting in the waiting room. They looked subdued or possibly overmedicated. The room was done in varying shades of beige, probably intended to be soothing, but actually, I felt, quite depressing.

Unframed abstract art hung on the walls, and the only touch of color was a large, hulking plant in the corner.

The waiting room was not very inviting, and neither was Dr. Lochner's office, which was also done in tones of beige. The focal point of the room was a mantel where clocks of all types were ticking away, which added to my anxiety.

In person, Dr. Lochner looked quite different from the photo in the *News and Schmooze* ads, where he had his hand on his chin, in the manner of Rodin's *The Thinker,* which made him appear thoughtful and sympathetic, not to mention a few decades younger. Despite a dark brown hairpiece and what looked like a botched eye lift, the years had not been kind to Marvin Lochner's face, making him look perpetually pissed.

"So, what seems to be the problem?" he asked, leaning back in his leather chair.

I took a deep breath and hurriedly went through the highlights (or were they lowlights?) of my new life in South Florida and how, in the past couple of months, I had not been feeling like myself.

Dr. Lochner scribbled something on his pad.

"As I told Dr. Ross—well, actually his nurse practitioner—it's not as if I feel sick or in pain. Something just isn't right somehow," I explained. "I get shaky and nervous. And I feel hot all the time."

"Hot? In Florida?" Dr. Lochner's lips twitched. "Who would think?"

"Well, and my mind is always racing," I continued. "And lately sometimes I come out with really smartass comments."

He nodded sagely. "You're depressed. Very, very depressed."

I shook my head. "I don't think so. I mean, I know what being depressed is like. I felt depressed when I was having problems with my husband and I went to a therapist, but the way I feel now is different."

"Well, of course, you're depressed." Dr. Lochner told her. "You're old, you're alone, you live in Palmetto Pointe. Who wouldn't be depressed?"

"Well, if I wasn't depressed before, I sure am now," I muttered under my breath.

"What's that?" He cocked an ear toward me.

"Nothing." I sighed. "It's just that I thought I was doing so well. I started a whole new life here. I found a place to live, I work, I made friends, and now—"

"You're in denial. I see many patients who are depressed. Even more depressed than you." He scribbled something on a prescription pad. "I'm putting you on the Prozac generic. It will energize you and help you feel better. But you also need to keep busy."

"I am busy. I go to work, I go out with my friends, I belong to a creative writing group."

Dr. Lochner made a face. "No, no, what you need is a hobby, something you can do with your hands, like needlepoint." He pointed to a framed wall hanging in black and white. "My wife did that."

He continued talking about his wife, the glamorous receptionist. Estrella was terrific at decorating and an antiques collector. "You see all these clocks? Estrella collects antique clocks."

Right on cue, the big grandfather clock near his chair struck the half hour. "The session is over," Dr. Lochner said. "Make an appointment for next week." He handed me the Prozac prescription and bolted out of his chair like a jack-in-the-box, looking only too happy to escort yet another depressed patient out of the office.

After stopping at Walgreens to fill the prescription, I was starving, so I picked up dinner from Chipotle and wolfed it down as soon as I got home. Just as I finished my last bite, Maria called. "So tell me, how was your session with Marvin Lochner, Psychiatrist to the Stars?"

"Well, it was kind of like speed dating," I said. "Only this was—you know—speed complaining. Next visit maybe I'll write out a script so I don't waste any time. Our HMO only pays for a limited number of visits."

"And I bet he put you on Prozac."

"How'd you know?"

"That's his drug of choice. Prozac is great for older women. You don't put on weight and it lowers your sex drive. What could be better?"

I laughed. "Wow. No wonder he's Palmetto Pointe's Favorite Psychiatrist."

We said our goodbyes and I thought about Dr. Marvin J. Lochner as I straightened up, made some calls, and got ready for bed. Something kept bothering me as I pictured him, sitting in his big, expensive leather chair   that look on his face—was he annoyed, impatient, angry? What?

There's something about Marvin, I thought, but I can't figure out what it is. Still, maybe he can help me.

And then, as I was flossing my teeth, the answer came to me.

The favorite shrink of Palmetto Pointe, Dr. Marvin J. Lochner, was *himself* depressed. Very, very depressed.

"Oh, crap." I had to laugh. "Just my luck."

CHAPTER 39

I smiled and thanked the server as I placed a napkin on my lap.

The ocean breeze made it just cool enough to sit outside in my sundress without needing a sweater, and to my right was a view of seemingly never-ending water.

Joe had finally come back from his tournaments and we had made a date for dinner.

At seven on Saturday night, even out of season, The Fish House was packed. I wasn't familiar with it, since I rarely went out to fancy restaurants, but Maria and Fran assured me that it was one of the top restaurants in the area for seafood.

Joe sat across from me, smiling. He was wearing khaki pants and a button-down shirt. I was pleasantly surprised to see that he had a full head of gray hair. I had only ever seen him wearing shorts, t-shirts, and baseball caps, but he cleaned up well.

The server poured us water, and asked if we had had time to review the wine list.

"What cabernets do you recommend?" Joe asked.

"Joe, we don't have to order cabernet," I interrupted. "I do like other wines. In fact, I'd like to try something different tonight, with you."

"If you're having seafood, we have several nice white wines," said the server.

"Give us a few minutes, please," said Joe.

"Certainly."

Joe looked over the list and asked if there were any particular type of white wines I liked.

"Not really," I said. "I've always been a red wine girl. I haven't had many white wines, other than champagne, which I love. But I guess I need to expand my horizons. You choose."

"Okay, I think you might enjoy this," he said, waving the server over and pointing to the menu.

A few minutes later, the server appeared, showing the bottle to Joe, and offering him a taste. After he agreed, the server poured each of us a glass.

"*Cin cin*," said Joe.

"Cheers," I said. We clinked glasses and I took a taste of my drink.

"It tastes like champagne, but lighter," I said.

"Exactly. It's called prosecco."

"It's yummy," I said.

"Let's order a couple of appetizers," said Joe. I was so glad, because I was starving.

"How about the calamari?" he asked.

"Not a fan," I said. "But you can go ahead and get that. I'd like the burrata with balsamic tomatoes."

"Sounds good," he said.

After we placed our appetizer order, I asked how his pickleball trip went.

"It was a lot of fun. The weather was cooler than here, and the people we played with were super nice."

"Did you win?"

"Actually, we won the gold in one of the tournaments, and a silver in another."

"Congratulations. Do they give you medals?

"Sure do. I'll be happy to show them to you later." Hah, I thought. What a smooth way to say he'd like me to come over to his place later. I liked it.

"Do you want to try some of my appetizer," I asked Joe, after the server placed our dishes on the table.

"Nah—I make it all the time, but thanks. Do you want to try the calamari?"

"No, thanks. But in a future taste test, I'll be happy to compare this burrata with the one you make all the time."

We laughed and he raised his glass.

"You know, laughing is underrated," Joe said.

"I couldn't agree more," I said, smiling at Joe.

"So tell me what you've been up to," said Joe.

He listened intently as I told him about the Mello family dinner, work, meeting Joyce Davis, and the writers' group.

"You're a great storyteller, so I bet you're a terrific writer," Joe said.

"Thank you," I said. Maybe it was the wine, or the summer evening, or the company, but I felt a flush of happiness. It had been a long time, so long I couldn't even remember when, that I had enjoyed myself this much on a date. I wasn't used to talking this much about myself, either.

"Enough about me," I said. "Let's get to the most important conversation we need to have tonight."

Joe leaned toward me, looking nervous.

"What did you think about the last episode of *Fauda*?" I asked.

Joe laughed.

An hour later we had finished our snapper and grouper dishes.

"Would you like to see the dessert menu?"

"Actually, I don't think so," said Joe.

I was annoyed. Joe knew I loved dessert, and I had looked longingly at desserts at other tables throughout the night.

"I know you love dessert, Debbie," said Joe, as if reading my thoughts. "So I made some tiramisu for you, since you liked it so much. I have coffee, too."

Wow, I thought. Forget the medals. I would have followed almost anyone back to their house for tiramisu as good as Joe's.

At the valet stand, Joe helped me get into his blue Hyundai Elantra.

"I forgot to ask earlier—did you just have this cleaned?" The inside was spotless, the polar opposite of the car Jim Tierney picked me up in.

"Actually, I like to keep my car clean," he said.

"Loves to cook, keeps his car clean. Are you going to turn into a pumpkin at midnight?" I joked.

He turned to me and smiled. "You'll have to see for yourself."

~

When we got to Joe's place, I felt like I was in a dream.

"Can I help you with anything?"

"Nope, just relax. I'll just be a minute. Oh wait, here are my medals," he said, handing them to me.

While Joe made some decaf coffee and put the tiramisu on serving plates, I sat on his couch and looked at the medals.

"Joe Moretti and Betsy Jamieson, Gold Medal Winners," read the inscription on the back.

"I didn't realize your tournament partner was a woman." Her name was familiar too, but I couldn't place it.

"Yeah, she plays here all the time. She really wanted me to be her partner and actually footed the whole bill."

"Here you go," said Joe, sliding everything onto the coffee table. "A decaf coffee with cream, and a slice of tiramisu for the lady."

"To laughter," I said, clinking my coffee cup to his.

"To laughter," he said.

Then it hit me.

"Betsy Jamieson. Does she have a really nice condo?"

"Actually, yes, she renovated it last year."

"Aha, I knew I knew her name from somewhere. When I rented my condo, the pictures online showed a beautiful place with light, bright furniture and stainless-steel appliances. My rental is nothing like that, and someone said that the rental company sometimes uses Betsy Jamieson's interior photos because hers are so nice."

"It that legal?" Joe was outraged.

"That's what I said. But hopefully I'll find another place soon, one that I can own."

"Well, I'm happy to help you look," he said.

"Unfortunately, I won't be able to get anything as grand as Betsy Jamieson's place," I said. "She must be loaded. And paying for the airfare and two hotel rooms must have been outrageous."

"Well, just one room, actually," said Joe.

"What?" I asked.

"We roomed together."

"Huh," I said. Then I was silent and looked sadly at the tiramisu before abruptly standing up.

"I need to get going."

"What? What's wrong?"

He leaned back when he saw my fierce gaze.

"I'm not interested in being a member of your harem," I said. "I'm looking for a one-woman guy."

Joe looked confused.

"Harem? What do you mean?" A look of comprehension slowly passed over his face.

"You think Betsy Jamieson and I—"

"Thanks for dinner, Joe," I said, gathering up my things.

"Debbie, that's ridiculous. We had separate beds—"

"Yeah, right. Men and women don't share bedrooms, Joe, unless something's going on."

"Debbie, please. Betsy and I are just friends."

"Yeah, that's what my ex-husband said when he went on weekend fishing trips with his *best friend*, Kelly. They shared a room, too. They've been married for years and have two grown children."

"Friends, my ass," I mumbled. "Maybe friends with benefits." I opened the door. "I'm walking home."

CHAPTER 40

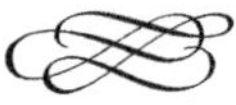

It was one of those dreams where you know you're dreaming, but you can't seem to break out of it.

The late August sun is beating down and the water is impossibly blue. Everybody seems to be swimming, and the pool is filled with young people. A blonde, golden-skinned girl in a white bathing suit is sunning herself. A good-looking young man with dark, close-cropped hair is poised on the side of the pool, looking hesitant. Everyone is watching him.

"Be careful—it's shallow here," somebody calls out. Then another voice—a girl's voice—yells, "Jump, Danny! Don't be a sissy. Jump!"

The others take up the chant: "Jump, jump, jump!"

I wake up from the dream, my body soaked with sweat, my face streaked with tears.

CHAPTER 41

"So. How are you feeling?" Dr. Lochner asked.

"Well, I feel like a hot mess. I had a fight with a man yesterday who I really liked. I thought he might even be boyfriend material."

He didn't answer. But apparently, what I just said must have been important because he began to scribble on his notepad, so I continued.

"And last night I dreamed about Danny again," I said. "Maybe the fight with Joe, coupled with seeing Kay recently, got me started again. You remember, I told you about Kay and Danny, right?"

"Uh-huh," Dr. Lochner continued writing.

"I always used to wonder how my life would have turned out, if Danny hadn't died," I said. "If he had been around to help Mom after Daddy's stroke, maybe I could have stayed in New York. Maybe I would have gone on to have a successful advertising career, or become a famous journalist. Found a nice guy and raised a couple of kids in the suburbs."

Dr. Lochner nodded and continued writing.

"Oh, and I'm still feeling pretty shaky. Yesterday at the bank I could hardly sign my name on the back of my check because my hands were shaking so much. What are the symptoms of Parkinson's?"

That got his attention. "You do not have Parkinson's." He put down pen and paper and examined his thumbs.

"And I'm so irritable lately," I went on. "The way things come out of my mouth—maybe it's Tourette's Syndrome." I wanted to add that I didn't look like myself either, but that would sound crazy and I didn't want to annoy him. As it was, he seemed to be in dire need of a nap. Everyone knew that he desperately wanted to retire, but the new Mrs. Lochner would not hear of it. No way was she going to derail the Gravy Train.

"Are you taking your medication?" he asked, staring up at the ceiling as if it were the Sistine Chapel.

"For whatever it's worth, yes."

With that, he resumed his frenzied writing. What was that about? I wondered. Once and for all, I had to find out.

"Dr. Lochner," I said timidly, "I'm curious. What did I say just now that was so important you took notes about it?"

"Why do you ask?" he countered.

"Enquiring minds want to know." I tried to make a joke of it. "Seriously, I always wondered about that."

Dr. Lochner seemed uncomfortable. "I was not taking notes."

"Then what is it you're always writing?"

He was silent for a moment. Then he said with a shrug, "I'm not writing anything. I'm just"—he held up the yellow-lined pad, "scribbling, doodling."

"You're what?" I strained to look at the pad.

Sure enough, it was filled with various doodles—Dr. Lochner's monogram, and what looked like women's breasts, some perky and some pendulous, all over the page.

Bad enough he hasn't even been taking notes about me, but apparently I'm so dull he had to doodle tits through all these sessions. What a jerk he is. I ought to dump him.

"So, how are you keeping busy?" he asked.

"The usual. Going to work, going to the pool, seeing my friends, going to the creative writers' group."

He tore his gaze from the ceiling and stared at me. "You know, you're doing much better, actually, than many of my depressed patients." He sounded almost accusing. "You hold down a job, you made friends, you're even writing. I don't feel you're as depressed as you think."

"But I never thought I was depressed," I reminded him. "It was you who said—"

"So's you don't need to come so often. Every four weeks would be enough unless you have a crisis."

"What?" Even though I had just been thinking about dumping him, I didn't see this coming. I felt jilted. It was like dating somebody you weren't all that crazy about—and all of a sudden he says he doesn't want to see you so often. I want to be the dumper, not the dumpee!

Suddenly I heard a sound so unexpected and startling that I nearly jumped from the chair.

"Cuckoo."

"What the f—" I cried.

"Cuckoo, Cuckoo."

"Oh, my God, I don't believe it." I burst out laughing. "A cuckoo clock."

"That happens to be a very valuable antique. My wife got it at an estate auction."

"I know your wife collects clocks, but come on," I said between fits of giggling. "I mean you're a psychiatrist, and here you've got a cuckoo clock in your office. How weird is that?"

Dr. Lochner stood up to signal the session was over. And what better way to tell your cuckoo patients that their time was up than to have a cuckoo clock remind them?

I was still laughing as I stumbled out of his office. The two patients in the waiting room stared at me. The woman was doing needlepoint and the man was knitting. "That's right, folks," I called to them, "you gotta keep those hands busy. Just what the doctor ordered."

Mrs. Lochner, sitting at the reception desk, nearly dropped the stick of gloss she was applying to her lips.

"Ciao, Estrella," I waved. "I'll call for an appointment. Oh, and I just love your newest timepiece."

But as I got in my car, I stopped laughing. Now what? I was back to square one.

CHAPTER 42

What to do?

Dr. Lochner certainly wasn't helping me.

Dr. Warren Ross wasn't any help either, since I could never get in to see him. And his nurse practitioner, Ludmila, simply pooh-poohed me as just another whiny older woman who was "losing it."

As for changing to another medical practice within my HMO, it seemed too complicated, and since I was feeling so jittery and nervous, this was not a good time to make any major changes in healthcare providers.

I repeat: What to do?

I would have to become my own healthcare advocate.

I would have to let the Internet help diagnose what was wrong with me by consulting with Dr. Google. Or, better yet, Dr. ChatGPT.

But first things first. Sweating and starving, I turned up the air conditioner and then gobbled down a dinner of microwave teriyaki chicken, a peanut butter sandwich, and three chocolate chip cookies.

I chatted briefly with my daughter, then called Maria to tell her about Dr. Lochner and the cuckoo clock. As always, Maria was a great audience. But then she mentioned she had spotted Kay driving a different car, this one a sedate black BMW. "She's a real mystery woman, that one," Maria said.

"Apparently Kay is still in Palmetto Pointe," I said, "even though she told us she was only here temporarily." I wanted to add: "Forgotten but not gone."

Later, as I took off my makeup, I stared at myself in the glaring light of the bathroom mirror, trying to decide exactly what it was that made me look so different lately. What was it about my face, my eyes? I had recently tried some new drugstore cosmetics—a navy-blue gel eyeliner, a mascara, and a bronzer, but they didn't seem to help.

Well, I thought, it's a good thing I hadn't said anything to Dr. Lochner about looking different lately. He would probably have snickered and said something like, "Hello, it's called getting old."

I was ready for my medical consultation. One symptom at a time. I typed in "causes of shakiness," among which were atrial fibrillation, hypoglycemia, internal tremor, and anxiety. That made me feel even shakier.

As I skimmed over the various websites ChatGPT suggested, one caught my attention. It suggested seeking medical attention if I had any of these symptoms: sudden or confused thinking; confusion about time or place (disorientation); or sudden personality or behavior changes, such as becoming aggressive.

My head was reeling. Did I, in fact, have confused thinking? Or a personality and/or behavior change that was making me aggressive?

Could Ludmila and Dr. Lochner be right after all? It was too much to comprehend, so I logged off the computer.

And I decided to call Maria back. "Are you free to go to the pool tomorrow?" I asked. I could definitely use a distraction.

CHAPTER 43

It seemed as if everyone in Palmetto Pointe had decided to go to the pool. I had never seen the place so crowded. Most of the chairs and lounges displayed colorful beach towels draped over the backs as proof of occupancy. Luckily, Maria had arrived early and saved me a seat.

Tommy, the security guard, was handing out copies of the *News and Schmooze*, calling out "Extra, extra—read all about it. Hot off the press. And it's free." He spotted us and brought over copies of the paper.

"Hi Miss Debbie, Miss Maria, how are you today?"

Maria and I smiled warmly at him.

"Great. You?"

"The sun is shining and I am in the company of two beautiful women," he said in his deep voice. "What could be better?"

"Uh, Tommy, this is kind of a personal question," said Maria.

"I'm an open book," he said, smiling.

"Are you Christian?" she asked.

"As a matter of fact, I am," he said. "I go to church every Sunday, too."

"Really? Hmmm—I noticed you're not wearing a wedding ring. Are you married?"

Like a deer in the headlights, Tommy seemed frozen in place. "No," he said softly.

Maria laughed merrily.

"I'm just teasing you, Tommy," she said. "Although if I was twenty years younger, I might have pounced. Unless you like cougars?" Maria's eyebrow arched suggestively.

Speechless, Tommy chuckled and walked away.

I looked at Maria and shook my head in wonder.

"What?" Maria shrugged. "I wanted to see if he met my boyfriend-list criteria. What do you think?"

"I think your pickup lines need some work," and we both laughed.

"It's nice to hear you laughing for a change," said Maria. "You've been so down since your fight with Joe."

"Yeah, well, I guess if something seems too good to be true, it usually is. Anyway, let's see what's happening in the latest *News and Schmooze*."

When I opened my copy, my eye fell to a page with some condos for sale.

"Just what I needed to see," I said. "Condos that I can't afford."

"Did you hear back from the Altmans?" Maria asked.

"Not yet. And I'm getting nervous."

"Let me ask Joyce Davis. She might know of some good deals that aren't even listed yet."

"Thanks, Maria."

"Here, have some homemade lemon cookies," Maria said, reaching into her tote. "They'll make you feel better."

And they did.

After a full day, I was ready to get home. As I got out of the car, who should come running over but Mister Highpockets' sister Freda, waving a small piece of paper.

"Look, I've got a two-for-one coupon for Vinnie's. You and Stanley could have a nice meal cheap. But you have to get there early because it's always crowded."

"Thank you," I told her. "But I am not interested in going out with Stanley. Not now. Not ever."

"So what are you saying?" Freda demanded. "Yes or no?"

I was so depressed about the astronomical condo prices that I didn't even bother telling Lori about my latest Freda encounter.

CHAPTER 44

"Hey, Debbie, you're talking to yourself again." Ursula's mean office manager face was on.

I bit back a retort and kept on typing the holiday camp schedule draft that Brad, the new assistant recreation director, needed ASAP. As usual, I seemed to have the only set of fingers in the recreation office. Ursula was taking the afternoon off, and Charmaine was at lunch, or socializing, or whatever suited her fancy.

Brad was hovering over me. "Can you read my handwriting?" he asked anxiously.

"Sure." I knew how important this was to Brad. He had just gotten promoted, so he wanted to make a good impression. And the poor guy had trouble getting his thoughts down using a computer keyboard, so he wrote everything in longhand.

I read the words aloud as I typed, a habit I had picked up over the years. I always kept my voice low, and nobody had ever made fun of me before until Ursula picked up on it.

"See that, Brad? She's doing it again," Ursula chortled. "Hey, Debbie, how come you like to talk to yourself?"

"Because that way, I tend to associate with a better class of people," I shot back.

Brad laughed. Ursula shrugged and said, "Half the time I don't know what she's talking about. Anyhow, I gotta run. My husband's outside waiting for me."

"Going to a lunch seminar?" Brad asked.

"Huh? No, I'm going to Costco." Ursula took her purse from her desk drawer. "See you tomorrow. And don't forget," she called over her shoulder, "Charmaine is in charge when I'm not here."

"Seriously?" Brad asked. "Charmaine is in charge? What's her job anyway?"

I had wondered the same thing myself. So one day I did a little research and found out she had the same title as me—administrative assistant. Except that her typing was terrible, and whenever she was on the computer, she searched for elephant figurines, which she said represented good luck. Charmaine had fifty of them in her house and was always adding to her collection.

But I just shrugged, because I liked Charmaine and didn't want to get her in trouble. "Don't ask me—I'm just the part-timer." I kept typing away. My major talent—from the days of the Royal manual to the IBM Selectric to the computer keyboard—I could type like a bat out of hell, fast and accurate, yet still take part in a conversation. And even though my hands were shaky lately, somehow my fingers were always sure and steady on the keys.

"I don't want to stand over you and make you nervous," Brad said. "I'll be in my office—I mean my cubbyhole. Call me if you can't decipher my handwriting."

I had no problem reading what he had written. After proofing and printing out the schedule, I brought it to Brad. "Oh, wow—so soon? Debbie, you're amazing."

"Nah—just an old typewriter jockey. You're so young I bet you probably don't even know what a typewriter is," I joked. "Anyhow, look it over and make any corrections."

A few minutes later, he came out, beaming. "Perfect. I just want to add a paragraph on the last page. Here. I wrote it in red."

I made the change in well, seconds flat, and handed him the corrected version. "The big boss will be duly impressed."

"You think?" Brad asked.

"I know for a fact." Actually, I didn't know any such thing, but Brad was a sweet guy, and as the new kid on the block, he needed reassurance.

"Thanks. I'll give it to him as soon as he comes back," Brad said. "Speaking of coming back—look who's here—the one, the only, the charming Chow Mein Cutler." Brad was the only one who could get away with calling her Chow Mein.

"I'm b-a-a-c-k, did anyone send me flowers?" Charmaine sat down at her desk and whipped out a mirror from her purse. She frowned at her reflection and chanted in a singsong voice, "Mirror, mirror on my desk, why is my hair such an awful mess?" She stood up. "I can't believe what I look like. I have to go to the ladies' room and fix it. I won't be long. Oh, and if anybody sends me candy, well, you can have the top layer."

Brad and I watched her tap dance out of the office. "Fixing her hair will take her at least twenty minutes," I said. "One thing's for sure, Charmaine is not going to die from overwork."

Brad grinned. "You are one funny lady. Who would I have to talk to if you weren't here?"

"This place is just a stepping stone for you," I told him. "You'll put in your time here, and it'll look good on your resume. You're meant for better things."

"And speaking of better things, how is the Princess of Palmetto Pointe? I haven't had a chance to find out what's going on in your hood these days?" Brad, too, was becoming an avid fan of hearing the latest Palmetto shenanigans.

"Every day a new adventure," I said, and told him about Freda's offer.

Brad erupted in laughter. He had such a great laugh. I liked the looks of him, too—sandy hair, blue eyes, and a tanned face that was slightly pitted, probably from teenage acne. Another Paul Newman type; I was about to tell him he reminded me of him, but Brad probably didn't know who Paul Newman was. Or maybe he did, if he was familiar with the salad dressings and pasta sauces that bore his name.

We bantered back and forth. "Why can't I find a girl like you?" he teased.

"Where were guys like you when I was young?" I countered.

His blue eyes stared at me, and I knew, in that brief moment, Brad had really seen another Debbie—not the senior citizen Debbie of Palmetto Pointe, but instead the young, fresh-faced La Deborita of the East End Hotel for Women.

At home that evening, I worked on something to read at the Palmetto Pointe Creative Writing Group.

Coming of Age

I was nothing special as a kid or an adult. But I think I'm pretty good at being a senior citizen.

For some reason, I do old quite well. People tell me I don't "seem old," that I take things in stride and don't complain as much as most seniors do. I think I know why: I've always had to drive old, high-mileage cars, so I'm used to things going wrong and parts needing to be replaced and stuff getting rusty.

Which probably puts me somewhere between "Grow old with me, the best is yet to be," and "Getting old sucks."

Now that I've gotten the hang of it, I realize that the business of living isn't all that complicated. Still in all, it would be nice to press the backspace key and start all over. Wouldn't life be so much easier if we could just cut and paste?

How come, now that I'm out of the running, I can talk to guys so easily? How come it took me so long to find out that the most important thing when you get old is a sense of humor? How come—

CHAPTER 45

I was up early Saturday morning. Since I had already written something for the writers' group, I decided to write to Lori.

Subject line: Stuff I Keep Forgetting to Tell You About the Palmetto Pointe Sunday Morning Water Aerobics Class.

1. Last week Maxine, the Aerobics instructor, had a big argument with an elderly man named Jake. Seems that Maxine had told him it might be better for his feet if he wore pool shoes. So Jake went into the water in his brown leather, laced-up Florsheim's. Halfway through the class, Maxine noticed and yelled, "Jake, what's wrong with you? I meant rubber shoes, the kind you use in the pool." And he yelled, "Well, you didn't explain that, so you have to pay for a new pair of shoes. I'm taking you to court." Will keep you posted on this important litigation.

2. Oh, and a little while later, we had a surprise visitor in the pool. A snake chased a frog into the water, and what a commotion. The snake bit a woman, and they called 911. The EMTs wanted to take her to the hospital but she wouldn't go because she had a canasta game afterward. As it turned out, the snake wasn't poisonous. Somebody threw it back into the bushes.

3. But what happened this morning is the best. After we finish exercising, we always form a circle, socialize a bit, and Maxine asks if anyone has good news to share. Well, some guy pipes up, "Yes, I had an erection this morning." Silence. Nobody knew what to say.

Anyhow, that's the report from Crazyville.

Lori e-mailed back, "What kind of chemicals are they putting in your pool? Viagra maybe?"

I chuckled and got ready for the meeting.

"Well, this never happened before," Norman told the writers' group. "Nobody brought in anything to read. Didn't any of you sit down and write this week?"

Even the always-prolific Eunice shook her head. "It just wasn't a good writing week," she said. Several people murmured their agreement. I didn't want to share what I wrote, so I nodded my head in agreement, too.

"Couldn't think of a thing to write about," Howie said. "I don't know why."

"That's because Mercury is in retrograde," said Astrid, the astrologer.

"I don't care if Mercury is in Fort Lauderdale," Norman said irritably. "We are all writers and writers write—right?" He smiled at his little play on words. "Well then, we're all going to do some writing here and now." He glanced at his watch, "Something, anything. Even if it's just a paragraph."

"Give us some topics," Astrid suggested.

"Okay, here are a couple of thoughts," Norman said.

"How has technology changed us? How do we feel about getting older? When did you know you had gotten old? Or any subject for that matter. Now remember—just write, don't edit. This is a freestyle writing exercise."

I drew a blank at first, then remembered a recent incident with the Comcast rep. I started to scribble quickly across the lined pages of my notebook.

After a while, Norman announced it was time to read and critique the writing. Astrid wrote a funny piece about her seven-year-old nephew listening to elevator music and announcing, "Auntie, that's dead people's music." Astrid concluded drily, "And that was the day I knew I was old."

Eunice read her usual self-promoting dribble about how she always thinks young and never intends to get old.

"As long as there are plastic surgeons in South Florida, she'll get her wish," Howie muttered.

Consuela had nothing to read. "I am steel theenking. I weel bring sometheeng next week."

Then it was my turn.

I was having problems with my TV when Comcast first took over. So they sent this nice young man to check it out. He told me what I needed to do, and I wrote the information down, most of it in shorthand because I was a secretary for years and, of course, it's so much faster.

The Comcast guy stared at me and said, "Where are you from?"

"Massachusetts," I told him, figuring he was wondering about my accent.

"No, I mean what country are you from?"

"I was born in this country," I told him. "Why do you ask?"

"Because," he said very seriously, "you're writing in another language."

"Another language?" I looked down at my notes and smiled. "Oh,

no, that's shorthand, Gregg shorthand, see?" I held the paper up to show him.

He looked at me blankly.

"You don't know—you've never heard of shorthand? We studied it in school. We had Gregg shorthand, Pittman—"

He shook his head.

And then it occurred to me that this young guy—maybe twenty-two years old or so—had no idea what I was talking about. To him, shorthand was the equivalent of buggy whips from my time. Shorthand was irrelevant, so last century. And so was I. And that was when I knew I was old.

I concluded and put my paper down. There was an immediate reaction but, as usual, not exactly the reaction Norman wanted.

"That Comcast—they're dumb shits."

"What—AT&T is any better?"

"I hated shorthand," Eunice declared. "And I hated typing. I never wanted to be a secretary. I got married after my first year at college."

"I remember hearing about a website called 'Comcast Must Die,'" Howie mused. "I wonder if they still have it."

Norman stood up and banged the table with what looked like a gavel. "We're getting off the subject. Let's stick to the writing. Did Debbie state the facts clearly and—"

"I took Pittman in school," Astrid broke in. "They used to say it was harder to learn than Gregg. But I never used it. I went into retail instead."

Howie said, "Retail? Not readings?"

"Astrology was kind of a sideline back then," Astrid explained. "Now that I'm retired, I'm into charting people's lives, giving advice." She fished around her purse and handed out some business cards. "Also, I do parties. Sweet sixteens. Bar and bat mitzvahs. Anniversary parties. Whatever."

Bang. Norman's gavel came down heavily. "Please—we're getting off the—"

"What's with the gavel?" Howie cried. "Are we in family court or something?"

Consuela spoke up. "I like what Dabbie wrote. Dabbie makes me to laugh."

"There she goes again," Eunice sniped. "It's Debbie, Not Dabbie. And I'll bet you didn't even understand what she wrote."

Norman quieted the two of them down. "We have to move on. But I do want to tell you, Debbie, that, as always, I enjoyed your little vignette. Your writing always seems to liven up the group."

I basked in his approval. My writing is getting better. And I'm feeling better, too. I had nothing to worry about.

Famous last words.

CHAPTER 46

I hadn't seen Dr. Lochner in a while, and I was starting to feel like maybe the symptoms I mentioned weren't really that worrisome.

That shakiness, for instance. It seemed to occur more often lately, but maybe, I reasoned, that's just part of getting older. I'm not as steady as I used to be. And always feeling so hot—well, didn't everyone say that the temperatures in South Florida were higher than usual this year?

As for being irritable and snapping at people, well, duh, that's what senior citizens do in South Florida.

But an incident at Publix made me stop and think. I kind of lost it at the checkout when the cashier asked, "Would you like some help to your car?" She gestured to the bagger, an elderly man.

I replied, as usual, "No thanks. I'm good." I don't know whether the man didn't hear me or what, but he grabbed my shopping cart and started wheeling it to the door. I was so upset I yelled, "Bug off," so loudly that the store manager hurried over from Customer Service to see what the problem was.

"I don't like it when they keep pestering me like that," I told the manager. "If I need help with my groceries, I'll ask for it."

"It's the Publix policy to offer assistance to our customers," he said soothingly. "And Tim here—" he patted the bagger's arm— "Is happy to be of service."

I couldn't let it go. "Well, to me that policy says you think I'm so old and decrepit that I need help from Tim the bagger, who, by the way, is no youngster himself." He was also, although I didn't say it, bent over and didn't look too healthy.

Tim straightened up as best he could and skulked away. Customers and cashiers nearby watched and listened.

The manager assured me that Publix offered the service to all customers, pointing to a nearby checkout where a young mother with a toddler was being helped to her car by another bagger. "People find this service very helpful. In fact, they love it."

"Well, I don't," I said. "I am perfectly capable of wheeling this shopping cart out to the parking lot and putting the bags of groceries in my trunk."

Out of the corner of my eye, I saw that one of the onlookers was Kay. Oh, great. Of all the people to witness this, it had to be her.

I hurried out of the store as fast as I could, my face burning like a tower of fire ants with embarrassment.

What the hell did I just do? And *why?* What's the matter with me?

In this moment, I finally admitted to myself that things that had never bothered me before now loomed as major grievances—a slow driver, a not-so-great haircut, a shopper in the express line who had more than ten items.

I was simply not myself.

What to do?

When you're crazy, who ya gonna call?

Who else but Dr. Marvin J. Lochner, psychiatrist to the stars.

I WAS SURPRISED TO SEE THAT THE DOCTOR'S TROPHY WIFE was not at the reception desk. And the cuckoo clock was not on the mantel in his office. Which was good because just the sight of that clock would probably make me laugh uncontrollably like a cuckoo.

The tone of the session was different this time, too. Dr. Lochner had a new tactic, at least with me. Apparently, he was so tired of listening to patients that he decided to do the talking instead, most of it bragging about his wife. "Estrella went on a day trip with her lady friends to a museum. Estrella is very involved in the arts," he added proudly.

I was in no mood to hear about Estrella who, according to local gossip, made a shameless ploy for Marvin Lochner even before his poor wife passed away. Estrella purportedly maxed out her previous husband's credit cards for a nose job, facelift, and tummy tuck, then dumped the poor bastard. As the second Mrs. Lochner, she insisted on moving to Boca Raton where she reinvented herself further, claiming she was an interior decorator who came from Scarsdale, even though everyone back in Banyan Beach knew she hailed from Brooklyn.

And that ridiculous name Estrella, my ass, I snickered to myself. I know an Esther when I see one.

"So, when did your wife change her name?" I asked outright.

Dr. Lochner's mouth dropped open. He fixed me with a how-dare-you look, and I was certain he was going to tell me to leave and never come back.

But instead, he shrugged his bony shoulders and sighed. "When we bought our place in Boca. She thought Esther made her sound too old."

"She's got a point," I agreed. "Esther is not a 'now' name and it's not a Boca name. But enough about her. I'm worried about me—I feel even more shaky than before. And lately I've been saying such awful things to people. I just snap at everyone."

"That's part of depression and anxiety," Dr. Lochner yawned loudly and didn't bother to hide it.

"You know, I was thinking," I said slowly, "maybe all this has something to do with that woman, Kay. I happened to see her a while back. I didn't know she was still down here. Remember I told you about Kay—the one who—the one I knew from high school?"

"What? You think she put a hex on you? Or a voodoo curse?" Dr. Lochner snorted.

"No. I mean I think I was okay until I bumped into her. Do you think that maybe seeing Kay again brought up things that were never resolved?"

For an answer, Dr. Lochner picked up his yellow pad and began doodling, which meant he was bored and I needed to change the subject.

"Oh, another thing." I said, "Last night I checked ChatGPT for 'causes of shakiness,' and one thing led to another, like 'confusion or personality changes.' It said to seek medical attention for things like changes in mood and behavior and suddenly becoming aggressive."

"Changes in mood and behavior can be for a number of reasons," Dr. Lochner said. "Dementia, brain tumor."

"Oh, my God—brain tumor" My heart, which always pounded loudly these days, seemed to be on the verge of exploding. "Do you think—?"

Dr. Lochner stood up to signal the end of the session. "I think we need to up the dosage of your Prozac."

Brain tumor. Just the mention of those words was enough to terrify me. But I don't have headaches, I reassured myself. And I don't really have memory problems—well, no more than anyone else in Palmetto Pointe.

Despite my worry, I was nonetheless able to scarf down two turkey and provolone sandwiches when I got home, but that did nothing to allay my fears. The condemned man ate a hearty meal, I thought ruefully.

Wouldn't that be a bitch? After I start to make a new life in Florida, I find out I have some deadly medical condition.

I went to the ChatGPT and, unable to stop myself, typed in "What are symptoms of brain tumor?" My eyes blurred as I skimmed over the comments "Mood and personality changes … memory problems … seizures …"

Seizures? I read on: "Up to a third of people report having seizures prior to being diagnosed with brain tumor. Seizures cause the body to shake and tremor in varying intensity. They can also cause one to stare for several minutes and to have visual disturbances."

Just this morning at work, Charmaine had remarked, "Debbie, do you know you have a funny stare?"

Oh, that's enough. I'm really making myself crazy. I

closed the tab. I checked my messages and to my surprise, I found an email from Roz. The subject line said: "Funny—You gotta read this." Well, I can use a laugh, I thought ruefully as I opened the email. It read:

A doctor had sex with one of his female patients and felt guilty all day long. No matter how much he tried to forget about it, he just couldn't. The guilt and sense of betrayal of his patients were overwhelming. But every once in a while he'd hear an internal, reassuring voice in his head that said, "Don't worry about it. You aren't the first medical practitioner to have sex with a patient, and you won't be the last. And you're not married. So, let it go."

But invariably, another voice in his head would bring him back to reality, whispering, "You're a veterinarian, you sick bastard."

I burst out laughing. That was just what I needed. I've said it once, I'll say it again. And probably again: thank goodness for friends.

CHAPTER 47

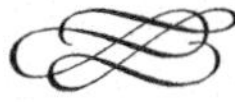

"'Never look back.' You know whose motto that is?" I asked Lori.

"I give up," she said.

"Never look back is the motto of all the old fart drivers down here. They never look back when they pull out of a parking space. I nearly got clipped just now at the market."

"Mom, please be careful," Lori said, sounding worried. "Those people shouldn't even be driving."

"Duh" I snorted. "But you'd have to pry the car keys from their cold dead hands before they'd give up driving. Anyhow, don't worry. I do try to be careful. I drive defensively and I walk defensively, especially in parking lots. Today it was like a zoo because there's another tropical storm brewing so everyone was out buying water."

"What's that banging noise?" Lori asked. "Is someone at your door?"

"Oh, that's Ira, Fran's friend. Remember I told you that no one's doorbells work, so he has to bang on the door. He's here to change my light bulb. Even with the step stool, I still have trouble reaching it. In my next lifetime, I want to be a six-foot-tall volleyball player."

Lori laughed.

We hung up, and I let Ira in. He had become the unofficial "boyfriend" of all three of us. Fran was his lady, of course, but he was also on call for Maria and me if we needed him. He put air in my tires. He fixed the leak under Maria's sink.

"Handy is dandy," Maria declared. "Ira is a gem."

"He sure is," I agreed and told Fran, "You better treat Boyfriend right or you'll have to answer to us." From then on, Ira's new name was "Boyfriend." He seemed to like the name. When he called Fran, he would say, "It's Boyfriend." And when he went to fix something at Maria's or my apartment, he would knock on the door and call out, "Boyfriend's here."

It had become an accepted fact that Fran and Ira were a couple, although she made a point of telling him that her two friends were very special and she needed to spend time with them. Accordingly, Ira saw her just twice a week, on Wednesday and one weekend night when we didn't have a meeting of The Cabernet Club.

Everything seemed to be going so well at first but now—

"I don't know what's happening lately," Ira blurted out as soon as he changed the light bulb. "Fran has changed—just like that. I keep asking if it's something I did or said, and she tells me 'No' but something just isn't right."

"What do you mean?"

"She's—oh, I don't know—it's as if she's hiding something," Ira said. "We used to watch the news on TV after I took her home, but now she just shoos me off. And she's always playing music lately. Really loud, like she's covering up some kind of noise. She seems very secretive."

"You know, Fran hasn't been available much lately," I said, frowning. "I thought she was spending more time with you."

"No," he said. "In fact, she seems to have even less time for me lately."

"This doesn't make any sense," I said. "Want me to check it out?"

"Would you? I'd really appreciate it. I'm worried about her."

"Matter of fact, I think I'll pay her a visit right now," I told him. "I'll let you know if I find out anything."

After Ira left, I called Maria and told her about his concerns. "Let's you and me go over to Fran's and see what's up."

"Okay, give me ten minutes." Maria said. "And now that I think about it, whenever I call Fran lately, the TV is always so loud. That's not like her. And it's not as if she's got a hearing problem."

"Okay, Sherlock, let's solve this mystery," I said. "Poor Boyfriend is really down in the dumps. Oops, I should have put that a better way."

We could hear music coming from Fran's condo, a loud, crashing classical piece at high volume. It took a good deal of pounding before she came to the door, which she opened only a crack. "Oh, hello. I—uh—wasn't expecting anyone," she stammered.

"Aren't you going to invite us in?" I pushed past Fran,

looking around to see if there was anything unusual. I noticed a couple of Fran's expensive dolls strewn carelessly on the floor.

"Didn't that doll cost you a bundle?" Maria asked, pointing at one of the dolls on the floor.

Fran just stood there, looking agitated.

"And for God's sake, lower that damn music or shut it off," Maria said as she and I sat down on the sofa. "So what's the big mystery here? What's going on?"

Fran lowered the volume. "I don't know what you're talking about."

Maria folded her arms across her chest. "Do you have a guy here or something?"

Fran started to protest when suddenly we heard a strange sound coming from her bathroom. A plaintive cry that sounded like, Mrow. Mow. Meow.

"Oh, Jeez, is that a cat?" I cried.

"Shhh—no it's not—yes, it is." Fran burst into tears.

"You mean that's the big mystery? You've got a cat?"

"And you couldn't tell any of us about it—not even Boyfriend?" Maria demanded.

"If the management finds out, they'll make me get rid of Kitty," Fran wailed. "You know how strict they are about the no-pet policy in Palmetto Pointe. I'm so afraid of somebody finding out."

"Where'd this cat come from?"

"The shopping center. She kept following me, and she was so scrawny and tiny and—" by now Fran was sobbing. "I was only going to take her home for a little bit and feed her and she just kept meowing and purring. I love Kitty. I never had a pet before. My mother didn't think animals were clean, and you know George was allergic. I won't give her up."

"Come on, Fran, stop crying," Maria patted her shoulder. "And don't worry. They can make an exception. What you do is get a letter from a doctor saying you need a service animal for your emotional health or depression—whatever. Actually, a letter from a shrink would be better."

"Really?" Fran sniffled. "But I don't know any shrinks."

"Woo-hoo, have I got a shrink for you," I said. "Dr. Lochner has a nice sideline writing 'Cats and Dogs for Crazies' letters." I got up from the sofa and carefully opened the bathroom door.

"Mrow?" There was the small, skinny gray-and-white cat whose domain consisted of a litter box, food, and water, with Fran's Princess Di doll that apparently served as a kitty toy.

"Hey, kitty," I crooned. "What's the matter? You want to come out?" I bent down to pet the little cat, who rubbed against me, purring. "I had a kitty like you when I was a kid."

I scooped Kitty up and carried her into the living room.

Then everything happened so fast.

A knock at the door startled everyone. Fran went to open it, and Ira was standing there, looking worried. In a fraction of a second, Kitty managed to squeeze from my arms and bolt out of the condo, a ball of gray-and-white fur, racing madly down the stairs and disappearing into the night of Palmetto Pointe.

Fran screamed, "Kitty got out. She's gone."

Ira, stunned for the moment, collected himself and ran after the cat. "I'll get her," he yelled, hurrying down the stairs with the three of us following.

"Hey—what's going on here?" As if it weren't enough of a circus, I was chagrined to see Kay open the door of her condo.

"Fran's cat got out." Maria gasped. "Ira ran outside to find her."

"He'll never find Kitty. It's getting dark outside and she runs so fast." Fran kept wringing her hands. "If anything happens to Kitty, I'll die."

We all stood frozen in place, not knowing what to say or do. Amazingly, with all the commotion, not one neighbor came out to see what was going on. Finally, we heard the sound of footsteps. From the corner of the building, Ira emerged, huffing and puffing, with an indignantly meowing Kitty in his arms.

"It's a miracle. Oh, Ira, you found her," Fran cried. "Thank you. Thank you."

"Way to go, Boyfriend," I applauded.

"Ira, you'd better put Kitty back in the bathroom and shut the door," Maria advised. Ira nodded and marched up the stairs.

Weak with relief and joy, Fran whispered to the women, "I never thought Ira could move that fast. I mean, at his age."

"He could have hurt himself," I agreed. "It's getting so dark outside."

"Well," Kay drawled as she walked into her condo, "like I always say, some men will do anything to get a little pussy."

CHAPTER 48

I was scarfing down my scrambled eggs, reading the latest *Woman's World* magazine and half-listening to the television weather report. "Disturbance forming south of Jamaica … developing tropical system … we will be watching …"

The telephone rang. It was Lori, sounding worried. "Mom, what's happening down there? I was just watching the news. Are you guys getting a hurricane?"

"Oh, please, we're always getting a hurricane," I said. "That's what helps TV ratings in Florida. The newscasters who scare you the most get the most viewers."

"No, seriously. I don't like to think of you all alone there. Do you have flashlights, batteries, water?"

"I bought all of them the first time we had a hurricane scare, in August, so don't worry," I reassured her. "I'm heading to Publix soon anyway to get some extra supplies."

"Well, okay." Lori sounded doubtful. "Be safe. Love you."

"Love you, too."

Like everybody else, I rushed out to Publix, only to find the shelves nearly empty and the checkout lines long and frustrating. I decided to stock up on all things chocolate to give me comfort during the storm.

As I stood in the "Express" line, I spotted Norman, the writers' group director. "Hi, Norman, what's the latest word on the hurricane?"

He stared at me for a moment, then said, "Oh, Debbie, I didn't recognize you."

"That's because I'm standing up," I joked. "You usually see me sitting down."

"Did you—" he adjusted his glasses, "have you lost weight lately? You look—different."

I didn't answer. I knew Norman was right. I had been too afraid to step on a scale but could not deny that all my clothes were baggy. And I did look different, although I couldn't exactly put my finger on what it was.

The fear surfaced once again but I pushed it aside. I had more pressing things to worry about right now. This line, for instance. Was I going to have another rage fit at the local grocery store? I certainly hoped not.

CHAPTER 49

The management at Palmetto Pointe hustled into emergency mode.

They put up notices throughout the development, knocking on doors to warn second-floor residents that they were in danger of more structural damage and urging them to stay with a downstairs neighbor during the hurricane, if possible.

Many of the residents didn't know their next-door neighbors, let alone their downstairs neighbors.

Everyone seemed to be in a high state of tension. Banyan Beach was in the path of the hurricane. People taped their windows and brought plants and furniture in from their patios. TV newscasters nattered endlessly about hurricane survival—making a closet into a safe room, filling up plastic bottles with water for flushing toilets, cooking any frozen foods that could spoil during a power outage.

My daughter kept calling as the weather reports became more ominous. "I think you ought to go to a shelter, Mom. I worry about you being alone."

"I'm not going to any shelter," I scoffed. "I don't want to get lice or crabs or whatever." I didn't tell Lori about the Palmetto Pointe alert advising residents to stay with a neighbor on the ground floor.

"Couldn't you stay with Maria or Fran?"

"Maria and her mom don't have any room," I said. "And Fran is going with Ira to his daughter's house. But you don't have to worry. I'll be fine right here."

A few minutes later, Lori called again. "Mom, Zoe wants to talk to you."

"Hi, Grandma," Zoe said in that sweet little voice I loved. "I'm worried about you. I want you to be safe because you need to be around for my bat mitzvah. You're the only grandma we've got," she added. "Here's Mommy."

"Wow," I said when Lori took the phone. "You sure know how to lay on the guilt. The torch has been passed to another generation."

"When it comes to guilt," Lori said, "I learned from a master. But seriously—we'd all feel so much better if we knew you weren't going to be alone."

My call waiting beeped. "Maria's on the other line. Let me see what she wants. I'll call you back."

Maria's message was terse. "You've got to go," she insisted.

"The heck I will," I retorted. The two of us argued back and forth.

"She's expecting you. I told her you'd be down around six thirty," Maria said. "Don't make a fool out of me."

"There's a lot you don't understand," I started to say, but Maria cut me off.

"Then tell me about it after the hurricane is over. At

least you'll be safe there. Promise me you'll do it," Maria said and hung up.

I called my daughter back. "Okay—you got your wish," I said reluctantly, "I won't be alone. I'm staying with a neighbor."

"That's great. Who are you staying with?"

"That woman—you know—Kay Caldwell." The name was like glue on my tongue.

"Oh, the one from back home?" Lori sounded relieved. "That was nice of her to invite you."

"Hah," I snorted, "Kay didn't exactly invite me. Maria arranged the whole thing. She bullied Kay into it."

"Whatever it takes," Lori said. "At least you won't be alone and I'll have peace of mind."

THE WIND WAS PICKING UP AS I WENT DOWNSTAIRS TO GET what would probably be the last mail delivery for at least a few days.

The good news was that I had gotten the latest *People* magazine and *Reader's Digest* (Lori always got me subscriptions as gifts), so at least I'd have something to read. The bad news was that Freda was yoo-hooing me. "Oh, dearie, Stanley and I want you to stay downstairs with us. I moved his clothes out of the way and we can all sit in the closet and ride out the hurricane."

"Thanks, Freda, but I already made plans," I said.

"Oh, yes, be sure to bring in all your plants," Freda agreed. "Otherwise they'll blow away."

"No, I said plans. I've got other plans."

"Well. Good luck to you, then," Freda said huffily. "The

condo director—Harriet what's-her-name—asked if she could come down and stay with us, but Stanley says he'd rather have you."

What a choice I've got, I thought. Kay Caldwell or Mister Highpockets.

I hurried upstairs, thinking of what I needed to do and what stuff I needed to take with me. The hurricane was supposed to make a landing sometime around 2 a.m.

It was going to be a long, uncomfortable night in Kay's condo.

But it would be even longer and more uncomfortable to ride out the hurricane with Mister Highpockets and his sister, Freda, in a dark, musty walk-in closet that smelled of old men's clothes. Oh, to be a moth flitting around there.

Good luck to you, Harriet Bertulli, I thought and laughed out loud.

CHAPTER 50

"Hello?" I answered my cell phone as I walked back into my condo.

"Hi Debbie, it's Joe."

I hadn't had time to look at the caller ID, and if I had, I probably wouldn't have answered it. We hadn't spoken since our blowup last month.

"Hi Joe," I said coldly.

"I wanted to make sure you're okay for the hurricane."

"I'm fine, thanks."

"Well, you know I live on the first floor, and I wanted to offer you a place to stay. I have a pull-out couch in the living room and you can stay in my bed, or on the couch, whatever you prefer."

I had to admit that was a nice offer and, in almost any other circumstance, would be better than staying with Kay. But I wasn't interested in a relationship, or even a friendship, with a "player."

"That's very kind of you, Joe," I said formally, "But I already have somewhere to stay."

"Okay," he said. "But if your plans change, let me know."

"They won't, but thank you."

"I know you're still mad at me, Debbie, but really, it's not what you think. I wish I had a way to explain everything—"

"Joe, I really need to get going. Goodbye."

CHAPTER 51

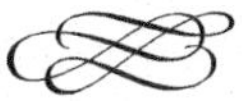

I was contemplating what to pack when Roz called.

These calls were getting exhausting, but I couldn't blame Roz for being concerned about the hurricane, too.

But no such thing. Roz wanted to vent about her boyfriend, Cy.

"You want to talk about Cy now? With a hurricane on the way?" I asked.

"Oh, that's right," Roz said, "I forgot. It's what—a Category Three? Well, anyhow, I had to call because you're the only one who understands. My daughter-in-law, Bonnie, got me all upset and I need to get it off my chest. Is this a good time to talk?"

"Oh, sure, I'm getting ready for what might be my last night on earth," I said. "The timing couldn't be better."

"Okay, so here's what happened," Roz went on, "I was talking to Bonnie the Bitch and I mentioned that I was sick and tired of hearing Cy's stories, over and over. It's driving me crazy. All he wants to do is sit at the kitchen table and talk. No sex, thank goodness, but the same old shit I've been listening to for years."

I laughed. "I bet by now you could dance to those stories. Cy loves to stroll down Memory Lane."

"Well, let him stroll there by himself," Roz said hotly. "Anyhow, Bonnie Big-Mouth just snickered and told me, 'That's what you get for being a Restaurant Whore.' Well, actually, she said 'Ho—Restaurant Ho.'"

"Bonnie called you a Restaurant Ho?"

"Can you imagine?" Roz was indignant. "Bonnie, the beauty, says that's the price I have to pay. Cy buys me a hamburger and a baked potato at Wendy's, so I have to sit and listen to those goddamn stories about when he was a kid, and his old Hebrew school teacher, and how he met his wife, let her rest in peace."

"I wouldn't call you a Restaurant Ho," I said, "more like a Fast-Food Ho."

"Stop with the jokes." Roz sounded like she was about to cry. "But listen to what my daughter-in-law from hell comes out with—oh, I can't even say it—you know what it means, don't you, when they say 'giving head'?"

"Uh—yes." Where *was* this going? I wondered.

"So, that bitch says to me, 'Well, Ma—some women give head. You have to give ear."

I giggled. "Hey, guys—Roz gives ear—I love it. That's the best laugh I've had today. So, are you going to keep seeing good old Cy?"

"Well, of course. At least I've got someone to be with. And I don't have to sit alone at bar mitzvahs and weddings. I'm not like you, Debbie. I don't like being alone."

"There are worse things than being alone," I said pointedly, "but listen, Roz, I have to finish packing and—"

"Packing? Where are you going with a hurricane on the way?"

"The management wants people to stay with a downstairs neighbor." I was about to tell Roz I would be staying with Kay Caldwell, but caught myself. Roz would never shut up about it, and I would not be able to get off the phone. "I'm just not sure what to bring," I added.

"Well, some clothes, clean underwear, maybe a raincoat in case the windows blow out," Roz suggested. "Oh, and bring the lady you're staying with something nice—candy or wine—you don't want to go empty-handed."

"A hostess gift in a hurricane? I'm thinking flashlights and bottled water."

"And don't forget your prescriptions," said ever-practical Roz. "And in case your condo gets destroyed, take some things you can't replace—photo albums, sentimental stuff."

I groaned. Bad enough I would be staying overnight with Kay, but I would go there looking like I was moving in.

"Look, Rozzie, it's getting late and I have to go before there's a power outage. I'll be in touch when it's over. Thanks for calling."

"That's what friends are for," Roz said. "I called because I was worried about you."

Yeah, right. I had to chuckle as I hung up and finished packing, taking more clothes than I originally intended, just in case. I filled a small cooler with bottled water, crackers, peanut butter, cookies, chocolate bars, and two bottles of cabernet. I certainly did not want to ask Kay for anything to eat or drink.

I clicked on the TV to check the latest developments.

The newscasters spoke in hushed tones, with scenes of past hurricanes and destruction. I quickly shut the TV off.

Did I forget anything? Prescriptions, toiletries, towels. What about the photos, as Roz had suggested? I took my daughter's wedding album and a box of snapshots of the grandkids. And what about the irreplaceable, sentimental stuff? I decided to pack the two brass Sabbath candlesticks my grandmother had brought over from Russia.

One last glance around. The mint chocolate chip ice cream in the freezer would probably melt anyhow, so I finished it all off. I unplugged the appliances. What else? It seemed to take forever until I was done. I brought everything over to the full-length mirror in the foyer and took a last glance at myself.

Oh, dear God, I look like a refugee fleeing from the enemy. All I need is a big, black cooking pot on top of my head.

I lugged all my stuff into the hallway, locked the door, and schlepped everything downstairs to Kay Caldwell's apartment.

CHAPTER 52

From the moment Kay opened the door, I wished I had never agreed to stay there. My face burned with embarrassment as I brought in all my stuff. What was I thinking? I looked like a bag lady.

To make matters worse, I realized I was holding a candlestick in each hand. How crazy-looking was that?

I tried to make a joke of it. "You know how they say you should never go to someone's house empty-handed."

The joke went over like a pregnant pole-vaulter. Kay didn't laugh. She just gave an impersonal "Hey" by way of greeting.

Glancing around, I noticed the entire condo was mirrored, floor to ceiling, elaborately furnished, and decorated in the once-popular Florida colors of pale pink and green, "Wow," I breathed. "This place is something. What do you call this style of furniture?"

"I call it Early Whorehouse," Kay said with a shrug. "Not my taste. But what the heck, the place is free so I can't complain."

Damn right you can't complain. I felt resentful. How come rich people always have friends who let them use their places for free? It's just not fair.

"Make yourself comfortable," Kay said, jutting her chin in the direction of the guest bedroom. "The cleaning girls came this morning, so there are fresh sheets on the bed and towels on the dresser. I'll probably just watch TV in my room while we've still got power. There's a TV set in your room, too," she added pointedly.

I forced a smile. "No problem. I'll be fine, thanks." But inwardly I seethed, You snotty bitch. Who wants your company anyhow?

"If you need anything—flashlight, water, something to eat—just holler," Kay told me.

"I'm good." That was all I could think of to say. Earlier, while packing my go-bag, I had brainstormed a couple of conversational topics in the event I had to make small talk with Kay, but now I was so flustered I couldn't remember them.

I brought my things into the bedroom. It was going to be a long, uncomfortable night, riding out the hurricane. God, I hope it's only one night, I prayed.

It took me a few minutes to figure out how the TV worked. I was damned if I'd ask Kay for help. It made me nervous listening to the newscasters talking about the hurricane, and nothing on cable interested me. I took the *People* magazine out of my tote bag, but it was hard to concentrate.

Outside, the rain beat a steady tempo. I jumped when I heard a deafening clap of thunder, followed by flashes of lightning. The lamps in the bedroom flickered, went dark, flickered on again briefly, then went completely out. I reached for my flashlight and turned on the battery-operated radio. "All nonessential vehicles off the main roads … power outages reported in …"

I tried to fall asleep, but as usual, sleep would not come. Outside, it grew more ominous. The rain turned torrential and the wind howled. Not wanting to stay in the bedroom where lightning kept flashing through the windows, I grabbed the radio and flashlight and carefully made my way into the living room, surprised to see Kay stretched out on the sofa.

"Oh, hi," she said, sounding somewhat friendlier than she had earlier. "This reminds me of the hurricanes we had back in Winslow. Remember that big one in the sixties?"

"Oh, God, yes. I remember they called out the National Guard," I said. "But that hurricane didn't do all that much damage. Not compared to what they say can happen down here."

Kay yawned. "I wish the damn thing would make landfall. The waiting can drive you nuts."

In the background, the radio droned on, "Heading toward South Florida."

"Hey, do you remember Billy Wong's back home?" Kay asked suddenly.

"The Chinese restaurant downtown? Sure, I do. What made you think of it?"

"I don't know. I just got this crazy craving for a chow mein sandwich. "

"You're making me hungry." My voice softened. "My aunt Evvie used to take me to Billy Wong's when I was a kid. Chow mein on a hamburger bun and orange soda to drink, right?"

"Oh, yeah. I don't think you can get them anywhere but

Winslow," Kay said. "When we lived in San Francisco, I asked for a chow mein sandwich at a Chinatown restaurant and they thought I was nuts."

"And how about coffee syrup?" I asked. "Hardly any place outside Winslow ever heard of coffee syrup."

"You know," Kay said dreamily, "looking back, Winslow was a nice place to grow up."

"Not for me," I said, biting off each word.

The silence seemed to last forever. Finally, Kay spoke. "Look, I'm really sorry about—about everything. He was such a great guy."

"Oh, so you do know who I am."

"Of course I do. Danny's sister. I recognized you right away. You look the same as you did in high school."

"Really? You never acknowledged me back then, never said a word to me, nothing."

Kay sat up. "What could I have said? What could I have done? Think about it."

"Oh, I've thought about it plenty, believe me. It destroyed my family."

"I can't even imagine what you went through," Kay said. "I had nightmares about it."

It was easier for me to speak up while we were sitting in the dark, while hurricane winds raged outside. "Yeah, I bet you had nightmares. I heard you were the one who kept egging Danny on to dive. You kept telling him, 'Jump, jump, jump.'"

"I swear to God, that wasn't me," Kay's voice cracked. "I was talking to a guy I liked."

"If it wasn't you, who was it?" I asked.

"A girl named Ginny Wilson. She used to spend summers in Winslow. People said we looked alike. I know the story went around that it was me, but it wasn't," Kay said. "I swear it on my son's life. I'll even take a polygraph, for God's sake."

She continued, "I really liked Danny. We all did. I wish I had paid more attention to how deep the pool was, but I didn't. And I'm so sorry."

The words landed like a punch to the gut. I wanted to reject them, to hold on to the anger that had kept me upright all these years. But beneath the shock, something in me knew—Kay was telling the truth. And that truth burned hotter than the bitterness I'd been carrying for decades.

"Your family never called or sent a sympathy note or anything," I lashed out. "It was as if he never existed."

"I didn't know that," Kay said slowly. "I'm really sorry. Right after it happened, my father sent Caroline away to a relative in California. He forbade her to talk about it to anyone. My father should have—"

"Your father," I broke in, "was a bigot. My aunt told me he was a real anti-Semite."

"Oh, yeah, that was Daddy all right." Kay didn't sound at all surprised. "An equal opportunity bigot—he didn't like anyone. But here's the kicker. Remember when I told you Caroline got married and converted to Judaism? Daddy ended up living with them in his last few years and he got to love my brother-in-law, if that makes you feel any better."

"It does not make me feel better," I said as I fiddled with the buttons on the radio. "And how come blonde *shiksas* always marry Jewish doctors? I don't see you grabbing off Jewish shoe clerks or cab drivers."

Kay laughed. "That's because *shiksas* have all the luck."

The talking stopped for a while as we listened to the

heavy rain. A fierce gust of wind caused a tree limb to break loudly and fall, startling both of us.

"That scared the hell out of me," I gasped.

"Me, too," Kay said.

We were silent until the wind quieted down. "Oh, hey," I said, "I'm sorry about your husband. When did he pass away?"

Kay chuckled. "Rick Jason, aka Jackrabbit Jason, is alive and well and living outside of Atlanta with his third wife."

It took me a moment or two to digest the information. "You mean you're not a widow? You're—"

"Divorced. I moved back to the Boston area to be near my sister."

"I can't believe it." I could hardly wait till the storm was over and the phones were working so I could call Roz and tell her all about this.

"Jackrabbit Jason," I sighed. "He was so gorgeous. And I never saw anybody run so fast."

"Guess what? That's not the only thing he did fast," Kay said and we both laughed.

I shut off the radio. "You know, Danny wasn't even eighteen when he died. He missed out on so much—going off to college, getting married and—So… I used to wonder if Danny had—uh—sex with your sister. Or did he just die and never have the chance to—you know—"

"Get laid?" Kay prompted.

"Right. I mean, at least if he did—even once—I think I'd feel better."

Kay cleared her throat. "Let me put your mind to rest. I happen to know for a fact that my sister and your brother had sex. And plenty of it."

"How do you know?"

"Because," Kay said, "I heard them. And I know Caroline. My sister would screw a rattlesnake."

Just then, as if for emphasis, there was another deafening clap of thunder and a zig-zag of lightning.

After a moment, I whispered, "Okay, thanks." I pulled myself up from the chair. I needed to process all of this. "I think I'll go back to bed now and try to get some sleep."

CHAPTER 53

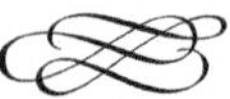

I woke up to the quiet of a Florida morning and dazzling sunshine filtering through the vertical shades of the guest bedroom. Hard to believe that only a few hours earlier, everything had been enveloped in darkness as torrential rain and screaming winds pummeled the area. I glanced at my watch on the nightstand and was glad to see it was nearly 8:00 a.m. The hurricane, which had been scheduled to make landfall around 3:00 a.m., was over. Looking around the room, nothing seemed to be broken, leaking, or waterlogged. I hoped the same was true for my place upstairs. And I hoped Maria and Fran were all right, and that their places were intact.

For some reason, I felt curiously refreshed even though I'd only had a few hours of sleep. I got out of bed and tiptoed into the living room where Kay was listening to her radio. "Well, you sure were out like a light," was Kay's greeting. "You missed the best part, right before landfall."

I hurried over to the window that overlooked the parking lot and peered outside. A couple of trees were down and branches were strewn around. Some flower beds were torn up, and the hubcap of a car was in the shrubbery. "But Palmetto Pointe is still standing," I marveled.

"Our section wasn't hit too badly," Kay said, lowering the volume on her radio. "But the main clubhouse area is a mess apparently, and we have quite a few damaged roofs, but no major flooding, no fatalities. Of course, the power is out everywhere. They don't know when it'll be restored. And God, am I dying for a cup of coffee."

"Me, too. I haven't had a day without coffee since I had to prep for a colonoscopy five years ago." I shuddered. "I need my caffeine."

"Chocolate has caffeine," Kay pointed out. "I've got some candy bars if you like."

"I love candy bars but not first thing in the morning." I said. "Oh, damn. And we can't make tea or cocoa either. I don't know what to drink." I noticed that Kay was sipping bottled water, which was probably warm now and not very appealing.

"I've got an idea." I went into the bedroom and emerged with some paper cups and a bottle of cabernet.

Kay rolled her eyes. "You're kidding. You won't eat candy on an empty stomach, but it's all right to drink wine?"

"Wine is fine," I declared. "Oops—I forgot something." Another trip to the bedroom, this time returning with a jar of peanut butter, a box of crackers and a plastic knife. "I need to eat something first. Want some?"

Kay put down her bottle of water. "Well, aren't you the resourceful little Girl Scout? You certainly came prepared."

"That happens to be the Girl Scout motto, 'Be prepared.' A lot of people don't know that," I said. "Anyhow, this is the kind of cheap-ass wine you don't need a corkscrew to open. It doesn't taste all that great, but it's better than nothing." I carefully placed some napkins on the small table next to her, spread peanut butter on the crackers, and poured the cabernet into a paper cup. "Want some?"

"Peanut butter, Ritz crackers, and cabernet for breakfast? Seriously?" Kay shook her head. "And you were such a quiet little thing back in school."

"Who knows? Maybe this will start a new breakfast tradition. It's got protein and carbs, and the wine comes from grapes. Actually, pretty healthy, right?"

I took a sip of the wine and made a face. "It's not coffee, but I need to fortify myself before I go upstairs and see what my place looks like."

To my surprise, except for a few minor things, my condo seemed fine. A lamp near the living room window was tipped on its side from the force of the winds shaking the building. Some knickknacks were on the floor, but I didn't see shattered glass or water marks. I checked the closet—everything seemed OK. I went back downstairs to Kay's condo to get my things.

"They don't want anyone driving around," Kay reported over the drone of the radio. "The power lines are down, and traffic lights aren't working. So, how does your place look?"

"No major damage, thank goodness." I replied. "I'll pack up my stuff and—" I broke off, noticing that Kay had poured herself some cabernet.

"You just might be on the cusp of a new trend," she told me.

I laughed and went into the bedroom to strip the sheets

and pack up my things. Suddenly I yelled out, "*Galumph!* The word is *galumph.* I can't believe it took me so long."

"What the hell are you yelling about?" Kay called from the living room.

I realized how crazy I sounded. "I just figured out what the pangram is for today's New York Times Spelling Bee," I said sheepishly, coming back into the living room. "Lori got me a New York Times online subscription and I always play the Spelling Bee. Thank goodness our Internet is still working. If I can't figure out the pangram, which uses all seven letters at least once, I worry that it's bad luck. I'm so superstitious."

"Me too," Kay nodded. "That's why I had my sister overnight express me my rabbit's foot, for good luck."

"Oh, like you need good luck," I couldn't help myself. The words just tumbled out.

"You've always been lucky." I plunked down on the overstuffed chair and poured some more wine into my paper cup. "Back in high school, you reminded me of Nancy Drew."

"Nancy Drew?' Kay repeated. "The only mystery I knew about was algebra, and I never solved that."

"No, I meant that you had the perfect life, just like Nancy Drew. You were blonde and pretty, you lived in a big, beautiful home with a housekeeper who let you do what you wanted," I rattled on, "and you had your own car, too. Hardly any kids in Winslow back then had a car."

"Well, it wasn't a yellow roadster," Kay pointed out. "That's what Nancy Drew had. I drove whatever car my big sister was tired of."

"Aww, you poor thing, getting cast-off convertibles." I snickered.

"FYI, it wasn't all that perfect. Mrs. Wickham, our housekeeper, was Satan on steroids, a nosy old witch and a terrible cook. Daddy was either drinking or looking around for another rich woman to marry, and I didn't really have close friends, just people to go places with. I never kept in touch with anyone from high school."

"Really? I still talk every week to my best friend, Roz, back in Winslow," I said, then realized I sounded like a pompous jerk.

"Well, maybe now I envy you," Kay said.

"Me?" I was incredulous. "Why the hell would you envy me?"

"Because you're in charge of your life. You're independent, you've got friends, you're close to your daughter. Me—I feel—aimless. Except for my sister, I don't feel connected. And I can't remember the last time I heard from my son." Kay refilled the wine in her paper cup. "I don't think I know how to be a parent. How did you figure it out?"

I paused, surprised by her display of vulnerability. "I don't know. I just brought Lori up the way I wished I'd been brought up. I guess you either copy your mother or you do just the opposite."

"That's the thing," Kay said softly. "I never knew my mother."

"Oh, God, that's right. I'm sorry." I had momentarily forgotten that rich, beautiful Bootsie Caldwell died when Kay was very young. The local gossip around town was that Bootsie drank herself to death.

As if responding directly to my private thoughts, Kay said, "Everyone in Winslow was convinced my mother was an alcoholic, that she hardly ever left her room because she always had a hangover, and she let Mrs. Wickham and babysitters take care of Caroline and me. What they didn't know was that Mom had breast cancer that spread to her brain. The last few years of her life she mostly stayed upstairs in her room, because she had loss of balance and terrible headaches. She didn't want anyone to see how she looked, and she didn't want anyone to know she had cancer."

I couldn't think of anything to say. She finished the wine in her cup and poured some more.

"It's funny," Kay went on, "I only learned about Mom recently when Caroline told me. Everything was always so secret. I guess I'm a lot like my mother that way. I don't want people to know either."

"Know what?" Despite the wine, my mouth felt dry.

"Why do you really think I'm staying here?" Kay asked with a wry smile. "I figured who the hell would know me in a place like Palmetto Pointe? It's true that I'm building a house in Banyan Falls, but I don't need to check on the construction."

In a daze, I listened to Kay's story. "A while back, I had this heavy feeling in my right breast, no lumps or anything, it just seemed to be heavier than the left one. I went to a few doctors, I had tests, but they couldn't find anything. Finally, I decided to come down to Florida and consult with my brother-in-law's cousin, Aaron Isaacs."

"Is he a specialist or something?" was all I could think of to ask.

"Actually, Aaron is an internist. He's what they call a 'doctor's doctor.' He's an amazing diagnostician. He listened to me, and he steered me to the right people. He's overseeing my treatment. Surgery, chemo, reconstruction—all that good stuff."

"Chemo? But you didn't lose your hair. You still have—"

"Best hair money can buy," Kay reached up and pulled off a blonde wig, revealing a bald head with gray stubble.

"Oh, my God," I kept saying over and over. Then I had a thought. "When I saw you at Publix on Yom Kippur, had you just had a chemo treatment?"

Kay nodded. "The day before." Then Kay adjusted her blonde wig. "Let me tell you what I learned from all this. If you think something is wrong, listen to your gut. Don't let doctors tell you there's nothing wrong and that—oh, Jeez, what the hell's the matter with you?"

I started to bawl.

"What's with those crocodile tears?" Kay barked. "Like you're really worried about my health?"

"No, I'm worried about *my* health." I could hardly talk, I was crying so hard. "If someone like you can get cancer, anything can happen to ordinary people. I know in my gut something is wrong with me, but my doctor doesn't listen and sent me to this crazy shrink, and I'm scared, and I don't have a Dr. Isaacs like you do and—"

If I hadn't had so much wine, I could never have blurted this out.

Kay stared at me. "I think there is something going on with you," she said after a moment. "You seem—I don't know. But don't worry. As soon as the roads are clear, I'll take you to see Dr. Isaacs."

I was so stunned I stopped crying. "You'd do that for me? Why?"

"Damned if I know," Kay said with a shrug. "Call it reparations."

CHAPTER 54

Just about everybody in Palmetto Pointe had a "before, during, and after the hurricane" story.

A few days earlier, another storm had been brewing between condo board director Harry Belson and Joyce Davis. Harry paid Joyce a visit and begged (according to him), or demanded (according to her), that she stay in a condo on the first floor during the hurricane.

"You want me to leave my apartment?" Joyce turned to Barbara, her next-door neighbor who had stopped by to find out why Harry Belson was there. "Barbara, tell Mr. Belson the only way I'll ever leave my apartment is when I'm dead."

"Poo-poo-poo," cried Barbara, so as not to attract the evil eye. "Mr. Belson, I can't tell Joyce what to do. I invited her to come with me. I'm gonna stay with my sister in West Palm Beach. She's got a big house and hurricane shutters."

"Be reasonable, Mrs. Davis," Harry said in a soothing voice. "This is a major hurricane. We're concerned for your health and well-being. And really, it would do you good to step out of your house and get a breath of fresh air."

Joyce, wearing a frayed sweater over her housecoat, looked up from the pot of fish soup she was stirring. "I haven't budged out of this place since I came home from my husband's funeral. So, if I don't go out to a doctor or a dentist, why the hell would I go to somebody else's condo?"

"The place you'd be staying in is lovely," he assured her. "It happens to belong to relatives of mine; they're snowbirds. You'll be safe there. And very comfortable," he added meaningfully, wiping rivulets of sweat from his forehead.

"Listen, mister," Joyce snapped, "when I call for toilet paper, then you can come rolling in—got it?"

"I give up." Harry replied. "You're my witness," he told Barbara, who was trying not to laugh. "If anything happens to Mrs. Davis, Palmetto Pointe is not responsible."

"Don't let the door hit your fat ass on the way out," Joyce cackled, waving her spoon.

"Some mouth on you for a woman your age," he shot back. "And why are you sitting around this sweat shop all these years? What—you're afraid to leave because you think your husband is gonna come back like Houdini?"

Barbara gleefully reported the encounter at the last canasta game before the hurricane, and the story spread quickly. Joyce stayed upstairs in her sweltering condo, enjoying her fish soup, and rode out the storm with no problems. Nothing got damaged, and she was perfectly fine the next day.

But any stories paled in comparison to the love connection that ignited in Stanley Stein's closet where he, his sister Freda, and condo director Harriet Bertulli waited out the hurricane. You might expect that the next day, three dead bodies would be sprawled in a mess of wire hangers, baggy trousers, and Stanley's orthopedic space shoes. But somehow, confined to such close quarters, both Stanley and his sister had no difficulty hearing what Harriet was saying, namely the details of her recent breakup with Barry. They were enchanted with her, although privately, Freda admitted she had a terrible headache from the condo director's heavy perfume.

Afterward, Harriet declared in a tone of wonder to anyone who would listen, "There I was, looking for the Bluebird of Happiness when all the time, it was right in a closet."

The reason I liked hearing all the stories is that they kept my mind off what was coming up—the appointment with Aaron Isaacs, Kay's doctor. "He's on vacation right now," Kay told me, "but he should be back in about a week or so."

"No rush," I said. "I've waited this long."

Actually, it was scary to think that Dr. Isaacs might discover something seriously wrong. But it was equally scary to think that I might be wasting valuable time not getting early treatment for whatever my medical condition turned out to be.

So I kept busy straightening drawers and getting my records all in one place so there would be less for Lori to contend with in the event I had to undergo emergency surgery, or died on the operating table, or whatever other awful possibilities were lurking.

In the meantime, Palmetto Pointe received some much-needed assistance a couple days after the hurricane from State Representative Murray Finkel, who brought a truck-load of sandwiches, ice, bottled water, coffee, and prune

Danish, knocking on doors and distributing the bounty to all the residents, earning their gratitude and most likely their votes on election day.

This act of kindness, however, drew the ire of condo board president Harry Kaplan, who hated Representative Finkel and had even written a letter to the editor of *News and Schmooze* back in August that said, "Finkel is not a friend of Palmetto Pointe. We'll remember in November."

But here it was, in October with the election less than two weeks away. "Oh, that *momser*, that bastard," Harry cried when he saw, driving into the main entrance, a familiar white van with its horn tooting nonstop and bright red lettering that read: "The Finkelmobile Is the Real Deal."

Harry knew what Palmetto Pointe residents would remember in November when they went to vote at the clubhouse. They would see that familiar white van with red lettering in the parking lot and remember that it was Rep. Murray Finkel who came through for them with food and drink in those long, dreary days after the hurricane when they were power-deprived, pissed off, and plugged up.

Sometimes I half-hoped Kay might have forgotten about the whole thing—the whole thing being my mystery illness and possible demise. But I did want to know, once and for all, what was wrong with me and if that called for Kay's intervention, so be it. I wouldn't be a hero.

The matter was resolved a day later when Kay called.

"He's b-a-a-c-k," she told me. "I got you an appointment with Dr. Isaacs at ten o'clock this coming Tuesday."

CHAPTER 55

"I'm still in shock about all this," Maria shook her silvery curls as if to clear her head. "So that's why you called an emergency meeting of The Cabernet Club."

"You never said anything about feeling sick," Fran added.

"It's not that I've been feeling sick exactly, but I know something is wrong. I mean, I eat a lot of food, and you've seen my hands shake," they nodded.

There was of course also my new habit of flying off the handle, but I had kept most of those incidents to myself.

"And no matter what Dr. Lochner says," I continued, "it's not depression. Anyhow, I really appreciate you coming over. You guys are such good friends."

"That's what friends are for," Maria and Fran said in unison and we all laughed, "Uh-oh. I think we're seeing too much of each other," I teased. "But seriously, I'm kind of worried about what this Dr. Isaacs might find."

"He might not be able to tell you anything then and there," Fran pointed out. "I mean, he might have to do tests and stuff. But it was nice of Kay to get you in to see him."

"I haven't even told my daughter about this. I didn't want to worry her." I leaned forward. "Tell me the truth—I look different lately, don't I?"

"Well, maybe a little," Maria admitted. "Your eyes or something. But hey, we're all getting older, right?" she added hastily.

"My eyes. Yeah." I seized on that. "I was thinking brain tumor but maybe it's an eye tumor."

"And you do look like you've lost weight," said Fran.

"But I'm sure it's just the excitement and stress of all the changes you've gone through since moving to Florida," said Maria. "You're gonna be fine, Debs. I know it." She came over and hugged me and for the first time, Fran, not one to show affection, did, too.

"Someday, this will all be over, and everything will be back to normal," said Maria.

"Someday." I forced a smile and pushed aside the little voice that whispered, What if something is really wrong with me and there aren't that many somedays left?

Just then Alexa beeped. I stood and headed to the microwave, where I was warming up takeout from China Palace.

"Ladies," I called over my shoulder, "dinner is ready."

"I'll probably put on two pounds after eating this dinner," said Maria, eyeing the barbecued spare ribs and fried rice. "I don't know how you stay so slim, Debbie—oops sorry."

"Maybe I just have a tapeworm," I said, half seriously.

After a couple of glasses of wine, I felt comfortable enough to tell Fran and Maria about Danny and my mistaken long-held grudge against Kay.

"I'm so sorry, Debbie, I had no idea," said Maria.

"Me too, Debbie," said Fran.

"And on top of that, the Altmans are still deciding what to do with the condo and Joyce Davis hasn't heard of any great deals. I've been scouring the listings, but nothing."

"How is your writing going?" asked Maria, obviously trying to change the subject.

"Actually, I just wrote something for the writers' group. Since I might not have much longer to live, and since you're always asking me to share what I wrote, do you wanna hear it?"

Fran and Maria looked at each other, shaking their heads. "You'll be fine, Debbie," said Fran. "And yes, we'd like to hear it."

"Okay. Here goes."

When a Friendship Fades

I was going through some old papers the other day when I found an address book from years ago when I lived in New York City.

Leafing through the pages, I realized how filled with names it was, how many people I used to know back then. And although I still keep in touch with one or two old friends, most of the names in that address book are not in my life anymore—casualties of geography or circumstance.

And that is the natural order of things. When our lives change, we may no longer have anything in common with a high-school pal or a co-worker or a neighbor. We accept the loss of these casual friendships and move on.

What is not so easy to accept is the loss of a deep and longtime friendship. This is especially wrenching if it happens when we are older, and the friendship that withstood time and tribulation begins to fade away.

Even though we realize that nothing lasts forever, somehow we expect a friendship of long standing to be one of the constants of our golden years. But alas, even then, life has surprises in store—a long-married couple divorce; a sister and brother stop speaking. And even though we always said you can't pick your relatives but you can pick your friends, nonetheless the friendship that spanned decades no longer works.

Perhaps it can be salvaged by sitting down and taking things over. Perhaps it has become more of an obligation or habit and needs a new direction. Then again, maybe the people themselves changed and/or outgrew each other. After all, the things you needed from a friend forty years ago may not be what you need today.

And it's something that's happened to virtually everyone. Whatever the reason, when a friendship of long-standing withers away, we lose not only the familiarity and comfort of shared history but a part of ourselves as well. And that loss, especially when we're older, leaves a hole in our life.

Hopefully, we have other people in our cheering section to fill the empty space and help us move on. And although we may not realize it at the time, sometimes the end of a friendship may be the beginning of a new direction, the catalyst that forces us to seek out new interests and new people to fill the void.

I remember the words of a girl I worked with years back in New York City. She had just broken up with a guy she'd been dating for a while but who could not commit to marriage. "Well," she said philosophically, "at least he helped get me through February."

Those words apply to friendship as well. Instead of feeling hurt and resentful, instead of feeling our time was wasted when a friendship fades, we need to remember the good times and the good things we got from that friendship when we needed them most—and be grateful to the people who helped us get through the Februarys of our lives.

"Before you say anything, I hope you're both my friends until we take our last breaths," I said.

Maria had tears in her eyes, and even Fran looked choked up.

"That was beautiful, Debbie," said Maria. "And I feel the same way."

"Me, too," said Fran.

"Okay, well, does anyone have anything fun to share?" I asked. "Let's lighten up the mood."

"I saw something funny in one of the senior Facebook groups I'm in," said Fran. "Let me look it up."

She took out her phone. "Ah, here it is," and she read,

I've sure gotten old.

I've had two bypass surgeries. A hip replacement. New knees. Fighting diabetes, too. I'm half-blind. I can't hear anything quieter than a jet engine. I take forty different medications that make me dizzy, winded and subject to blackouts.

Have bouts with dementia.

Have poor circulation, hardly feel my hands and feet anymore. Can't remember if I'm eighty-five or ninety-two. Have lost all my friends.

But, thank God, I still have my Florida driver's license.

We all burst out laughing.

After that, the evening turned out to be a lot of fun, with good-natured joking and teasing and an even stronger bond of friendship, possibly one of the liveliest meetings of The Cabernet Club yet.

I was surprised to find myself still smiling as I cleaned

up after Maria and Fran left. Thanks to my friends, I had gotten through Friday night.

Just Saturday, Sunday, and Monday to go.

And then Tuesday. D-Day. D for diagnosis.

CHAPTER 56

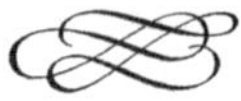

Maria called me at 9:00 a.m. on Saturday. "I wanted to catch you before you went to your writers' group."

"Oh, we don't have a meeting today. The air conditioning in the clubhouse is out, and why do you need to catch me?"

"Because I'm taking you and me out for a nice, relaxing pedicure," Maria told me. "It's my treat, and I won't take no for an answer. This is a 'good luck' gift. I know you're nervous about seeing that doctor on Tuesday."

I, always superstitious, couldn't say no because that would be bad karma. And besides, I'd been thinking how awful my feet looked. Scenes flashed in front of me. Dr. Isaacs orders an immediate MRI, and the technician gasps when she looks at my rough, callused feet. Another scene: I am rushed to the hospital where the Haitian aides whisper in Creole about the crazy lady whose long, unkempt toenails make holes in the sheets.

"This is so relaxing," said Maria, who was seated in the pedicure chair next to me. "Don't you just love this?"

"Oh, yeah," I said, but in truth, I felt restless and didn't like all the fuss and bother. I would be happy to simply have my toenails cut short, filed down, and polished. Just dip 'em and clip 'em, I wanted to say. I had no patience for lotions, massages, and hot towels, not to mention a lengthy, clunky, multi-lingual conversation with the sweet ponytailed nail technician.

I don't have patience for anything lately, I thought.

Sunday was Fran's turn to babysit me. "No ifs, ands, or buts," Fran said. "I'm taking you to lunch at the mall."

"You guys are too much," I said, pretending to sound annoyed but secretly happy to be coddled. I had been dreading a long Sunday, but lunch and shopping would help fill the time.

As we strolled through Macy's, I suddenly announced, "I need to buy some new, pretty underwear. I want to look nice when I see Dr. Isaacs." I picked out a silky lavender bra and matching panties.

"You're going to a doctor's appointment, not a honeymoon," Fran reminded me. "And the things you picked out aren't even on sale. That's not like you, Debbie. You're the queen of sales. Let's go for lunch now. I'm starving."

My mind was racing as I ate my Reuben sandwich and sweet potato fries. There were so many things I wanted to buy, so much I suddenly wanted to do.

"Oh, Debbie, I forgot to tell you. I saw Betty Jamieson at Sushi Yama the other day."

Like a scratch on a record player, my thoughts came to a screeching halt.

"Oh, was she with Joe?" I asked, sarcastically.

"No," she said. "She was with another woman. I was picking up my takeout order, and they were at a table in the back, talking and laughing. I recognized Betsy's voice, and I started walking over to say hello, but Betsy was feeding some edamame to her friend. It felt kind of strange."

I nodded slowly, processing this information. Then I felt a pit at the bottom of my stomach. Had I been wrong this whole time? Could the two women be more than friends? Is this what Joe had been alluding to?

My thoughts kept running faster and faster, but I couldn't focus on Joe right now. My health was my number one priority. And keeping myself busy until my Tuesday appointment.

"Fran, do you mind, there's a Supercuts nearby, and my hair looks so ratty. I could use a shaping. It won't take very long."

"Sure," said Fran.

After a brief wait at Supercuts, I told the hairdresser that I just wanted a shaping. "Please don't take off too much." That was something you should never tell a hairdresser, because it always seems to trigger a cutting frenzy.

Finally, the woman finished. She twirled my chair around to the mirror. "So how do you like it?"

"Well, it's kind of short," I said. "I look like an old boy."

The stylist huffed, "Short hair is best for women your age. And it makes your eyes pop."

It makes my eyes pop?
That was the last thing I wanted to hear.

CHAPTER 57

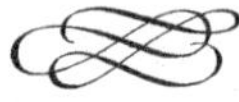

One day to go.

Luckily, Monday flew by at work.

Then I had an early-evening appointment with Dr. Lochner that I had forgotten to cancel. Besides, I wanted to tell him about my appointment with Dr. Isaacs.

As I walked into his office, Dr. Lochner gave me his "Oh, crap, you again?" look.

I took a deep breath. "Well, I finally did it. I'm getting a second opinion. I have an appointment tomorrow morning with someone who's supposed to be a top diagnostician."

"Well, if you want to throw your money away," he shrugged. "But I'm telling you you're depressed. And what, may I ask, is the name of this big-shot doctor?"

"Dr. Isaacs in Boca Raton. Aaron Isaacs."

"You're seeing him?" Dr. Lochner sounded impressed. "He doesn't take new patients."

"Yeah, well," I said loftily, "I've got connections." I glanced around at the walls and saw strips of different colored paint. "What—is Esther redecorating the office again?"

He was only too happy to do the talking. "Yes, my wife, *Estrella*—he emphasized the name—thinks the office décor needs a tweaking. She's tired of all the beige. She wants to set the mood with varying shades of gray."

"Gray," I murmured. "Well, that ought to make the place jump out at you."

Dr. Lochner went on to complain about how much everything was going to cost because his wife wanted new furniture and accessories, of course, but what could he do? When Estrella wanted to decorate, that was it. Being able to talk instead of having to listen seemed to make him more cheerful than usual. He wasn't even upset when I told him I'd forgotten to bring my checkbook but would put the check in the mail.

"Don't worry about it," he told me graciously. "You can bring the check to us tomorrow on the way back from Dr. Isaacs."

He even wished me good luck and grudgingly admitted that Isaacs was considered brilliant.

Driving home, my heart raced and I felt shakier than ever. Well, soon I might learn what was wrong with me.

I called Kay to make sure that everything was set for tomorrow. "You're on," Kay said. "I'll drive. Let's plan to leave about 9:15 a.m."

I set my alarm later that evening, wondering if I would be able to fall asleep. I tossed and turned, but I finally did.

And before I knew it, it was Tuesday.

CHAPTER 58

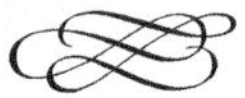

"How come you're so quiet?" Kay asked as we drove to Boca Raton. "Are you nervous?"

"Me? No, I was just dozing off." That was an outright lie because I was wide awake, busily praying and bargaining with God (*If you let me get a hopeful diagnosis, I promise to be a kind and honest person*). And now, here I was already defaulting by telling a lie. Well maybe just a little fib, but still, I was already defaulting by telling a fib—or was it two fibs? I had fervently promised to become what I might have been if, by some miracle, Dr. Isaacs would tell me I was going to be all right.

"Don't be nervous about Aaron. He's like a medical detective," Kay said reassuringly. "Do you remember Mrs. Marchand, our English teacher back in Winslow? She developed some really weird condition and went from doctor to doctor but nobody knew what it was. Aaron diagnosed it right away—something very rare. It's written up in medical journals."

"Mrs. Marchand." I smiled. "I really liked her. She always encouraged me to keep writing."

"Yeah, I remember you used to write for the school paper," Kay said. "You were a smart kid. How come you didn't go to college?"

"Because we didn't have the money."

"Oh, Jeez," Kay breathed. "I'm sorry."

"Hey, it all worked out," I said, putting on my cheerful voice. "I stayed in Winslow and went to Hollis Secretarial School—remember them?" I went on. "Anyhow, I learned typing and I always had a job, so that was good."

From the rich Oriental rugs on the gleaming floors to Mozart in the background and the pale-haired receptionist who looked like she should be playing a harp instead of sitting at a desk, the office of Dr. Aaron Isaacs was, to say the least, impressive.

Even the magazines in the office made a statement. Not a *People* or that free *Nostalgia America* to be found. Instead, I saw magazines about tennis and sailing, along with *Architectural Digest* and *Fortune*. And no diplomas on the walls. Only tasteful sketches and watercolors.

With shaking hands, I filled out the long, detailed Patient History form. One question surprised me. It was something I had never seen before, "What do you think is wrong with you?" I mulled that one over, then scribbled "Possible brain tumor or dementia or maybe an undetected tapeworm." I completed the form and returned it to the receptionist.

After a while, the door to the inner office opened and a

young man wearing a blue turban and a white lab coat came into the waiting room. "Miss Deborah, please? Dr. Isaacs will see you now."

Knees weak and hands still shaking, I stood up.

"I am Dr. Singh." He held the door open for me.

I grabbed Kay's arm. "You need to come in with me," I said urgently. "That way, if I don't understand things or—" I was too nervous to finish the sentence. Kay followed us inside.

Aaron Isaacs looked like a doctor you might see on TV —tall and lean with close-cropped silver hair and deep-set dark eyes behind rimless glasses. He was flanked by Dr. Singh and a young woman, also in a lab coat, who was introduced as Dr. Chang.

Kay went over and hugged Dr. Isaacs, who assured her she was welcome to stay during the exam. Then he turned his full attention to me, staring at me intently. He came over and grasped my hands firmly, never taking his eyes off mine. Dr. Singh and Dr. Chang were busy reading my Patient History form, nodding and whispering to each other.

"So, Debbie, suppose you tell me about the problems you've been having." Dr. Isaacs motioned for me to take a seat.

In a rush of words, I told him about the tremor in my hands, the constant sweating, the nervousness, the weight loss.

Dr. Singh and Dr. Chang came over. Once again, Aaron Isaacs took my hands and stared intently at my eyes. "Now swallow, please. That's it." He murmured something to Dr. Singh, who bobbed his turban in agreement. "All right, Debbie, now breathe in and out."

"Swallow again, atta girl." He said something to his two worshipful disciples but I couldn't hear because my heart was pounding so loudly.

Dr. Singh and Dr. Chang each took one of my hands. This is weird, I thought, what are they going to do, sing "Kumbaya"? Dr. Singh nodded and Dr. Chang said "Ah."

More whispering. Dr. Singh spoke up. "Do you have trouble sleeping, Miss Deborah?"

"Well, yes, but—" I explained that my psychiatrist, Dr. Lochner, said my insomnia was caused by depression and that most people my age had insomnia, even though I insisted that this was recent and I never used to have trouble falling asleep.

"So—you feel often warm. You perspire more frequently," Dr. Chang said. It was more of a statement than a question.

Dr. Isaacs leaned over to me and whispered, "Are you having more frequent bowel movements?"

"Yes," I whispered back, embarrassed. "I'm going broke buying toilet paper."

"Hard to concentrate, too, I imagine. And do you find yourself anxious, irritable, short-tempered?"

"Ha." From her seat in the corner of the room, Kay snickered.

"I tried to tell all that to my doctor, Warren Ross." I couldn't stop babbling. "Only I never really get in to see him. He's got this pit-bull nurse practitioner who won't listen to me. She kept saying I'm depressed and sent to me to a shrink, who put me on Prozac but it's not helping and," my voice trembled, "I'm scared."

"Don't be scared." Dr. Isaacs patted my hand. "You're going to be all right." He went over to confer with

Doctors Singh and Chang, who were hopping with excitement.

I could only hear snatches of conversation. "Exophthalmos … thyrotoxicosis … enlargement of—"

He came back and sat down. "My two young colleagues concur. We believe we know what is wrong, and we believe with treatment you're going to be fine."

"You d-do?" I stuttered. "I am?"

Dr. Isaacs smiled. "I had a professor years back who used to say, 'If a patient is going to have something wrong, this is a pretty good thing to have.' With treatment, it's very manageable." Dr. Singh and Dr. Chang nodded vigorously.

He took off his glasses and rubbed his eyes. "We believe you have Graves' disease, a form of hyperthyroidism or overactive thyroid," he went on. "Your primary care doctor will conduct thyroid-function tests and handle your treatment or refer you to an endocrinologist. You might recall that some years back the first President Bush's wife, Barbara Bush, developed it later in life and as it turned out, so did he."

I only heard the word "thyroid" and was confused. "I don't understand. My friend Roz back home takes pills for her thyroid but she wasn't like me. She was always cold and dragged around and she gained weight."

"Your friend is hypothyroid," he corrected. "That's much more common than hyperthyroid. You have the classic symptoms—shakiness, anxiety, rapid heartbeat. You're always hungry and need to eat frequently, but you're losing weight. Graves' has an effect on people's moods and physical appearance. The eyes protrude and have a glassy stare."

"Ha. I kept thinking my eyes looked weird," I said, "but

I figured it was because I was getting older and needed an eye job or something."

"Graves' disease gives the patient a staring, bug-eyed look," Dr. Singh offered.

"Well, that certainly makes me feel a lot better," I said under my breath.

Dr. Isaacs wrote something on his pad. "So you need to see your primary doctor as soon as possible. After he tests you and gets you to the right level, you'll need to take a pill once a day. In a few weeks you'll be feeling a lot better."

"But the problem is, I can never get in to see my doctor," I explained. "His NP is convinced I'm crazy, and he seems to go by whatever she tells him."

"Give my receptionist your doctor's name and I'll call him myself," Dr. Isaacs said. "You need to get treated right away. And he'll need to wean you off the Prozac because anti-depressants exacerbate your problem."

"So I was right after all," I felt triumphant. "I kept telling Dr. Lochner that the Prozac wasn't helping, and he wanted to up the dosage. He said that doing needlepoint or something with my hands would calm me down."

"Dr. Lochner? Marvin Lochner? I know him. He used to practice family medicine before he decided to go back and become a psychiatrist. I understand he has a huge practice in Banyan Beach."

"Hey, Aaron," Kay piped up, "I know I'm just a layperson—no jokes, please, but if this Dr. Lochner practiced family medicine, how come he didn't pick up on Debbie's symptoms? I mean, I'm no MD, but I could see something wasn't right physically."

Dr. Isaacs gave a "What can I tell you?" shrug. After a moment, Dr. Singh and Dr. Chang shrugged, too.

Kay got up and chatted briefly with the three physicians. I didn't hear a word they were saying. All I could think of was I'm going to be OK. Thank You, God.

"Come on," Kay said, motioning to me, "we've taken up his time long enough." She gave Dr. Isaacs a hug. I rushed over and planted a kiss on his cheek. "Thank you," I said. "Oh, and thank you guys, too," I told Doctors Singh and Chang. "So then, I'm going to be okay, right?"

"A little nutsy for a while till you come down." Dr. Isaacs told me. "But yes, you'll be okay."

"How can I ever thank you?" I gushed as we walked out to the parking lot.

"Don't thank me," Kay said. "Just get back to normal. You're as high as an elephant's eye."

"Thank you, Dr. Isaacs, thank you Doctors Singh and Chang," I clasped my hands. "Oh, my God, I just realized I walked out without paying. Nobody asked me for my insurance card or—I'm so mortified."

"It's all taken care of," Kay told me. "Don't worry about it. What did you think of Dr. Singh and his magic turban. Pretty hot, huh?"

"Oh, yeah," I agreed.

As quiet as I'd been on the way to Boca Raton, that's how talkative I was on the way back. "Recalled to life," I kept saying, "that's how I feel. It's like that phrase from *A Tale of Two Cities*, when what's-his-name says 'recalled to life.' Remember how Mrs. Silva used to make us act out those stories?"

"I don't remember," Kay said. "Anyhow, you were the brain, not me."

"I just feel so happy," I said, getting into the car. "I won't let anything bother me again. I'm so happy and grateful."

We stopped for lunch—I insisted on treating. Back in the car, my mood changed. "You know, now that I think about it, I'm really angry. Nobody believed me. Not Ludmila, not Dr. Ross. And all these months, that quack Dr. Lochner, the Prince of Prozac, looked at my eyes bulging and, like you said, he should have picked up on that."

"Let it go," Kay told me. "At least you found out what you've got and it's treatable and you're going to be all right."

But I was still pissed and felt I needed to do something, *now,* while I was still on this crazy thyroid high. But what about all those promises I made to God only a few hours ago? Well, hey, what I'm going to do is *tikkun olam*—repairing the world, in Hebrew, or at least my corner of it. God would understand.

"Kay, I have to ask another favor," I said. "When we get to Banyan Beach, I need to make a couple of stops. It shouldn't take long. And I need you to come in with me."

"You're up to something," Kay glanced at me. "What is it?"

I sat up straight. "Let's just say I have promises to keep and miles to go before I sleep."

A little smile played on my lips.

CHAPTER 59

Predictably, the waiting room at Banyan Beach Medical Associates was packed. "I'm Deborah Gordon," I told the girl at the front desk, "and this," I pointed to Kay, "is my healthcare advocate. I need to make an appointment asap with Dr. Ross. Tomorrow, actually."

"Dr. Ross is booked solid. He doesn't have an opening for two weeks. But his nurse practitioner can—"

"We do not want to see the nurse practitioner." Kay broke in. She had put on tortoise-rimmed eyeglasses, which made her look very intelligent, and she was impeccably dressed in a linen suit that somehow never seemed to wrinkle. "My client, Ms. Gordon, was seen earlier today by Dr. Aaron Isaacs in Boca Raton, who insists that her primary, Dr. Ross, must see her immediately."

I restrained a smile. Kay was pretty damn impressive.

From out of nowhere, Ludmila appeared, looking grumpier than usual, especially when she spotted me. "Oh, it is you. You will have to—"

"Excuse me," Kay pushed forward. "I am Deborah Gordon's attorney."

I squinted, trying not to look at Ludmila's eyebrows, which seemed to be moving around wildly. At the word *attorney*, Ludmila blanched. "You come inside and—"

"That is not acceptable," Kay said. In her heels, she was intimidating, not to mention considerably taller than Ludmila, who seemed to be shrinking. "My client needs to be seen by Dr. Ross first thing tomorrow morning. Apparently, nobody in this office noticed that she has Graves' disease. How did that happen? Look at her eyes. Touch her hands. Feel her neck. Yet you kept insisting she had mental issues, but—" she let the sentence hang.

"Who are you?" Ludmila stammered.

"I am Kay Caldwell Jason of the law firm Jason & Jason. Please give my client the first appointment tomorrow morning with Dr. Ross," Kay ordered. "She'll need thyroid-function tests and a possible referral to an endocrinologist."

"But she cannot see Dr. Ross. I am the one she is supposed to—" Ludmila started to say.

At that moment, a young woman wearing the powder-blue Banyan Beach Medical Associates uniform hurried over. "Dr. Ross just got a call from a Dr. Isaacs about her," she pointed to me.

A moment later, Dr. Ross appeared. "Hello, young lady," he smiled at me with forced heartiness. "I had a chat with Dr. Isaacs. So we're going to see you tomorrow first thing, around 8:15 a.m., okay? And nothing to eat or drink after midnight."

He motioned for Ludmila to leave and she hurried away in a huff.

The patients in the waiting room watched with interest.

"Dr. Ross," Kay said, in an imperious voice, "with all due respect, my client has concerns, and rightfully so, that she will be seen tomorrow by your nurse practitioner, Ludmila, which is unacceptable."

"No, no, I will be doing the complete examination and overseeing the tests," he assured her. He turned to me and said almost pleadingly, " Ludmila is very capable. I don't quite understand the problem."

"With all due respect," I said, "I don't think Ludmila knows her ass from her eyebrows."

Back in the car, I high-fived Kay. "You were terrific. I couldn't have done it without you."

"That's enough for one day," Kay said as we drove out of the parking lot. "I'm all doctored out."

"Please, just one more stop," I begged. "This shouldn't take long. I have to settle my account with Dr. Lochner. His office is right near here."

"You're really milking this thyroid thing," Kay told me.

"I'm on a roll," I said. "Oh, hey. Did I ever thank you for the time you told off that mean guy from New Jersey who took my parking space? You were—the word would have to be masterful."

Kay laughed. "I think I hear a big sucking sound. You are such a little suck-up."

"Seriously, I want you to come in. Besides, it's worth the trip, just to see Dr. Lochner's trophy wife. She's the poster lady for plastic surgery. Her face is tighter than Premium Saran Wrap."

"Once again curiosity trumps common sense," Kay said.

As we walked into the office, I whispered, "See what I mean?" Esther aka Estrella Lochner had apparently undergone even more facial rejuvenation since my last visit. Mrs. Lochner now had full, perfect, teenage lips except they looked like they had been pasted on her mature face, as if a cosmetic surgeon had played a macabre game of Pin the Tail on the Donkey.

She flashed me a baleful glance and probably would have pursed her lips, if only she could.

"Oh, and look—you have paint samples," I turned to Kay. "Did you know Mrs. Lochner decorated this whole office?"

"All by myself," Esther preened. "I'm planning to freshen it up a bit. I got tired of the beige motif. I'm going into soft grays." She's trying to impress Kay, I thought, probably wondering what someone like Kay is doing with someone like me.

"Oh, this is my attorney, Kay Caldwell Jason," I said.

"Your attorney?" Esther looked bewildered, then nervous. "Oh, yes, my husband said you were going to drop off a check. I can—"

"We want to give it to him personally," Kay interjected. "Now."

"You can't go in. He's got a patient with him."

"This is a legal matter," Kay said as they strode past the reception desk to his office. "Of utmost importance."

Esther trotted after us. "You mustn't—"

"Now don't give us any of your lip," I said merrily, yanking open the door of Dr. Lochner's inner office.

He looked up, startled. "What is the meaning of—"

"I told them they're not supposed to," Esther whined. "But they wouldn't listen."

Dr. Lochner's patient, a heavy-set woman, was cowering on the sofa. "Please," she begged, "take my jewelry and my wallet, but don't hurt me."

"Oh, for God's sake," I said, "this is a confrontation, not a home invasion."

Kay made her presence known. "I am Deborah Gordon's attorney, Kay Caldwell-Jason of Liggett, Goldberg, and Jason. And you are Dr. Marvin Lochner, a well-known Banyan Beach psychiatrist, who previously practiced family medicine."

"And," I put in, "you ditched your first wife for Esther when the big bucks started rolling in."

That was just something I made up, but apparently it had some truth because it seemed to hit a nerve.

"I am so sick of hearing that." Esther stamped her foot. "Marvin was already separated. We were introduced by mutual friends."

"You need to leave my office this minute," Dr. Lochner demanded, "or else."

"Or else what?" Kay sat down leisurely on the sofa next to the terrified patient. I flopped down as well. "You have no excuse. All these months, you could see that my client complained of feeling nervous and agitated. Her hands shook, she was always sweating, her eyes bulged out. All visible symptoms of Graves' disease, but you just wrote it off as depression and put her on Prozac, which exacerbates the problem."

"Dr. Lochner is a psychiatrist, not her primary provider," Esther put in.

I whirled around to face her. "He never even looked at me. He looked at the ceiling, he looked at his notepad, he looked at his thumbs or his crotch, I don't know which. But he never looked at me. If he did, he'd have noticed the obvious symptoms."

Silence. Then I stood up and said to Dr. Lochner, "You are a quack." I flapped my arms, imitating a duck. "Quack, quack, quack."

Dr. Lochner's patient jumped up and ran out of the office crying hysterically.

"Now look what you've done," he said. "That poor, fragile woman—"

"Fragile my ass," I said. "All you need to do is increase her dose of Prozac or whatever meds you put her on. Or maybe she should take up something to keep her hands busy."

"Didn't you say you wanted to leave a check?" Esther ventured.

"Oh, that's right. I nearly forgot." I pulled the check out of my purse. "You might have a problem with it though."

Esther blanched. It read, "Pay to the order of Dr. Quack."

"We can't cash that."

Kay stood up. "In summary, you need to be more mindful of your patients," she told Dr. Lochner. "You need to see them as individuals, not dollar signs. At the present time, we do not plan on taking legal action, but be aware of your transgressions." It was all she could do to keep a straight face.

Dr. Lochner's mouth dropped open.

"Let's go," Kay whispered. "You made your point."

Out in the waiting area, a woman was doing needlepoint and a man was working on an embroidery hoop. "Good job, you two," I sang out. "The doctor would approve."

Across from them was an elderly man with curly white hair, lethargically picking his nose. "Pardon me, sir," I said, "but when Dr. Lochner says you need to keep your hands busy, I don't think he means you should put them up your nose."

"Come on. Let's get out of here." Kay grabbed my arm and marched me out of the office. "We've had enough crazy for one day."

CHAPTER 60

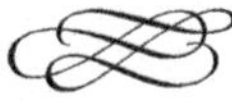

"I can't believe you never mentioned any of this," Lori said.

"I didn't want to worry you. And anyhow, it's all good and I'm going to be fine. Dr. Ross couldn't have been nicer. He sat me down and told me about thyroid treatment, which I actually knew because I looked it all up online last night."

"That's not the point, Mom. All this time you never said a word about not feeling good. You don't need to protect me. Look, I understand where you're coming from, why you're always joking around. Your friend Roz told me."

"Roz? What did she tell you?"

"What it was like for you growing up in a house where your mother never opened the shades, never stopped crying for Danny," Lori went on. "Roz told me about the time Grandma sent your friends home from your birthday sleepover because she couldn't stand hearing them laugh when she was in such grief. Roz told me you once said you felt like the consolation prize after Danny—"

"Please, honey, let's talk about this another time," I was anxious to change the subject. "Hey, can you believe we'll be seeing each other next month?"

"Mom, you're not listening. Don't you get it? Your health is important to me, and I'm always worried about you, because Florida is where people go to die," Lori was crying now. "I don't want you to die."

"Omigod, Lori, please, I'm not planning to die anytime soon."

"And I miss you," Lori choked out the words. "You're my best friend. That's why I've been hounding you to move to Delaware. Yes, I worry about you, but I'm also selfish. I want you here with me, so we can do stuff together, like we always did."

She took a breath, and so did I. Lori was right. I hadn't been listening lately. But as I read between the lines, I knew I needed to respond as a parent, not a friend.

"Lori, I love you, and you're my best friend, too. But I probably didn't do you any favors by keeping you so close to me." I paused. "And I'm not going to be around forever. You're making a new life, in a new place, with your family. We'll always be best friends, but you can have a variety of friends, especially people that live near you, so you can do things together."

I didn't know if I was saying this right, because Lori was still silent.

"Lori, are you still there? Are you okay?"

"Yes," she said. "But mom, I've been having trouble making friends here."

"Well, why didn't you tell me?" I asked.

"You've been so caught up in your new life, and I was so

focused on getting you to move to Delaware, that it never came up in conversation."

"I'm all ears, Lori. What's going on?"

Lori told me how hard it was to make friends at this stage in life, and in a new place. The kids were making friends, but the other moms seemed to already have their own friend circles.

"Lori, I'm so sorry. I had no idea. But of course it makes sense. I had the same problem after I got divorced. Do you have a few minutes now? Let's brainstorm."

I felt Lori's smile through the phone. "Yes, Mom. That would be great."

Later on, when Maria stopped by to find out how the visit to Dr. Ross had gone, she remarked, "By the way, I saw Kay this morning. She was leaving for Boston."

"Boston? She never said a word about going to Boston."

"Well, she had a suitcase and she was getting into the airport limo."

I started to laugh. "Oh, my God, it's true. I got this funny email the other day about the difference between gentiles and Jews. It said gentiles leave and never say goodbye; Jews say goodbye and never leave."

Maria laughed, too. "Kay didn't say when she was coming back, and I didn't ask."

As the days passed, I started feeling better. I was calmer and not so shaky. Now that I was able to concentrate, I started taking books out from the library. Maybe, if I made amends, I'd even be able to share book recommendations with Joe.

CHAPTER 61

I walked over to the pickleball courts on Wednesday night, after the beginner clinic. I spotted Joe, speaking to a couple of people.

When he was finally alone, I walked up to him.

"Debbie, I'm surprised to see you. How've you been?"

"A lot better," I said. "And I owe you an apology, I think."

Joe looked stunned. "Okay."

I explained how Fran had seen Betsy Jamieson with another woman.

"Was that what you were trying to tell me?"

He nodded slowly. "Yes, but I couldn't tell you, because it's not my story to tell. Betsy's private life is really private. I didn't know how to tell you without telling you." He sighed. "Men really aren't great at conversations, are they?"

"Um, that's an understatement, especially in this case," I chuckled. "But I also jumped to conclusions. Some of that was based on first-hand experience with an unfaithful husband, but part of it may have been due to my medical mystery, which has now been solved."

"Really?" he asked.

I explained my thyroid issue and all its unpleasant side effects.

"But I'm already feeling better, since I've been taking medication."

"That's terrific."

"And pretty soon I might be able to take that pickleball lesson you promised, if the offer's still good," I said.

Joe smiled broadly. "Absolutely. Oh, and will you still have a good appetite once your thyroid is stabilized?"

"Definitely. Why?"

"Well, we need to have that burrata contest. I guarantee you that mine is better than The Fish House."

"It's a deal," I laughed.

CHAPTER 62

"Okay girls, I have some big news," I said, taking a swig of cab, as Fran and Maria looked at me expectantly.

"I made up with Joe. You were right, Fran."

"I knew he wasn't a cheater," said Fran. "He's just a really nice guy."

"So his doubles partner was not into guys, huh?" asked Maria.

"Right," I said. "But she isn't really 'out,' and he didn't feel right telling me. So, don't tell anyone else, please."

"Oh brother," said Maria, shaking her head. "Men." Then she looked at me. "So, did you have a make-up kiss?"

"Ooohhhh," said Fran.

"Oh God, you two are as bad as Lori," I said. "And no, we haven't even had our first kiss yet, let alone a make-up kiss."

"Well, remind him that you're not getting any younger," said Fran.

"Really?" said Maria. "And what base have you and Ira gotten to?"

Fran began blushing furiously.

"Okay," I said, changing the subject. "Any funny stories to share?"

"Me, me, me," Maria said, raising her hand.

"Little Joyce Davis finally left her apartment for the first time in decades. And you'll never guess why."

"A romantic liaison?" I asked.

"Nope. A visit to a gynecologist. Little Joyce had a terrible itch in her vee-jay-jay, of all things. And none of the over-the-counter creams worked."

"Wow," said Fran.

"Anyhow, Joyce's neighbor, Barbara, took her to the doctor and went with her into the examining room. After it was over, Joyce sat up and yelled to the doctor, 'Does your mother know what you do for a living?'"

We all laughed. Fran opened another bottle of cabernet and we proceeded to give a toast to Joyce Davis.

"Okay so this isn't a funny story to share, but I thought it would be interesting to discuss," said Fran. "One of the volunteers at We Care brought up this question. If you could have dinner with any person, living or dead, who would you choose and why?"

"I'd pick Joan Rivers," Maria said. "Because she'd have me in stitches."

"Andrea Bocelli," Fran said promptly. "Because I love his music."

"I don't even know if she's living or dead," I said slowly, "but I would want to have dinner with my Aunt Evvie. I called her my sister-aunt, because she was only ten years older than me and she lived with us. My mother and Evvie had an argument, and Mama threw her out of the house. We never saw Evvie again after that." I sighed and poured more wine into my glass.

That night I dreamed about Aunt Evvie and Mama.

"Why is Debbie crying?" Evvie asked. "Why did you send her friends home?"

"I couldn't stand listening to all that silliness and laughing," Mama said.

"They were just being kids, Sylvia. Debbie needs to have some fun."

"You're worried about what she needs? Nobody worries about what I need," Mama said bitterly.

"I can't even imagine how you feel, Sylvia. But Debbie is your child, too. She needs to get out and—"

"No!" Mama thundered. "You're the one who needs to get out. Get out of this house and never come back. Not until you've lost a son, Evvie. Then maybe you'll know how I feel."

Aunt Evvie started to cry.

I would have that dream over the years. Sometimes Evvie would go into the bedroom and pack her suitcases. Sometimes she walked out of the house and Mama would close the door behind her.

But this time, the ending was different. Suddenly my brother Danny was there.

"Why doesn't Aunt Evvie live here anymore?" he asked.

"Mama got mad and threw her out. None of the other relatives come over either."

"Is it because of me—because I died?"

Not wanting to hurt my brother's feelings, I didn't answer.

"That's not right," Danny said.

When I woke up, my mind replayed the dream. After Evvie left, we never heard from her. Some years later, I heard that Evvie had married a man named Scarpitti and they were living in the Chicago area. Later I heard they had twin boys.

Danny's words from the dream kept echoing, "That's not right." It was as if he was trying to tell me something.

Before I moved to Florida, I had located my aunt online. But I had been afraid to call her. Suppose Evvie was angry with me and slammed down the phone. Or suppose, God forbid, Evvie had died. And if I did contact Evvie, would that be disloyal to Mama's memory?

But Danny had given me the key.

And, I realized, moving to Florida and finding happiness wasn't just about drinking wine and going to the pool. Finding happiness meant dealing with my demons and unfinished business.

"That's not right," Danny had said. But now, I can try to make it right.

Yes, right now. It was 8:00 a.m. Chicago time and I hoped it wasn't too early, but I just couldn't wait.

I punched in the telephone number I had written down nearly a year ago. The phone rang twice, three times—well, at least the phone hadn't been disconnected—and then a few more rings.

"Hello?" The woman's voice sounded sleepy and

worried. After all, who would be calling so early in the morning? I recognized the voice right away.

"Aunt Evvie," I began and started to cry.

"Debbie—is that you? Oh, dear God, all these years I kept hoping—"

We talked for over an hour, laughing and crying and catching up on all that happened, all that had gone unsaid. We promised to exchange letters, photos, emails. Now a widow, Evvie was anxious for me to come to Chicago and offered to send a plane ticket.

"I would come to visit you in Florida," she said, "but I had a knee replacement, and it'll be a while before I'm back to myself."

"I always wanted to see Chicago," I said, "but it's too cold now. I'll come in the spring, okay? Meantime, we can talk, and I'll send you pictures of Lori and the grandkids."

"And my boys and grandkids, too. Oh, Debbie, you don't know how happy this makes me."

I WAS LATE FOR WORK AND COULDN'T HAVE CARED LESS. Once and for all, I was ready to do battle with Ursula, who was obsessive about punctuality. But for some reason, Ursula didn't say a word, even though I annoyed her by whistling and singing, over and over, "Chicago, Chicago, that toddling town."

"Well, you've certainly been in a good mood ever since you saw that hotshot mystery doctor the other day," Ursula remarked. "What did he tell you?"

"Oh, good news. He says I'm not pregnant."

It was the first time I had ever gotten Ursula to laugh.

CHAPTER 63

I finished writing out my grocery list for tonight's celebratory dinner with Maria and Fran. To thank them for their support while I dealt with my medical issue, I was actually going to cook. I would have liked to have asked Kay, too, of course, but she still hadn't come back from Boston.

The phone rang, and it was Maria. "Are you sure you don't want me to whip something up? It's no bother," she said.

"No, but thanks," I said. "My meatloaf is the one foolproof recipe I have, and I'm happy to make it."

"Okay," she said, "but let me know if you change your mind."

I hung up and smiled to myself. Where was a friend like Maria when I was a single parent and Lori was growing up? Who knows how well we could have eaten? Maybe I could have traded help with technology for dinners. Or Lori could have helped her kids with math in exchange for leftovers. Or—

A knock on the door brought me back to reality.

The FedEx guy had me sign, and I took the envelope.

The return address was from the Altmans. Finally, I thought. I just hope the price they were asking for was in my budget.

I carefully opened the envelope and read something I wasn't expecting.

The condo was not for sale, and new renters would be coming in the second week of December. I needed to be out by the end of November.

"Oh no."

My backup plan, if I wasn't able to find any place to buy, was to renew my lease for another six months, even if I had to pay more money during the season. I had assumed that, if the Altmans didn't want to sell, they'd be willing to rent to me.

Why didn't I ask the Altmans that question?

I smacked the side of my head. I always told Lori that assuming made an ass out of you and me, and I'd made the biggest, dumbest assumption of all.

It was too much for me to deal with on my own. I picked up the phone.

"Maria, I need you and Fran over here, please. I have a housing emergency."

An hour later, Fran was at my door with a big brown bag stapled shut.

"I brought takeout for lunch."

"Bless you, Fran," I said, because despite everything, I was still hungry.

"I think better on a full stomach, too," said Maria.

After a few minutes of feeding my still bottomless appetite, I explained the situation.

Immediately Maria said, "Well, you just have to find another place to rent."

"I know, but I don't even know what's available at this point," I said.

"Debbie, you could always stay with me," said Fran. "I know I don't have an extra bedroom, but I have a pull-out couch."

I teared up. "That is so kind of you, Fran, but no."

"I wish I could offer you the second bedroom, but Mom is there," said Maria. "I have a pullout couch, too, though."

"Please, Maria. You have enough to deal with."

"How about your friend from up north—isn't she renting a condo in December?" Maria asked.

"Yep—another one bedroom."

"How about Joe?" Fran asked.

"I thought about that," I said. "But he only has a one-bedroom, too, and a pull-out couch."

"Well, you could share his bed," Maria said, with a wicked grin.

"Um—I don't think I'm ready for that," I said.

Maria stood and started cleaning up. "Okay, I'm going to call my friend from church, the realtor, and see if she knows of any rentals. I'll ask Joyce Davis, too."

"And let's look online for some rentals," Fran said.

I gratefully nodded at my two Cabernet Club friends, who were taking charge when I was not feeling up to it.

Three hours later, we were spent.

Maria's realtor friend had nothing available, Joyce Davis had no ideas, and there was nothing online.

"Debbie, you have a month to figure this out," the ever-cheerful Maria pointed out. "Something could open up at any time."

"I guess, but it seems unlikely," I said, my head in my hands. "Well, girls, it's been a great run, but I guess Lori was right, after all. I'll be moving to Delaware after Thanksgiving."

"Don't give up, Debbie. I'm sure we can find something," said Fran.

A wave of pain and exhaustion hit me. "Listen, do you mind if we cancel dinner for tonight? I'm really not up to it."

Both women nodded.

"I have a massive headache," I said. "I'm just going to lie down," I said, heading to the bedroom.

"We'll let ourselves out," said Maria quietly.

CHAPTER 64

I was putting a Macy's bag in my trunk when Kay's car pulled up.

"Hey, welcome back. I heard you went up to Boston," I said.

"I had some things to take care of. So, how's it going with you and Dr. Ross?"

"Great," I said. "I'm feeling better."

"Good. And where are you off to with all that stuff?"

"I'm off to return something to Macy's. Anyhow, what are you up to? I figured you'd stay in Boston seeing how it's nearly Thanksgiving."

"No, actually I'll be flying out to Denver on Monday morning."

"Denver? Oh, that's—" I stammered, not sure what to say.

"So tell me all about it," Kay said. "When did you call him?"

I leaned back against the hood of her car. "Oh, God, I still can't believe I did that. It was the day we went to see

Dr. Isaacs. I figured I already told off Dr. Ross and Dr. Lochner, and as long as I was still hyper, I might as well give your son hell, too."

"How did you find him?"

"Long story short, I went online and searched for Mitchell Jason in the Denver area," I replied.

"You didn't tell him I've got—" Kay started to say.

"Cancer? Hell, no. I have my own way of making a kid feel guilty," I decided not to mention what I said I would do to Mitchell's manhood if he didn't get in touch with his mother.

Kay laughed. "Apparently, it worked. We talked nearly two hours. I'm going to meet Mitchell's fiancé too, and we're going out for Thanksgiving dinner," Kay went on. "Oh, and thanks for looking up a good restaurant there. Mitchell made reservations for us."

"You're welcome," I said, with a sigh of relief. "And speaking of restaurants—that reminds me. Maria, Fran and I are going out for dinner Sunday night and we'd love to have you join us. We're going to Randy's place—remember him?"

"Who could forget?"

As we talked, we heard a loud, annoying sound. "What's that terrible racket?" I asked, and saw a familiar Camry chugging slowly into a parking space nearby.

"Sounds like Harriet Bertulli needs a muffler," Kay said.

"Yeah," I agreed. "And so does her car."

We watched as Mister Highpockets emerged from the front passenger seat and his sister, Freda, from the back. The two hurried over to open Harriet's door, as if she were a celebrity.

"Ah, young love," Kay said, with a mock sigh.

"I heard they were an item," I said. "And look how Freda steers them along, like a tugboat pulling two ships into port. Stanley is an old frigate, and let's see—what kind of ship is Harriet?"

"A tramp steamer," Kay suggested.

"As a great philosopher once said, 'Only in Palmetto Pointe.'"

Kay nodded. "This is one crazy place."

"Yeah, I'll miss it," I said.

"What do you mean?" Kay said, surprise in her voice.

I explained my situation.

"Why didn't you call me?"

"Well, we really don't know each other that well, and I didn't want to bother you."

Kay held up her hand. "I could have saved you a lot of heartache," she said. "I own this place. You can stay in the guest bedroom."

"What? You said a friend was letting you borrow it." I was confused.

She nodded. "Yep, not true. I bought it. I thought it would be a good investment. I just didn't want anyone to know that I bought it, because, well, you know Palmetto Pointe, right? I usually rent it out during season, but I didn't this year, because I knew I'd be staying here until my house is ready in Banyan Falls.

"I don't know what to say," I said. "Why didn't you ever tell us?"

"Because I don't like a lot of people to know my business. It's probably why I don't have many friends."

"Speaking of—how do you know we can get along?"

"Well, we survived a hurricane. And you're pretty entertaining. Plus, I'll be spending less time here once my house is ready in a few months."

I laughed shakily. "I don't know how to thank you. Of course, I'll pay rent, whatever you want—"

She shook her head. "Don't worry about that. We'll figure it out."

After a few moments of thought, I said, "Wow, okay. But I'm going to start looking now for something to buy. Hopefully, I'll be able to find something I can afford. Otherwise, I should have more time to find another rental."

Kay was quiet for a moment. Then she said, "You can stay at my place here as long as you want. Or if you want to buy it, I'll give you a great deal."

"Who are you?" I stared at her.

"Why not? I can afford it. Money isn't a big deal to me."

"Did you really make all that money from real estate investments?"

"Some. And my father left me money, too."

"Your father," I choked. "Your father would turn over in his grave if he knew you were so—so generous with his hard-earned money."

"Hard-earned money? Not to worry," Kay said with a wry smile. "Daddy made his money the old-fashioned way—he married it."

"So when do you want to figure all this out?" I asked.

"I know you were heading to Macy's. Let's talk more later."

I wanted to hug her, but she had already started walking off, with her suitcase.

And instead of going to Macy's, I decided to tell Maria and Fran the good news in person.

CHAPTER 65

"Good morning, everybody," Norman said. "We have a special guest today. This is Craig Robbins. If his name sounds familiar, it's because he's the editor of the Palmetto Pointe *News and Schmooze*." Several people nodded their heads in recognition.

Norman gestured to the smiling bald man, probably in his late seventies. "Craig, would you like to say a few words?"

"Sure, thanks Norman." Craig beamed at us. "It's nice to see such a thriving group of writers here."

"Are you gonna read anything?" Eunice piped up.

"Um—no. I'm just here to listen," he said.

"Very good," said Norman. "Well, let the games begin. Who wants to read?" Except for Eunice, not many hands went up; with Thanksgiving around the corner, the extent of everyone's creative writing was probably just making a grocery list.

So, Eunice proceeded to read yet another long chapter

of her ongoing memoir. So far in the story of her life, she had already received an astonishing number of accolades and awards for her looks, talent, and poise, and she was only up to age seven.

Eunice finished reading. Her efforts, however, were not well-received. Astrid remarked that the tone of her writing sounded rather one-dimensional. "Didn't anything not-so-wonderful or perfect happen in your life?" she asked.

Tapping her perfect teeth with a pencil, Eunice thought for a moment. "Yes, come to think of it, this really mean girl stepped on my beautiful pink dress and ripped the lace."

"Wow," Astrid said straight-faced. "That adds a lot of drama."

Howie raised his hand. "Eunice, I personally feel you have taken the memoir to a different level. You've launched a new genre, romantic self-love."

"Huh?" Eunice looked confused and Norman said hastily, "It's always difficult to critique a memoir." He glanced around the table. "Anybody else want to share? What about you, Debbie? One of your essays? We missed you last week. Were you ill?" For Norman, illness was the only acceptable excuse for not showing up.

"Yes, but I'm better thanks. Anyhow, I'm not sure whether this is a vignette or part of a memoir or what, but anyhow, here it is."

In the Time of the Monkey House

The other day, I was talking to my friend, Roz, from back home in Winslow, Massachusetts. Sometimes we brew a cup of decaf on our Keurig's and have a long-distance coffee klatsch. "Oh, gross," I complained as I sniffed the container of half-and-half which was past its expiration date, "this smells like the Monkey House at Briarwood Park."

Roz burst out laughing. She knew exactly what I meant. We both grew up in Winslow and vividly remember that small green building, long since gone, with its wall mural depicting monkeys cavorting in the jungle. As soon as you walked in, you were overwhelmed by the wild activity and the indescribable smell of animal and bird droppings. There were all kinds of monkeys in cages, screeching and scratching, as well as a variety of tropical birds, some flying over your head, so you had to watch out. As Roz and I reminisced, it was as if we were kids again, holding our noses in that noisy, smelly, but fascinating place.

Thinking about our conversation later that day, I realized that no matter how much we love being with our kids and grandkids, there is something special about staying connected to our peers, especially those who are not only from our time but from our place as well.

Now that I live in Florida, I have a deeper sense of appreciation for my hometown and for my friend, Roz. Roz told me that when she travels, she often wears the special t-shirt made by a shop back home that says "Winslow, Massachusetts" in bold letters and has sketches of well-known landmarks. A number of times, people have come up to her and said, "Hey, I'm from Winslow, too." And when that happens, it's such a magical feeling, a sense of belonging to a special club.

When we were growing up, the factories were humming and downtown was thriving. Winslow was in fashion and fashion was in Winslow, with numerous ladies' apparel stores that could rival those in Boston. We had a small but vibrant Jewish community then, with two synagogues, and Roz and I nagged our parents for new outfits to wear on the High Holidays.

All of that, along with the colorful parades and the elegant old movie theaters and Rita's Dance Pavilion, are just memories now.

Somehow, the older I get, the more I need to stay connected to those who came of age when I did and can travel back with me to the time of the Monkey House—when summer stretched endlessly ahead and Winslow was as big as the world needed to be.

As soon as I finished reading, Eunice was ready to pounce. "That's it? It's not very long."

"It's as long as it needed to be," Norman told her.

Astrid raised her hand. "I think that was very touching and real. I loved the end where you say 'Winslow was as big as the world needed to be.'" I smiled to myself as I heard murmurs of approval.

"Does anyone remember if there was a monkey house at the Bronx Zoo?" Howie asked, sparking some lively nostalgia about monkeys, zoos, and the Bronx.

Eunice seemed peeved that she was not getting much attention, especially since she had apparently gotten more hair extensions, which made her look like the senior citizen version of Rapunzel.

"I believe you should not simply tell," she declared, tossing her new hair. "When you say the Monkey House had a terrible smell, I believe you need to describe that smell."

"I believe for every drop of rain that falls, a flower grows," Howie intoned, which broke everyone up. Everyone but Eunice, who sat there sulking.

"Please everyone, let's get back on track with comments and suggestions about the writing itself," Norman reminded them.

"Well, I found it quite depressing," Eunice persisted.

"That's judgmental," Howie told her. "We all need to try new areas of creativity."

"Oh, yeah, as if you write anything else but letters to the editor," Eunice snapped.

Consuela shook her head and proclaimed, "Joonis is no nice."

Once again, Norman had to bang on the table. "Please, that's enough. This is a writers' support group and we need to support each other."

Consuela raised her hand. "Jes, and I liked Dabbie's story."

"Yeah, right," Eunice sneered, "I don't even think you understood what it was about."

"Who gives a chit what joo think?" Consuela spat out the words.

"What'd she say?" Eunice demanded.

Howie translated, "Consuela said, 'Who gives a shit what you think?'"

Norman intervened. "Craig, do you have any thoughts about Debbie's piece?"

"Yes," he said. "I thought it was a delightful piece of nostalgia, with the perfect amount of description, narration, and dialogue."

The room was silent. I was floating on air.

"Well, that about sums it up, folks," said Norman. "Nice job everybody, and we'll see you next week." Norman nodded to Craig and they both looked at me.

Craig walked over to my seat and I stood up. "Debbie, do you have a minute? I'd like to talk to you about something."

CHAPTER 66

"Actually, if you have a few minutes, let's take a walk," said Craig.

I frowned for a minute, but then figured that Norman wouldn't have invited a serial killer to the writers' group meeting, so I grabbed my things and followed Craig.

Craig opened a door a short walk down the hall from our meeting. The sign on the door said "*News and Schmooze* Office."

The office was small. It contained a desk, computer, a printer, and a couple of chairs. A small window behind the desk looked out onto the parking lot.

He gestured for me to sit down, across from him.

"Debbie, I think you're an excellent writer."

I glowed. "Thank you."

"I understand you also ran a legal office," he said.

"I did."

"So I'm guessing you're good at meeting deadlines."

"I am," I said. This was sounding like a job interview, I thought.

Apparently, I had said those words aloud.

"You're very perceptive, too," said Craig. "You're right. It is a job interview."

I looked around the office again.

"I don't see any space for another desk. Do you have other employees? What kind of office management responsibilities do you need help with?"

Craig shook his head. "Sorry for not communicating very well. I'm a much better writer than I am a speaker."

I frowned, still not understanding.

"So here's the scoop, pun intended," Craig laughed. "I've been the editor of the *News and Schmooze* for three years. Since every editor is a resident of Palmetto Pointe, most of us are interested in working for a few more years before we retire for good. I'm ready. We often find good candidates in the writers' group, and I'm also friendly with Norman. I'd like you to be the new editor."

My jaw dropped below my ankles.

"I'm guessing you didn't walk into the writers' group today expecting to end up with a job offer?" Craig said, chuckling. "Norman told me you that you currently have a part-time administrative job, so I was hoping you might be interested in one that could use your writing and organizational talents."

I finally found my voice and said, "But I've never been an editor before."

"Neither had I," he said. "I was a salesman who always enjoyed writing. I joined the writers' group five years ago, and the editor before me found me there, too."

I must have still looked uncertain, because he continued.

"The prior editor taught me how to use Google documents, and we have an outside graphic and printing firm that puts the paper together."

"I'm very experienced with Google Docs, but do you write and edit all of the articles?"

"No, that's the best part," he said. "I occasionally write some profiles, but most of the information is submitted by residents and clubs. My job is to edit everything and send it to the design firm."

"How about all the ads?" I asked.

"Oh, thanks for the reminder. We have a budget from Palmetto Pointe corporate that covers the editor's salary, design, printing, and distribution. Any ads we sell, we get to keep the revenue from."

"What?" I asked skeptically. "That seems pretty outrageous, since we have so many ads in the paper."

"We only had a few before I came," he said, smiling. "I'm a pretty good salesman. But any ad revenue you get from now on, including ads from companies I originally signed on, you get to keep."

My thoughts were whirling around in my head. What's the catch? This sounds too good to be true. Ah—the pay is probably peanuts, and the hours are long, I bet.

"So what are the pay and hours?" I asked.

"The pay is a monthly stipend of $2,000, and I put in about ten hours a week, sometimes a little less."

I did some quick calculating in my head. That was about fifty dollars an hour.

"Oh, and the ad revenue is about another $2,000 a month. And you can change the rates if you want, too.

They're pretty low, actually. Probably the best deal in town. I never raised them."

That brought the hourly rate to a hundred dollars.

"What are the hours?" I asked.

"You work whatever hours you want," he said. "The paper gets distributed on the fifth day of every month, so I just work backwards to make that deadline. Oh, and I hardly go into the office. I work from home most of the time. The office comes in handy to meet advertisers, though."

Was I dreaming?

"So, what do you think?" Craig asked.

"Well, I couldn't start until January."

"That's great," He stood up, and shook my hand.

"Congratulations on your new position, Editor Gordon."

When I got home, I was tingling with excitement and immediately called Lori. After telling her about the pop-interview, I confessed that I was nervous.

"Do you think I can do it?"

Lori took a few moments, then answered. "Mom, these last six months have really opened my eyes. I mean, I always knew you were good at so many things, and you never complained about anything when I was growing up. But deciding to move to Florida on your own and making a life for yourself made me realize that you can do anything you put your mind to."

My tears started to flow.

"You do understand what this means, don't you, Lori?"

"I'm not sure."

"Well, it means I'm committing to spending at least a couple of years at Palmetto Pointe, and I don't plan on moving to Delaware."

"I get it, Mom. And it's such an amazing opportunity for you. You'll finally get the recognition you deserve."

"Oh, and I forgot the best part," I said. "Craig said that nostalgia is something that's missing in the newspaper. He suggested I write a monthly column, along with my editorial responsibilities."

"I'm so glad, Mom."

CHAPTER 67

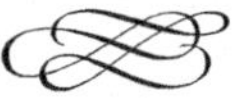

"Oh, no, not again."

The sign at Randy's restaurant said, "Under New Management."

The menu posted on the door showed specials that were entirely different, "Look, no Asian dishes," Maria pointed out. "Maybe this time Randy went belly-up."

"And I had my heart set on trying the Taiwan Tacos," Fran said.

Inside, nothing had changed, although Randy was nowhere to be seen "We're early, as usual," I said, glancing at my watch. "But I guess we should wait to be seated."

We stood there uncertainly, making small talk. "I can't believe it's only four days until Thanksgiving," Kay said.

"Oh, look," Maria said, "they've got something new—that statue of a pirate over there. It's so lifelike."

She went over to examine it and let out a shriek as the pirate statue turned to her and sang out, "Avast there, my pretties."

"Randy, you scared me. I thought you were a statue."

"One of my many talents. In my younger days, I had a job as a window mannequin, so I learned how to be semi-comatose." Randy was decked out like an extra in a *Pirates of the Caribbean* movie, with a colorful bandanna on his head, a big gold earring, and a black patch over one eye. He wore a gaudy waistcoat and shiny boots, and he brandished a sword, which turned out to be made of rubber. His hair, which had been black and cut in bangs the last time we saw him, was now long and brownish-red, and he sported a luxuriant mustache. "It's a wig, of course," he confided, "and the 'stache is a fake, too. My newest marketing campaign."

"Wow," I marveled, "from Shirley Temple to Prince Valiant to Johnny Depp. You never fail to amaze."

"How come the Asian specials you used to have are gone?" Fran asked.

"Because Sung is gone. Sung got married, can you believe it—to a woman—well, a girl, actually."

"A girl? You're kidding."

"Remember that little waitress, Wei? Sung told me she was his niece—hah." Randy was getting so worked up his mustache started to twitch. "Sung never told me he was promised to that little wench. It was one of those family-arranged things."

The women clucked in sympathy as Randy led them through the restaurant to their favorite table.

"And after all I did for Sung. I still can't believe how he lied to me," Randy went on. "I'm not even sure he was really—well, Sung is what I would call a fair-weather fairy."

"A fair-weather fairy?" Kay chuckled. "Well, that's a new term to me."

"Well, shiver me timbers," Randy broke into a big

smile. "Look who's here. Haven't seen you in ages." He pulled out a chair for her. "So, my proud beauty, would you like to try my new rum drink, Pirates Passion?" He began to chant, "Fifteen men on a dead man's chest, yo-ho-ho and a bottle of rum."

"Yo, ho, ho and a bottle of wine." Kay said. "Make it a good cabernet, Captain Brownbeard."

"Certainly, Miss Bitch. But you didn't even comment on my swashbuckling."

"In your case, more like swishbuckling," Kay said.

"Oh, I just love her," Randy said rapturously. "She really gets me. I mean, you all get me in different degrees—even Madame Fran, who, I'm pleased to report, is now tipping up to fifteen percent when she comes for lunch with the We Care group. However, Mistress Kay and I are truly kindred spirits. But enough of this. The cabernet is calling." He hurried off.

"So, catch us up on what's happening with you, Kay. Are you going up to Boston for Thanksgiving?" Maria asked.

"Actually, I'm flying to Denver tomorrow morning," Kay said. "I'm spending Thanksgiving with my son. And what's going on with you guys? How's your boyfriend, Fran?"

"Oh, poor Ira is in a rehab facility." Fran sighed. "I'm going to have Thanksgiving dinner with him there. He tripped over somebody's walker at Dunkin' Donuts and fractured his ankle in two places."

Kay laughed. "I can't help it—I'm sorry. But all those goddamn walkers and wheelchairs down here. They're dangerous."

"The funniest thing is that Dunkin' Donuts used to have a slogan 'It's Worth the Trip,'" I said, and they all laughed.

"And how's that little pussy of yours, Fran?" Kay asked, just as Randy arrived with the cabernet.

"Oh, what interesting conversations you ladies have," he said, as he poured the wine. "What's this about your pussy, Miss Fran?"

"No—uh—she's talking about my cat." Even in the dim light, we could see that Fran was blushing furiously. "Kitty is doing fine."

"So, I assume you ladies all have plans for Thanksgiving," Randy handed us the wine glasses. "Obviously none of you plan to dine here, although we're taking reservations," he added hopefully. "I've even got a couple of new waitresses, see?" He pointed to two young women wearing pirate hats, short skirts, and low-cut tops.

"I'm serving our annual Thanksgiving dinner for the homeless at church," Maria said. "It's one of the highlights of my year."

"Okay, you win the 'most impressive Thanksgiving plan' award Maria," I joked. "But I'm excited about seeing my daughter and her family. And—drumroll please—Joe is cooking dinner. For once my family will have a great meal, and I won't get stressed out making a crummy one."

"Wow, things sound pretty serious if you're letting him meet your family," said Kay.

"Not really," I said. "He told me that his kids aren't coming in for Thanksgiving, and he's visiting them at Christmas. He asked me if I had plans, and I mentioned that I'll be struggling through my one major family meal for the year, and he offered to do it instead."

"Let's have a toast." Maria raised her glass. "*L'chaim.* To life."

"To life," Kay repeated, not batting an eyelash. She had never told the other two about her breast cancer. When I asked why, Kay maintained that when people hear that you have a serious medical condition, they're never really comfortable with you.

"And to good health," Fran said.

"And good friends," I added. We clinked glasses and sipped the wine.

Fran recalled how, every year she was a teacher, she asked the students around her classroom's Thanksgiving party table say what they were grateful for.

"My favorite was from a little girl named Heather," said Fran. "She said she was grateful for lipstick."

We all roared.

"Let's do that now," said Fran. "You start, Debbie."

"I don't know where to begin, I have so much to be grateful for," I said. "My health is good, and I feel fine now, I'll be seeing my daughter and her family soon, and I'm back in touch with my Aunt Evvie in Chicago. My old friend Roz from back home is coming down after Christmas. Wait till you meet her. She's a pisser. I've made such great new friends here, Maria and Fran, not to mention the former Kay Caldwell, queen of the Winslow High School Senior Prom, who, as you know, has also offered me a place to stay for the season. And in January I'll be taking submissions for the *News and Schmooze.*"

"All hail Editor Gordon," said Kay, and everyone clapped.

"Oh, Debbie, here's something else you can be grateful

for. Fran and I voted you president of The Cabernet Club," Maria said. "And Kay—you're an honorary member."

"Wow. President of The Cabernet Club. I've never been president of anything. Thanks, guys," I said. "My cup runneth over, but… my glass is kind of empty." I reached over for the bottle of wine.

"How about you, Maria?"

"Well, you know how happy I am to have met you girls," she said. "A year ago, I wouldn't have had anyone except my mother to go out to dinner with. And she doesn't like cabernet." We all laughed.

"And you helped me realize that I've been there for everyone else in my life, and it's time for me now," she said, smiling broadly. "And I've made a decision."

"Really? About what?" I asked.

"Remember that guy from church who wanted to go to dinner with me as a friend? Well, his wife lives in a nice assisted-living facility, and I asked him to give me a tour, to see if it's a good fit for Mom."

"What? When did you talk with him?" Fran almost choked on her wine.

"After church the other day," said Maria.

"And?" I asked.

"Let's just say that I may have reconsidered going out to dinner with him as a friend. And I may even consider him a friend with benefits." She winked.

"TMI," Fran and I chorused, and Kay laughed.

"Well done, Maria," Kay said and clapped, and we joined in.

Maria took a bow then headed to her seat. "Fran, what are you thankful for?"

In a low voice, Fran said, "Well, I don't like to get too personal, but I will just this once."

We all leaned forward to listen.

"I never really had any friends as an adult," she said. "I did a lot of traveling, and played sports, and spent a lot of time teaching, but I didn't spend time with friends. My mom was really critical, and there weren't any women I looked up to."

"That's because you're taller than all of them," I joked, and we all laughed.

She took a sip of wine. "But I feel so lucky and thankful to have met all of you. Each of you is a role model to me. You helped me learn to take chances, had my back when it came to Kitty, and even helped me find a way to volunteer with foster kids," Fran said, smiling at me.

"You're forgetting that we helped improve your wardrobe," I said. "Now you look like a true Floridian," I said, and we all nodded.

"And we encouraged you to date Ira, a good boyfriend who might be able to show you what all the fuss about sex is about," Maria chucked.

Blushing furiously, Fran laughed and sat down. "How about you, Kay?" she asked. "What are you thankful for?"

"You know, I'm not good at this kind of stuff. But I can tell you a good joke, if you want to hear it."

"Yes, please," said Fran.

I barely listened as Kay told her joke. My mind was whirling. Only six months here in Florida, and what a trip it has been. Who could have imagined that wacky, tacky Palmetto Pointe would have turned out to be as comfortable and comforting as an old shoe with a hole cut out for a bunion? And the Florida condo lifestyle was like a cornucopia, filled with the fruits—and fruitcakes—of the harvest.

Anything was possible here. You never knew who might become a new friend or who would fall in love with you at the dumpster.

"Hey, Debs, how come you're so quiet?" Maria asked.

I forced myself back into the conversation, namely, what to order.

Randy was back at the table. "Ladies, have you reached a decision? I hope none of you are ever on a jury."

"I probably should get the tilapia because I'm watching my weight," Maria sighed, "but then I think about those rich ladies on the Titanic, getting into the lifeboats and thinking to themselves, 'Damn, I should have had dessert.'"

Kay nodded. "It's like that saying, 'Life Is Short—Eat Dessert First.'"

I sat up. "Hey, I know what I want. The gooiest, most fattening chocolate dessert you've got, Randy. I want ice cream on it and hot fudge and all that good stuff. For once, I'm going to eat dessert first. Afterward, I'll probably have the Boston scrod dinner. If I can't eat it, I'll take it home."

"I'll have what she's having," Kay quipped.

"Me too," Maria said.

"And me three—or is it four?" Fran giggled. "Except I want the Taiwan tacos—I mean Pirates Plunder."

Randy pulled the black patch off his eye and gawked at us. "What will my chef think when I tell him you're all having dessert first?"

"He'll think you've got some cool customers," Kay said and whispered something into Randy's ear. I had a hunch Kay told him to bring her the check. Randy nodded and went off to the kitchen.

Kay held up the bottle of wine. Was it the second, the third? "As an honorary member of The Cabernet Club, I make a motion that you guys finish this. I can't. I'm the designated driver."

"You talked me into it, you silver-tongued devil," I said. More warm laughter.

As we raised our glasses in salute to Kay, it was as if everything seemed to fall into place.

So, this is what they mean by the Golden Years, I thought. This bright and fleeting window of time when you can finally see what you never noticed before and be who you never were before. I can take classes, join a book club, be a volunteer. Now that I'm able to focus on my writing, maybe I'll write a novel and become the Grandma Moses of the publishing world. And maybe I'll finally meet my Mister Right, or maybe I've already found him.

After all, it is never too late to be what you might have been. That's what the fortune cookie said the last time we were at Randy's Rendezvous. I still had that message on my refrigerator.

"Here we go, my lovely wenches," Randy sang out as he set down a tray. "As Miss Kay so aptly stated, 'Life Is Short—Eat Dessert First,'" he added for the benefit of gawking customers at nearby tables.

The chocolate cake was gloriously rich and decadent, with a big scoop of ice cream, drizzled with hot fudge, whipped cream, and nuts.

"Oh, and ladies, you get fortune cookies, too. I saved them from the days of the Sung Dynasty," Randy tittered.

"Well, then, I guess we should read our fortunes first," Maria suggested. "Mine probably says 'You will put on five more pounds.'" Actually, it said, "The smarter you get, the less you talk."

Fran's read: "Time is a dressmaker, specializing in alterations."

"Hey, mine is deep," Kay said. "Don't let your future be based on someone else's past."

I caught my breath as I read my fortune cookie message. "You may not have gone where you intended to go, but you ended up where you needed to be."

"Oh, my God," Maria stage-whispered, "look who just walked in. The Palmetto Pointe Power Couple and Matchmaker Freda."

The Widow Bertulli, dressed in her trademark black, was chattering away, while Stanley Stein had his usual blank "Who, me?" look on his face. Freda spotted me and marched over, looking triumphant. "Well, Miss High and Mighty," she chortled, "you lost your chance. Stanley found someone better. And what a catch Harriet is, smart as a whip. She even has her own business."

"Harriet sells Avon," I pointed out, "Not exactly an entrepreneur."

"Yes, she's self-employed," Freda smacked her lips in satisfaction. "She and my brother are soul mates. You know what they say, 'For every pot there's a cover.'"

"And for every toilet, there's a lid," I shot back. My fellow Cabernet Club members woo-hooed and applauded. Freda slunk off in a huff.

Kay began to sing "This Nearly Was Mine," and Maria hummed along. Fran poured the last of the wine into her glass.

I dug into my dessert.

The fortune cookie message was right on target, I smiled to myself. This is exactly where I needed to be.

ABOUT THE AUTHORS

Rona S. Zable

"There wasn't a person out there who didn't love Rona. We all aspired to be like her."

Rona S. Zable was a beloved mother, grandmother, and friend. She loved cabernet, laughing, crossword puzzles, the pool, and any TV show on Bravo. She always loved writing, and her first poem was published at age 10, in the junior *Standard-Times* newspaper in New Bedford, MA.

Rona always said her life got better after 50, which is when she published three Young Adult (YA) novels with Bantam Doubleday Dell—*Love at the Laundromat* (nominated as an American Library Association Best Book and ALA Recommended Book for Reluctant Readers), *An Almost Perfect Summer*, and *Landing on Marvin Gardens* (a Junior Library

Guild selection chosen as an outstanding book for young adults and a *USA Today* selection as one of the best new books for YA readers), and a middle-grade novel, *Don't Get Mad, Get Even*, with Troll Press.

She wrote her books at night, and during the day she worked as the editor of *SeniorScope*, the largest senior publication in New England.

A native of New Bedford, MA, Rona passed away in February 2023.

Margie Zable Fisher

Co-author Margie Zable Fisher is Rona's daughter. Margie is a wife and mother, also loves cabernet and the pool, and competed in her first triathlon after age 50. She plays pickleball several times a week and considers it a good day if she achieves genius status playing the *New York Times* Spelling Bee.

Before becoming a full-time writer and author after age 50, Margie owned a P.R. agency for 20 years. Her articles have been published in the *New York Times, AARP, Fortune*, *Next Avenue*, and more.

She and her family live in Florida.

ACKNOWLEDGMENTS

Thank you to Alisa Kennedy Jones, Molly Zakoor, Erinn McGrath, and The Empress Editions team. I'm so grateful for your interest in this book and series, and for your terrific work on the cover art, editing, marketing, and so much more.

Thank you to my first publisher, Sibylline Press, and the Sibylline team, including founders Vicki DeArmon, Julia Park Tracey, Alicia Feltman, and Anna Termine, as well as my editor, Maureen Jennings, for helping bring this book into the world. Thanks also to the Sibylline community of women authors over 50 who supported me and *The Cabernet Club* through the initial launch process and beyond, especially Lisa Friedman Rosenberg.

Thanks to my friends, family, and colleagues who supported me throughout this writing and publishing journey, especially Fern Cole, Terri Sherman, Kevin Shuster, Sharon Saulenas, C.J. Tchozewski, Susan Olson, Lynn Miner-Rosen, Ellen LeBoeuf, Nancy Brice, Stacey Zable Robin, Sheila Zable Kopelowitz, Judy Joyce, Allyne Cole, Rona Lewis, Nikki Netburn, Laurie Weissman, Debbie Frimet, Robin Stevens, Robin Golieb, Sue Perets, Enid Weinraub, Pam Farnsworth Wilkinson, Kristen Bomas, Debbye Meehan, Bonnie Mason, Rich Eisenberg, Barb Cohen, Marilyn Scheck-DePlaza, Jeanne Gadless, Sheree

Goroff, Carmen Cuascut, Nancy Weiss, Sandy Levy Ramos, Ann Marie Pane Kuratnick, Suzanne Gurwitz, Sandra Rose, Andy Rose, Sherri Jaquays, Shoshanna Breitbart, Susan Nathanson, Sharon Sara Sabga, Patti Frederick, Valerie Staggs, Lynette Demar, Dale Miller, Tonya Jarvis, Melissa Hankinson, Jody Pflanzer, Rowena Deen, Lynne Pisano, Duffy Lieber, Wendy Howard, Linda Good, Ruth Furman, Joan Harris, Amy Soble, Linda Hensley, Bronya Zeitlin, Linda Waldon, Lana Rudner, Cami Popiel, Terry Wolfisch Cole, Esther Summer, Sue Schuman, Mickey Goodman, Nanette Saylor, Cindy Moss, Mim Van Orman, Marilyn Endo, Adina Moses, Ronnis Oher, Gigi Krauser, Patty Triplett West, Caitlin Alexander, Laurie Chittenden, and Don Silver.

Thanks to all the podcasts I listened to that were instrumental in helping me craft, pitch, and market this book. They include *The Creative Penn Podcast For Writers, Fiction Writing Made Easy, Novel Marketing, Book Marketing Tips and Author Success Podcast, and The Book Marketing Action Podcast.*

Thanks to Renee Weiss Weingarten, and Renee's Reading Club, the best Facebook reading club, for all of your support for *The Cabernet Club*.

Thanks to my husband, David, who read the book and listened to me talk about it endlessly. Your support means the world to me.

Thanks to my daughter, Zoe, who is always an inspiration.

And most of all, thanks to my mom, Rona Zable. You were my first and toughest editor and best cheerleader. You, and your writing, were a gift to the world.

Thank you so much, dear reader, for reading this book! Mom and I are raising a glass to you!

To receive a bonus chapter of *The Cabernet Club*, and learn about upcoming events, new books, sweepstakes, and more, please sign up for the VIP Club at my website, https://margiezfisher.com/.

You can also contact me there to book me for a speaking event, book club discussion, and more.

Last but not least, if you enjoyed this book, please help us out by leaving a review on Amazon, Goodreads, or any other online platform where you purchased *The Cabernet Club.* And if you borrowed the book from a friend or library, you can still leave a review on Amazon or Goodreads. Reviews help so much! Thanks in advance!

BOOK CLUB QUESTIONS

1. What was your favorite part of *The Cabernet Club*?
2. Which scene has stuck with you the most?
3. Who was your favorite character and why?
4. How did the setting contribute to the characters and the plot?
5. Were you surprised by any of the plot twists?
6. What are some common challenges older women face that are explored in this book?
7. How important is friendship as women get older?
8. What are some ways the women in *The Cabernet Club* are of service to each other?
9. What did you learn from the book or what did it teach you about yourself or others?
10. How did you feel about the ending? Was it satisfying or did you want more?

TO OUR FOUNDERS

Every Empress Editions book is a declaration: midlife women are not a demographic—they're a cultural force.

This revolution wouldn't exist without the founding vision and bold support of **Shannon Kennedy** and **David Roberts**. They believed in our mission before the ink was dry and helped us build a publishing house devoted to amplifying the voices of women in their prime.

Shannon brings fierce heart and strategic clarity; David, sharp insight and unshakable belief. Together, they lit the match that started this fire.

To our founding visionaries: thank you for helping us turn the page on what publishing can be.

With gratitude and a glint of rebellion,

The Empress Editions Team

If you've enjoyed this Empress Editions book, why not write or telephone us for a free catalogue—or visit TheEmpressAge.com to join our Substack and discover more bold, midlife voices rewriting the rules.

Our authors love book clubs—especially the kind with mocktails and candor. Books ordered directly from Empress support a living legacy of matrilineal storytelling, healing, and cultural visibility.

Empress Editions
303 Third Street Cambridge, MA 02142
Telephone: +1 617.580.5266
hello@empresseditions.net
empresseditions.io

MARKETING CAMPAIGN

- Digital Advertising
- National Television Interviews
- National Radio and Podcast Interviews
- National Print and Online Media Coverage
- Pitch Influencers on instagram and TikTok
- Prepublication Author Events
- Prepublication Online Buzz and Early Consumer Review Campaign
- Grassroots Outreach to Special Interest Groups
- Features in Brand and/or Imprint Newsletters
- Targeted Email Marketing Campaign Based on Consumer Browsing and Category Interests
- Social Media Posts on Empress Editions/Hachette Book Group Imprint Platforms
- Reader's Edition Available
- eGalley Available on Edelweiss and NetGalley

Fiction

February 2026

$18.99 US ($26.99 CAD)

380 Pages ~ 5.5 x 8.5

For publicity contact: hello@empresseditions.net